Meet the fighters of the Lucky 13th

Colonel Stossen is the only commanding officer the Lucky 13th has ever had. He doesn't always like what he has to ask his men to do, but he always knows they'll do it—or die trying.

Sergeant Joe Baerclau rarely shows any outward emotion. But when his gray eyes begin to smolder, his men know it's time to get out of his way—or follow him to where the action is.

Corporal Ezra Frain is a veteran at age twenty. The tall redhead had joined the 13th after helping fight off an invasion of his home planet. Now he's ready to give the enemy a taste of its own poison.

Private Mort Jaiffer is the "old man" of his squad at twenty-seven. A former college professor turned soldier, he turned down a chance at officer school to be a private.

Private Kam Goff had never seen combat before the landing on Porter. But before the end of his first day on the ground, he'd seen enough to last him the rest of his life.

UNTIL RELIEVED

RICK SHELLEY

2003
50TH
ANNIVERSARY

ACE BOOKS, NEW YORK

UNTIL RELIEVED

An Ace Book / published by arrangement with
Bill Fawcett & Associates

PRINTING HISTORY
Ace mass-market edition / March 1994

ISBN: 0-441-00019-3

ACE®
Ace Books are published by The Berkley Publishing Group,
a division of Penguin Group (USA) Inc.,
375 Hudson Street, New York, New York 10014.
ACE and the "A" design
are trademarks belonging to Penguin Group (USA) Inc.

PRINTED IN THE UNITED STATES OF AMERICA

10 9 8 7 6 5 4 3 2

PROLOGUE

The wall, ceiling, and floor of the circular room were a uniform pearl-gray. The ceiling was domed, and there was recessed lighting around the top of the wall, but at the moment, those lights were off. The only illumination within the chamber came from the spherical starfield projection that appeared to hover above a five-meter-diameter circular table in the precise center of the room, and from the monitors of compsoles. Those lights, though faint, reflected well from their surroundings. The room scarcely needed more light.

Each of the eight men (there were no women in this subcommittee, though there was approximate parity in the numbers of men and women in the Council from which they were drawn) seated around the table had a compsole screen embedded in the table in front of him. None of these men could be described as young. The youngest was nearly sixty years old, and the average was well over seventy-five, approaching middle age. Each man also had a personal compsole, for taking or reading notes, sitting either on his lap or on the table next to the built-in terminal. Each man also had one or two aides standing behind them, ready to run errands or to provide information that their principles had not thought to look for in his notepad.

Even the name of the planet on which this room could be found was classified information. There were at least a dozen identical rooms located on separate worlds. Meetings were sited at the whim of the chairman. The men sitting around the table had come from a half-dozen different worlds scattered throughout the Accord of Free Worlds of the Terran Cluster, often by circuitous routes. Once this conference ended, they would disperse just as widely, some to return to their own worlds, others to oversee the operation that this meeting would authorize.

There was little doubt of what would come out of this session. Hundreds of ships and more than twenty-five thousand soldiers were already traveling to their final staging areas, waiting only confirmation of their orders before moving into action. Only catastrophic news might cancel the Accord's first major counterstrike against the invaders from the Schlinal Hegemony. There would be no such news.

"We're going to put full assault teams on the ground on four planets," Encho Mizatle, the Accord's minister for Defense, announced without rising from his chair. He spoke softly, but a microphone in his compsole picked up his words, and speakers in the others compsoles relayed them to his colleagues.

Those others looked at the starfield projection or at their compsole screens, which displayed three-dimensional video of the speaker. Three of them could not have seen the minister if they had wanted to. The star globe hid him from direct view. They did not need to see him, however. They really had no need to even *hear* him—not unless Mizatle managed to say something novel, something not on the agenda. Otherwise, this session was merely pro forma, a matter of putting already-reached decisions on the—highly classified—record.

"The 9th Spaceborne Assault Team will land on Devon as the spearhead of our primary offensive. The 2nd and 12th SAT, as well as the 19th and 21st Mobile Infantry Divisions and the 31st Light Infantry Regiment, will also be committed to the fight on Devon, with the schedule of air and artillery units agreed upon in the General Staff meeting of eleven-seventeen. The reserve units also remain unchanged." The

minister simply did not recall the rest of the combat units
going into Devon offhand, and he did not want to waste
time reading it from his compsole. "The 6th SAT will land
on Kulik, the 8th on Hobart, and the 13th on Porter. The 6th,
8th, and 13th are intended to provide diversions to keep the
Hegemony from reinforcing their troops on Devon from other
garrisons in the sector. Some of these diversionary forces
might take heavy casualties, but overall, we expect that their
activities will lower the cost in lives to recover Devon. We
expect to save more lives than the diversions lose." That was
a touchy point. Even after the details of this operation were
eventually made public, the Defense minister's assessment
would remain classified. He was, after all, a politician.

"The units providing these essential backup missions will
be told to expect pickup within four or five days, but their
orders are to hold until relieved or recalled." The minister
shrugged. "Again, a necessary evil. Evacuation under fire
without reinforcement might be suicidal. They really have
little choice but to hold until we come for them. That is
why we're sending the best we have. They will have to hold
until we can free up sufficient forces from Devon to relieve
them."

"A question, Minister," Thomas Tompkins, the Accord
Council member from Earth, said. Tompkins was the only
one present who would have had the audacity to interrupt
the minister. Though Earth was no longer the most powerful
or most important of humanity's worlds, Terrans still tended
to regard their world as the center, the progenitor.

"Yes, Councillor?" Mizatle asked, keeping his voice impec-
cably polite.

"At need, just how long are these teams provisioned for? How
long *can* they hold out, assuming, of course, that they aren't
overwhelmed by the Hegemony garrisons on these worlds?"

Mizatle hesitated only briefly before replying although he
would have preferred to avoid the question completely. "Nominally, each assault team carries all of the supplies it needs for
unsupported action in the field for seven days—ammunition,
food, medical supplies, and everything else. That is a con-
servative estimate, of course. We can gauge the food demands
fairly closely. Expenditure of munitions is rather more difficult
to predict with assurance. It depends most significantly on the

level of enemy opposition. In the present instances, the three teams that will be operating solo ought to be able to stretch all of their supplies to last ten to twelve days, in a pinch."

"And what is the *soonest* we'll be able to relieve them, assuming that the invasion of Devon comes off precisely according to the mission timetable?" Tompkins asked.

Almost inaudibly, the minister replied, "Eight days."

CHAPTER
1

The only lights on in the troop bay of the landing shuttle were red and dim. The lander had already separated from its mother ship and was waiting for the rest of the assault boats to form up. Ninety soldiers, half of Echo Company, 13th Spaceborne Assault Team, had been crowded into the lander for nearly two hours already. With the visors of their combat helmets down, the men appeared faceless and might almost have been robots save for the small, random movements generated by nerves. Two thirds of these men had faced combat before, but that did not make the veterans any less nervous than the men who were going into battle for the first time. In some cases, knowledge was worse than imagination. The veterans *knew* what they might face.

Each man had his own personal reasons for fighting, weighty or trivial. There were no conscripts in any of the elite assault teams of the Accord of Free Worlds. Every man had volunteered for military service, and then volunteered for this duty—after he had been in uniform long enough to make an informed decision. Some fought because their homeworld asked. Others fought because they felt a personal call to the career, or to the crusade against the Schlinal Hegemony. And, naturally, there were some who never discussed their motives, some who might have had no real idea why they had enlisted.

Strategists rarely think of an army as a collection of individuals. Teamwork is much easier to attain than the spark of personal initiative, and generally more valued in an army. After all, a unit must function smoothly in combat to have any real chance of success, weapons and numbers notwithstanding. And soldiers have to be drilled until the instant obedience of any order becomes such a deeply ingrained habit that the order is not questioned until after it has been obeyed, if then. But any army is made up of the men—and occasionally women— who wear its uniform.

The first squad, 2nd platoon, Echo Company, was perhaps typical of the 13th SAT. On the regiment's Table of Organization, the squad was merely one sergeant, one corporal, and five privates. But the squad was more than just a collection of slots on a manning chart.

Sergeant Joe Baerclau was a veteran. Twenty-four years old, Joe had been a soldier for five of those years, first in a defense regiment on his native world of Bancroft, then in the Accord's Defense Force, the last two of those years in the 13th SAT. The landing on Porter would be his third campaign in less than a year. He was physically smaller than most of the men in the platoon, but he was a tough opponent in any sort of fighting, whether in actual combat or in training. An extremely private man, he rarely showed any outward emotion. At times though, one or another of the men in his squad would say that he could always tell when the Bear was upset; his gray eyes "smoldered." While the shuttle waited for the word to begin its descent, Joe was on his feet surveying the men of his squad, looking for any hint that any of his men might be less than ready for the assault. It was a redundant inspection. For the last two days there had been one equipment and weapons check after another. But concentrating on his men helped Joe suppress his own anxieties about the coming fight.

Corporal Ezra Frain, assistant squad leader, was still a month short of his twentieth birthday. Tall and thin with flaming red hair and green eyes, he came from a farming region on Highland, one of the worlds where Accord and local forces had defeated an invasion by the Schlinal Hegemony. At the conclusion of that fight, Ezra had transferred into the 13th. He doubled as the squad's electronics fix-it man.

The five privates in the squad ranged in age from nineteen to twenty-seven. Four of them were between nineteen and twenty-two.

Mort Jaiffer was the "old man" of the squad. He was also the intellectual, though no one would guess that to look at him, or to see him in action. He was large and burly, with rough hands. Although only twenty-seven years old, his hair was already thinning, with a bald spot like a priest's tonsure. Since he normally wore his hair cut almost to the scalp, he didn't bother to get the bald spot cured. He had taken to the military with as much dedication as he had taken to the study of history and political science. One fine spring morning at the end of the school term, he had resigned his associate professorship to join the Accord military. He had turned down the chance to become an officer and would have preferred to stay a private for as long as he wore the uniform. Despite his wishes though, he had already been tagged for promotion to corporal in the near future.

Tod Chorbek and Wiz Mackey had joined the Accord Defense Force together and had managed to draw assignment together after training, and even when they transferred to the 13th. They were both twenty years old, or would be as soon as Tod celebrated his birthday in two weeks. Both were tall, big-boned, and fair-haired. They had grown up living less than three kilometers apart, on farms, and both had opted for the military as being preferable to what they knew. They had been friends for as long as either of them could remember. Most of the time, the two seemed interchangeable. Even the men who knew them best sometimes confused their names.

Al Bergon and Kam Goff were the only two men in the squad who had never faced combat before, but each of them had at least a year in uniform. One or the other was required for assignment to any of the Accord's fifteen assault teams. Al was twenty-two, tall, thin, and dark. He doubled as the squad's medic. Kam was the youngest member of the squad, just barely past his nineteenth birthday. Blond and with a fair complexion that was almost albino, Kam looked as if he should still be in school, perhaps even several years from graduation.

Finally satisfied with the preparation of his men, Joe sat down and fastened his safety belt.

"Keep it loose," he whispered over the squad's radio frequency. Each man's battle helmet had several radio links. Though there were distinct channels, they were not assigned to constant frequencies. To avoid enemy interception, each channel was switched among a number of different frequencies. Computer chips in the helmet circuitry were synchronized to ensure that each helmet had the current frequency combination correct.

Two minutes later, the lander's pilot announced, "Everybody strap in. Here we go." The shuttle's artificial gravity was switched off as the craft changed attitude and accelerated, aimed almost directly at the sunrise line moving west across Porter.

Although detection at any significant distance from the planet was unlikely, the transports and escort ships had used Porter's sun to help camouflage their approach. Holding the ships directly between Porter's sun and the occupied portions of the world, the electromagnetic signatures of the ships—inherently difficult to detect because of the construction materials and methods used—were thoroughly blanketed. The landers would also be difficult for an enemy to discover before they got within easy visual range. By that time, the Schlinal communications satellites strung around Porter would be under attack. That was a matter of timing. It would never do to warn the enemy of invasion by going after their communications network too soon.

The fleet of landers accelerated toward the northern hemisphere of Porter, aiming toward the plateau northeast of the rift valley that held the bulk of the world's population, and the bulk of the occupying Schlinal Hegemony forces. Monitors spaced high on the curved bulkheads of the troop bay gave the soldiers a chance to see where they were going.

A "hot" landing raised havoc with the senses, destroying natural orientations. At its peak, acceleration made "up" toward the ground, and "down" toward open space. With the bench seats in the troop bay facing fore and aft, some men felt as if

they were being hurtled face first at the world, while the rest
felt as if they were "falling" backward. It would not be until
the last minute that "down" would be beneath the feet of the
soldiers and pointed toward the ground, when the shuttles went
to full power on their antigravity drives to land their passengers
softly. For a time, the men would be subjected to more than
three gees.

Joe Baerclau felt a familiar sour taste in his mouth and
throat as the approach upset his stomach. That happened every
time he went through one of these hot landings. He wanted
to close his eyes but did not dare. If he did, the sensation
of falling would be even stronger, and he doubted that he
could control his nausea then. He could already hear some
of the men in the bay retching into motion sickness bags, and
a faint smell of vomit started to overpower the more familiar
odor of lubricants. Even a veteran was susceptible. The human
body had never been designed for such rough conveyance.

To keep his mind occupied, Joe went over his squad's initial
movements once they disembarked. Again. Each squad had
its own assignment in those first seconds and minutes. There
might not be time to think through alternatives if the landing
was heavily opposed, and they would not know the strength of
the opposition until they reached the ground. Attacking across
interstellar space meant that they had no up-to-the-minute
intelligence on enemy strength and deployment. With luck,
they would have that information shortly after they landed.
Each of the shuttles was scanning constantly, and the transports and escort vessels would also be launching probes.

Breathe deeply, Joe told himself as he felt nausea rise again.
It did not seem to matter how many times he took rides like
this, or whether or not he ate before. His stomach always
objected. The lander stopped accelerating toward the ground
and switched the direction of its antigrav drives to brake.
That reversal almost made the difference. Joe's hand started
to slide toward the rack on the front of his seat that held the
airsick bags.

The shuttle started to vibrate from the surge of power and
from the buffeting of Porter's atmosphere. The landing craft
were built too sturdily for there to be the slightest danger of
it breaking up in flight just from shaking. Shuttles had even
been known to remain recognizable after three-gee crashes—

though the same could not be said for their occupants.

Joe noticed that the palms of his hands were sweating. He wiped them against the net armor of his combat fatigues, one hand at a time, using the other hand to hold his zipper, a Mark VI Armanoc wire carbine.

Over the platoon channel on his helmet radio, Joe heard the "lock and load" command from Platoon Sergeant Maycroft. Joe clicked back to his squad frequency and repeated the order while he charged his own rifle.

"Mind your safeties," he added.

Less than two minutes left, he thought. He took several deep breaths, making them as long and slow as he could while the feeling of weight built up. The monitors on the bulkheads showed a variety of views now. They were finally close enough to get a decent look at the terrain.

"It could be worse," Joe muttered softly after scanning several of the screens. There was enough open ground for the fleet of landers, with cover close enough for the men once they got away from the boats. Most importantly, there were no rocket trails visible, no sign of anything that might knock a shuttle out of the sky. The landers were vulnerable once they were seen. If an anti-air missile was launched at them, there was little the crew could do but drop chaff and decoys, and try to jam the missile's electronics. The shuttles could scarcely maneuver out of their own shadow coming in for a hot landing.

"Thirty seconds," the pilot warned as apparent gravity within the lander reached its maximum. Joe counted those seconds in his head. He looked around at his men again, then braced himself. Sometimes, landings were rougher than they were supposed to be.

This one, however, had a barely noticeable jolt. Before it had ended, Joe hit the quick release on his safety belt and jumped to his feet.

"Let's go," he said over the squad frequency. "Safeties off." He held his rifle in front of him as he ostentatiously switched off the zipper's safety.

The men of the 13th rehearsed combat debarkations with some regularity between campaigns. The goal was to get ninety men out of a shuttle and moving toward their initial positions in less than thirty seconds. The four large doors in the troop bay popped open as soon as the shuttle came to rest. Double lines of soldiers moved quickly to each exit. Each man knew which door he was to head for. There was no lagging, no stopping to chat. They were on the ground on a hostile world, with unknown opposition. Outside, away from the shuttle, the men would present smaller targets to the enemy, and they would be in a position to defend themselves.

Echo Company's 2nd platoon exited through the rear of the crescent-shaped lander, carrying all of their combat gear with them. Joe checked to make sure that his squad was with him and followed Sergeant Maycroft and Lieutenant Keye, the platoon leader. Joe's first thought as he left the shuttle was that they had set down precisely at the dawn line. To the east, everything was bright and sunny, but there were still deep shadows to the west.

"We're heading for the tree line," Maycroft said over the platoon frequency. He also pointed. West.

Joe nodded from reflex, although Maycroft was already five meters in front of him and twenty meters to the right. Joe also repeated the directions over his squad frequency. A touch of a control put a target acquisition overlay against the visor of his helmet. His sensors showed no targets in infrared or through electronic emissions anywhere in the 120-degree arc in front of him.

The last shuttles of the first wave were already landing. The landers that had touched down first were lifting off again. They would return to the ships in orbit, some to load up with supplies and return, the rest just to get out of the way of possible enemy fire. The vertical takeoff and landing capabilities of the shuttles made it possible to land them in close proximity, both physically and chronologically.

The 13th Assault was spread over three landing areas, but they were not all that far apart. The first order of business once the landing was secure would be to link up the three LZs. As soon as the recon platoons and the eight infantry companies were down, equipment shuttles would start landing the Havoc mobile artillery, the ground support for the squadron of Wasp fighter-bombers, and the rest of the 13th's support personnel and supplies. Under field exercise conditions, it was possible to have the entire regiment in position and ready to operate within twenty-five minutes of the first touchdown.

Under combat conditions, that time could be anywhere between fifteen minutes and never.

From somewhere toward the far side of the landing zones, perhaps fifteen hundred meters away, there were several short bursts of automatic fire from wire carbines. Joe heard two distinct sounds, the first—recognizable as the standard Hegemony wire rifle—pitched somewhat lower than the second, the Mark VI Armanoc.

"Keep your heads down," Joe warned his men. "They know we're here."

But there were still no targets apparent in the trees ahead of them.

CHAPTER 2

A good soldier always knows who the good guys and bad guys are. "We" are the good guys. "They" are the bad guys, whoever "they" are. The soldier has to believe that, *know* it so firmly that he never questions the right of what he is doing.

Sometimes knowing is easier than explaining. The "Why We Fight" lectures in garrison assume a lot, but they also include a lot that is not really necessary for the audience. For the outsider, well, the basics do not take long.

More than three thousand years have passed since the first men left Earth for worlds that orbit other stars. One history turned into hundreds of diverging histories as colonies were planted on more and more worlds. Inevitably, some of those colonies failed or lost contact with the rest of mankind. Individual worlds and groups of worlds have faced their distinct crises and triumphs. Civilizations have risen and fallen. Ages golden and dark have dawned and set. Empires and federations have supplanted and been supplanted by independent world states. During the first millennium of the stellar frontier, the human population went through an unprecedented explosion. From a peak population of 7.3 billion on Earth, mankind's numbers swelled to more than 800 billion at the time of the last relatively complete enumeration, 2000 years ago.

In the twenty-seventh century SA (Stellar Age), interstellar travel became rare in the Terran Cluster—generally, those worlds that had been colonized first, about seventy-five planets relatively close to Earth. A great plague traveled from world to world. The mortality rate reached as high as twenty-one percent on some planets. Even after the plague was conquered and immunity bred into the survivors, people in the Terran Cluster were slow to return to interstellar commerce, afraid of the possibility of other plagues.

But in the twenty-eighth century SA, the peoples of the Terran Cluster *did* return to that commerce, in ever-increasing numbers. The fact that no new plagues emerged gradually laid to rest the residual fears. New generations did not have the terrors of their parents and grandparents. But when the peoples of those worlds did venture back into interstellar space, they found changes. The great plague had not stopped travel in *all* of the settled regions of the galaxy.

From roughly 2700 to 2950 SA, the worlds of the Terran Cluster lived independent and peaceful existences. Commerce grew. There were no attempts to unify those worlds by force. When trouble finally came, it came from outside the cluster, from worlds that had not retreated from interstellar travel for a century.

Two empires had grown in the area beyond the Terran Cluster, on the side farther in along the spiral arm, bordering each other as well as the Terran Cluster.

The Schlinal Hegemony had spread across some fifty worlds, densely populated and heavily industrialized, with an average distance of little more than three light-years between inhabited worlds. The Hegemony was a tight dictatorship run from the world of Schline, fairly close to the border between the Hegemony and the Terran Cluster.

The Dogel Worlds were more feudal in nature. In theory, they were a loose confederation of about one hundred worlds, but in actuality, they were tightly controlled by a half-dozen extended families who worked in very close concert. The leaders of these aristocratic clans, the Doges, controlled—

owned—everything on their worlds. Those worlds were, on average, less industrialized and less heavily populated than the worlds of the Schlinal Hegemony, but there were twice as many worlds, giving the two empires a rough parity.

Beginning in the middle of the thirtieth century SA, both the Doges and the Hegemons started trying to upset that parity.

During the first years of war, the worlds of the Terran Cluster paid little attention to the fighting between their neighbors. It did not affect them, and as long as those neighbors were fully occupied with each other, they were not bothering the independent worlds of the Terran Cluster. Stalemate along the frontier between the two empires changed the situation though. Both sides looked for allies . . . or additional subjects. Most of the worlds of the Terran Cluster were heavily populated and nearly as industrialized as the core worlds of the Schlinal Hegemony. And the easiest routes for either the Hegemons or Doges to outflank their enemy ran though the Terran Cluster.

In the next several decades, the Doges and Hegemons expended as much effort on the independent worlds of the Terran Cluster as they did on each other. A dozen worlds fell to one side or the other—to military force if not to diplomatic suasion—and the diplomats of both empires made their rounds of the remaining free worlds, using whatever threats or cajolery they could to try to line those worlds up with their respective masters.

The threat was enough to drive the remaining independent worlds of the Terran Cluster to unite in the Accord of Free Worlds, a military and economic alliance that remained something less than a full union of the planets. For twenty years, the power of the Accord was enough to keep both the Hegemony and the Dogel Worlds away. But in 3002 SA, the Hegemons started a military drive into Accord space. Two lightly populated Accord worlds, Jordan and Porter, were conquered and occupied. There were several other skirmishes, and Accord forces repelled invasions on three other worlds.

Six months later, the Accord was ready to counterattack, to start taking back the worlds that had been lost to the Hegemons.

Lieutenant Zel Paitcher tried to watch everything at once, and it was already giving him a headache. This was his first combat drop as a Wasp pilot, and he had not learned how to partition his attention most efficiently yet. Coming down, he had projected all of his available sensor data on the heads-up display on the canopy—the ships of the fleet in orbit, the rest of his squadron, the landers, and the nearest of the Hegemony satellites. It made for a cluttered screen, and he also tried to keep a constant watch on the various electronic readouts provided on two monitors below the canopy, on the board in front of him.

It left him very little time to actually fly his fighter, but then, until things started happening, the Wasp scarcely required a pilot at all. Still, Zel flew his Wasp as if he were hardwired to it, the machine no more than an immense prosthesis. In the cockpit, it did not matter that Zel was only 150 centimeters tall, or that he weighed less than 50 kilograms soaking wet. Most Wasp pilots were below average in height and weight. A big man would find the control module of a Wasp much too confining for comfort.

The Wasp squadron had dropped ahead of the troop shuttles, but the pilots watched the landers accelerate past them. The Wasps could not be so profligate with energy. Until their ground support was established, the Wasps would be unable to land to get fresh batteries for their antigrav units. At best, they had only a little more than an hour's flight time before they needed to land to recharge or replace depleted batteries. If the landing failed or was aborted after the Wasps were deep in Porter's gravity well, the pilots would have no choice but to land and abandon their fighters. The Wasps would be unable to boost back to orbit without the jet-assisted takeoff rockets that their ground crews would provide for them.

But the Wasps were there, close, ready to defend the shuttles from any ground fire or enemy air response. When the troop shuttles finally started to land, Zel and the rest of the Wasp squadron's Blue flight were orbiting the LZs at an altitude of three thousand meters. The infantry was most vulnerable during the first few minutes of an operation. The Wasps could easily mean the difference between a successful landing and a catastrophe.

The Yellow and Red flights were higher, and farther away laterally, posted to intercept any enemy air attack, and when none appeared, Yellow flight landed for fresh batteries and then was vectored off to strike at the power stations ringing the planet's capital and primary city. Destroying the city's power system was secondary. The main reason for the raid was simply to give the enemy something more immediate to consider than the infantry landing on the plateau.

"Blue three, Blue four, ground support mission," the controller aboard the flagship radioed. "Your vector is zero-two-seven, 120 meters beyond the Alpha-Romeo beacon."

Zel waited until Blue three rogered the mission, then echoed it. He cleared his heads-up display of extraneous clutter and keyed in a transponder display to show the microwave AR beacon.

"Stay close, Zel," Slee Reston, Blue three, said. He was the veteran in this duo. He had seen combat twice before.

"I'm here, Slee. Let's do it."

The Wasps did not depend on aerodynamic design to keep them in the air, merely to minimize the power required to push them through it. If a Wasp lost power in atmosphere, the pilot's only option was to eject. The Wasp had roughly the glide characteristics of a sixteen-ton lead ball. Powered solely by antigrav engines, the shape of the fighter-bombers was dictated by mission . . . and by the whims of their designers. Radar neutral at any frequency, the Wasp was roughly kidney-shaped. The pilot sat in a confined cockpit at the center of the leading edge. In an emergency, the entire cockpit module could be jettisoned and brought to ground by parasail. The antigrav engines and batteries were outboard on either side of the Wasp, in bulging pods. The space between the propulsion units, except for the tiny cubicle that contained the pilot and controls, was given over to payload—with a wide variety of options. At present, the Wasps of Blue flight were each loaded with rockets and five high-speed cannons.

Zel thumbed his weapons selector to the cannons as his target acquisition system locked on, balancing beacon and offset. The 25mm depleted uranium rounds would each separate into five projectiles in flight. With each cannon firing sixty rounds a second, one Wasp could put fifteen hundred hypersonic projectiles—slivers fifteen millimeters long—into an oval five meters by three at a distance of five hundred meters in just five seconds. Not even the best personal armor could withstand that sort of onslaught.

Even as the two Wasps dove toward their initial run, they
received additional targets. Above and behind Zel, another pair
of Wasps were diving to follow them across the front.

Zel pressed the trigger for his first burst just before the
targets were centered on his targeting display. The fraction
of a second of reaction time meant that his first shots were
precisely on target. When Slee pulled up and rolled left after
the run, Zel followed automatically. It was his job to stay right
on Slee's wing, and Zel was *good* at that. He had no chance
to see what damage their cannon had done though. They were
traveling too rapidly, and never came within 350 meters of
their targets. There was no going back to make their own
damage assessment either. They were already moving toward
their next objective.

"I don't want any itchy trigger fingers," Joe warned his men
as they moved into the trees. "Just because you hear shooting
doesn't mean that you have to join in."

Joe felt the itch himself. In the four minutes since they had
jogged away from their shuttle, they had heard gunfire around
the LZ almost constantly, first from one area and then from
another, almost as if by turns. A couple of times, Joe had
heard the telltale sound of wire rounds cutting into the trees
overhead, from behind, but there was still no sign of hostiles
in front of them. The difference in sound between Accord and
Hegemony weapons was obvious to anyone who had heard
both. And the sound made by the cannons that the Wasps
carried was far removed from any of the infantry rifles—
deeper, louder, and far more intense—a metal tornado.

"Keep your heads down," Joe reminded his men. He was
not particularly worried about spent rounds passing overhead.
They were no real threat to net armor or battle helmets.

Once under the cover of the trees on the western flank
of the LZ, the platoon's advance slowed dramatically. Each
squad moved as a semiindependent unit, with one fire team
advancing cautiously while the other was on the ground in
firing position, ready to provide covering fire if necessary.
One team would move forward five to eight meters, then take
defensive positions while the other team leapfrogged them. It
was up to the squad leaders to make sure that they did not
stray too far from the squads on either side of them.

Dawn started to race past. The shadows under the trees lightened. There was little underbrush or ground cover in this forest. There seemed to be no true grass, just the detritus of leaves that had fallen through the years, with moss beneath that. As boots disturbed the surface, a musty smell rose, not especially unpleasant. These trees were native to Porter, different from any that Joe had seen before, but still generically *trees*, woody trunks and branches, green leaves—in this case seven-lobed leaves larger than a spread human hand. The lowest branches were more than three meters above the ground. The only distinguishing feature that Joe had noticed so far was that each tree seemed to rise from the peak of a cone of ochre dirt. Those cones varied from forty centimeters to more than a meter in height, and somewhat more in diameter. They did provide good cover for a prone infantryman. And the copse was dense enough that there always seemed to be one of those cones within two meters—diving distance.

"Okay, Joe, get your men down. This is our line for now," Maycroft said over Echo Company's noncoms' radio circuit.

"Find good spots," Joe told his men. "This is where we stop."

One of the larger tree cones, eighty centimeters high and a meter and a quarter wide, was right in front of Joe. He knelt behind it and looked to either side to watch while the men of his squad found their own locations. His fire team was on the right, with Kam Goff sharing his tree cone. Corporal Frain and his fire team were to the left.

"Get settled in," Joe said once he was satisfied with where his men were.

Joe took a long scan of the squad's front, moving his eyes—and the sensors in his helmet—from side to side, looking farther out with each pass. Although sunrise had already come, there were still deep shadows under the forest canopy. As the air warmed up, the infrared sensors in the battle helmets became less effective. It was summer in the northern hemisphere on Porter, and the plateau was well down in the temperate latitudes. The temperature was already 25 Celsius. By midafternoon, it would probably top 30. Hot. Joe looked more for hints of movement in the distance than for human forms. He still did not spot anything that looked even remotely threatening.

"Where the hell are they?" Ezra Frain asked over the squad frequency.

"Close enough, I imagine," Joe replied. "Cut the chat."

Joe looked around at the positions his men had taken again. Even without specific orders, each of the men was working at improving his cover. They dug in with entrenching tools, piling dirt around the holes as they provided themselves with shallow slit trenches. The longer they stayed in one place, the more care they would take with their defenses, using their idle moments to dig. After one more long look into the forest in front of them, Joe started scraping away ground cover and dirt himself. He worked more slowly than his men though because every few seconds he stopped to look out into the forest, anticipating the arrival of enemy troops.

He had scarcely excavated five centimeters into the ground before Sergeant Maycroft came down the line and flopped to the ground at Joe's side. Maycroft lifted his helmet visor.

"Saddle up," the platoon sergeant said in a voice that sounded infinitely tired. Maycroft always sounded that way in the field, whether or not he actually was tired. "We're moving up another hundred meters, and sliding over to the right to link up with Delta Company."

"Right, Max," Joe replied after he lifted his own visor, getting the microphone away from his mouth. "Any bogeys at all on this side?"

"Nobody's seen any yet, but that could change at any second. Five minutes," Maycroft added before he pulled his visor back down into place. He got up and moved back along the line.

"Put your shovels away," Joe said over the squad frequency once his visor was down again. "We're moving in five."

"Just when I was getting comfortable," Kam Goff whispered at his side, lifting his visor so that the microphone would not pick up his words.

Joe growled softly, then said, "Get that visor down and pay attention, rookie. Unless you want to die a rookie." Goff blanched noticeably at that, but he did pull his visor down quickly.

The order to move out came over the command frequency. Joe got his men up and moving as before, one fire team at a time. "Just like a drill," he whispered. He hoped, fervently, that it would remain that calm. They had worked hard enough at the training drills in the weeks before boarding the ships for the voyage to Porter. In training, even the new men who had never seen real combat had the moves down pat. If only they remembered that training once hostile wire started zipping past their ears.

The platoon had scarcely started moving when Joe and his men heard shooting off to their left for the first time. This was relatively close, but it still did not seem particularly threatening.

Less than two minutes later, the fight did reach them. A rocket-propelled grenade exploded ten meters in front of Joe. The timing was lucky for him. Joe and his fire team had just dropped to the dirt, and Ezra Frain's team had not got to their feet yet. Shrapnel from the RPG whizzed overhead and thunked into tree trunks. Close. Dirt and debris showered the soldiers.

Joe swallowed hard to clear his ears after the noise of the blast. *Too close*, he thought. *We would have been in the kill zone on that one*. He waited until the last of the debris had fallen before he lifted his head enough to look over the tree cone just in front of him. The visor on the Accord battle helmet was alleged to be able to stop anything short of a full burst from a splat gun at close range, but Joe Baerclau had not survived two previous campaigns by taking *any* unnecessary risks.

The forest floor was only a blur in infrared now. Joe switched off that part of his helmet sensors.

"Anyone get a look at where that came from?" he asked, knowing that it was a futile question. There were no replies from the squad. His men knew better than to clutter up the channel with unnecessary negatives.

Joe looked to either side. The rest of the platoon was to his right. Third platoon, the one squad of it that Joe could see, was also down, waiting to see if there would be more than the single grenade.

"Okay, Ez," Joe said after three minutes had passed without more incoming fire. "Move 'em out. Carefully."

There was little need for that warning. Ezra and his fire team moved forward in a crouch, keeping their heads down and their rifles up, ready for instant use. Joe's fire team was ready to lay down covering fire if they got any clue as to where the enemy was. Ezra's fire team was just passing the line of Joe's team when two more RPGs came in. These both exploded behind the lines, back near where Ezra's team had been just seconds before. The men went flat and brought their unprotected hands in under their bodies as the grenades exploded. The blasts were far enough away that their net armor and helmets were able to absorb the force of the shrapnel without difficulty. But two men had the wind momentarily knocked out of them by the impact.

"Crap!" an anonymous voice said over the squad frequency.

Before Joe could call for silence, the squad was under direct fire. Bursts of wire whizzed by, too close to be ignored. Joe turned his head to the side, hoping to see some clue as to the direction the fire was coming from.

"Stay put," Sergeant Maycroft told Joe over the radio. "Delta is moving around behind. They have a fix on the Heggies who have us under fire."

It's good to have someone else do the work for a change, Joe thought. "Don't shoot unless you have a clear target," he warned his men. "We're going to have friendlies moving in behind them. I don't want us to ace any of our own people."

There was one short flurry of fire from third squad, accurate enough to slow down the incoming for a few seconds. Still, nearly five minutes passed before Joe heard heavy fire from Mark VI zippers out in front and the unseen enemy soldiers turned their fire away from 2nd platoon.

"Okay, let's go," Joe told the squad after he had his orders from Maycroft.

This time they moved with their carbines firing, scattering short bursts ahead of them, aiming deliberately low. The men of Delta Company showed up as blue blips on visor displays. The men called those blips DSUs, for "Don't shoot us!"

Joe finally saw his first enemy of the campaign. There was movement eighty meters out, just slightly to Joe's left. At first, he only noticed the movement, camouflage that shifted quickly enough that it could not be natural. Joe directed his fire that way and the figure went down. Joe did not assume that that meant a kill. At eighty meters, the wire rounds of his zipper might have penetrated battle armor. Or they might not. As quickly as Joe had shot, there was even a chance that he had missed his target completely.

"Down!" Joe ordered, leading by example. "Keep moving, but down." Forward movement slowed considerably when it varied between crawling on hands and knees and slithering flat from cone to cone. Joe worked to keep as many of the soil buttresses between him and the spot where he had seen the enemy battle uniform go down.

There was a sudden explosion of gunfire from that area, from both Accord and Schlinal weapons, perhaps forty seconds of confusion. There was little, if any, truly *aimed* fire, but a lot of spools of wire were emptied. Then there was silence. Joe got his men up and rushing forward as soon as they had time to load new spools of collapsed uranium wire in their carbines, even before Maycroft passed the word that Delta Company had cleared the enemy position.

The squad stopped when they reached the four bodies— three of the enemy, and one soldier from Delta. Delta had also taken two Schlinal prisoners, both wounded. They stood back-to-back, helmets off, hands on the tops of their heads. Two soldiers from Delta were watching them, zippers at the ready. Joe walked past the dead Heggies without a glance, but he gave the captured enemy soldiers a close look as he went past them. They were young men, not unlike the men in his own squad. They looked sullen. One of them appeared to be in considerable pain. There was a large blot of wet blood on the left leg of his fatigues.

Kam Goff stopped and stared at the bodies on the ground. He had never seen a dead human before. One of these was in a particularly gruesome condition. His head had been completely severed from his body. A burst of wire had totally chewed away the neck, just below the bottom of the man's helmet.

After a moment Kam lifted his visor hurriedly and vomited.

"Keep moving, kid," Joe said, moving to get between the rookie and the corpse.

"Joe." He recognized Maycroft's voice.

"Yeah, Max," he responded over the noncoms' channel.

"You're getting close to the edge of the trees. Find good spots for your men. We may actually be staying put for a bit this time. We seem to be a little ahead of schedule. Time to let the rest of the regiment catch up."

"Okay by me." Joe switched channels and started positioning his men.

"You come with me, Goff," Joe said after everyone was in place. "I want to take a look out front."

Kam simply nodded. If he suspected that Joe had chosen him just to give him something to think about besides the corpses, he said nothing about it.

They moved away from the rest of the squad, darting quickly from tree to tree, weapons ready. Joe led the way. Kam stayed just behind him and off to the side, far enough away that a single burst of wire would be unlikely to nail both of them. They stopped frequently to look and listen, getting down on their bellies behind whatever cover was handy. The background noise of gunfire had moved well off again. It seemed to be coming from the far side of the LZs now, perhaps as much as four kilometers away.

The end of the wooded area was only thirty meters in front of the squad's positions. As Joe and Kam neared the border, they moved forward on hands and knees. Finally, they took up positions behind a cone at the very edge. Out in front of them was a grassy area at least two kilometers across, with grass that appeared to be waist high, and with only a few isolated trees—of a different variety than those they were under.

There were no enemy troops visible. But then, Joe had scarcely expected to *see* any. That would have been too easy. An entire regiment could hide in that tall grass.

CHAPTER

3

Blue three and four landed in the same tight formation they had held while flying, making their vertical landings within a few meters of their ground crew. Neither Slee nor Zel bothered to get out of their Wasps or even open their canopies. They communicated with their crew chief by radio, assuring him that both fighters were running smoothly. While that conversation was going on, batteries and ammunition were being replaced in both Wasps. The ground crew worked as much by feel as by sight. The matte-black color and the gently flowing contours of the Wasps made them look more like shadows over the ground than physical objects. The canopies reflected no light. The interior of the cockpits and the flight suits and helmets of the pilots were also a dull black. Staring at a Wasp gave some people headaches as they tried to derive reality from the optical illusion that the plane's designers had worked so hard to achieve.

As soon as the hatches were replaced on the battery compartments, the two fighters were back in the air. They had been on the ground for less than seven minutes. While Slee and Zel were climbing away from the LZ, the next pair of Wasps was coming in for servicing. The plan, as long as it worked and was needed, was to have no more than two of the fighters on the ground at one time.

Slee and Zel headed southwest this time, moving low and fast, scarcely above the treetops. Zel was thankful that flying his Wasp and watching for any hint that he was being targeted by enemy radar kept him too busy to pay much attention to how close the ground was. He preferred to have plenty of sky below him. When he followed Slee over the escarpment at the edge of the plateau, he felt more comfortable. The floor of the rift valley was three-hundred meters below the level of the plateau. Slee climbed for even more altitude. There was a trade-off. The lower the fighters flew, the less time any enemy on the ground would have to target them—but the more air there was between the Wasps and enemy fire, the more time their electronic countermeasures (ECM) would have to defeat incoming rockets.

"Targets of opportunity," Slee said with something approaching joy. Later missions would undoubtedly be laid out in greater detail, once the combat planners could identify proper targets, but in the meantime, the Wasps could still be put to good use.

"Preferably targets that don't give back more than they get," Zel said. They spoke over a tight light beam, a form of plane-to-plane communication that was virtually impossible for any enemy to intercept.

The two pilots divided their attention between the displays inside their cockpits and eyeballing the terrain. Neither man was particularly impressed at being in the sky over a world they had never seen before. Human-inhabited worlds did offer a certain measure of variety, but the essentials were generally rather similar or humans would not have settled them in the first place. Habitable worlds were far too plentiful for anyone to bother colonizing one that was marginal, or too far from human norms. Slee concentrated on the left and Zel on the right. Flying at eight-hundred meters, the ground seemed to race past beneath them. There were no roads visible. Even with a population of 750,000 before the Schlinal invasion, the people of Porter had not required a very extensive road net. The ground effect machines they used for most transportation did not need paved surfaces, just vaguely level or gently sloping land. According to the briefing the pilots had received aboard ship, the only real *roads* were to be found within Porter's towns.

"Dust at two o'clock," Zel announced when they were 280 kilometers from the escarpment. "Looks like several vehicles."

"Two, anyway," Slee said after he took a look. "Let's get closer."

"Roger." Even though the Wasp's sensors would almost certainly detect hostile air traffic sooner, Zel looked around to make sure that there were no enemies in the air. Once he was satisfied, he flipped the weapon selector switch to rockets. The rules of engagement for the Wasps were clear. If it was moving toward the 13th and there was no positive identification that it was friendly, destroy it. In any case, it was much too soon for help to come from the residents of Porter City.

Two vehicles. Slee lined up on the one farthest away. Zel took the other.

"I'm picking up active electronics," Slee announced as they closed to within six kilometers of the floater trucks. "Looks like soldiers. Let's take 'em out."

Zel's answer was a short whistle, a near duplicate of the sound made when his target acquisition system announced that it had a lock on a target.

"On lock," Zel announced.

"Ditto," Slee replied. "Hit it."

Two missiles raced forward. The Wasps banked left and moved lower before turning back to the right so that they could watch their rockets hit. Thin trails of smoke dissipated slowly. On the ground, the truck drivers spotted the rockets. In the few seconds they had, one turned left and the other turned right. Both vehicles accelerated violently as their drivers tried to evade the missiles. But even supersonic aircraft had difficulty doing that. Ground vehicles with a maximum speed of one-hundred kilometers per hour had no chance whatsoever.

Zel couldn't keep his eyes off of the rocket trails even after he could no longer pick out the missiles at the far end. His rocket hit almost simultaneously with Slee's, and both trucks erupted in boiling flame and smoke. There was no chance that any of the occupants might have escaped.

"That's a few Heggies who won't be killing our lads up on the hill," Slee said.

Zel did not answer. *Where the blazes is their air power?* he wondered. *They must have fighters of their own.* But he had seen nothing but Accord Wasps so far.

Headquarters for the 13th Spaceborne Assault Team was wherever Colonel Van Stossen happened to be at the moment. At the moment, he was within fifty meters of the front line, and he was not happy.

"Why in blazes are you sitting here with your thumb up your butt, Lieutenant?" he demanded, leaning forward right into the junior officer's face. "You're holding up the entire operation."

"I can't help it, sir," Lieutenant Jacobi replied, barely getting the words out without stammering. "We're taking casualties. Every time we start to move forward, the Heggies zero in on us. I've had three killed and a half dozen wounded already, and we haven't been on the ground thirty minutes." Jacobi was not yet thinking of a career that might be shattered. He had seen combat before, but this was his first time as a company commander, and all he could think about were the men he had lost.

"You've had half the Wasp wing strafing in front of you. If you could pinpoint targets, you'd have Havoc backup. But you're not showing me anything."

Colonel Stossen, the only commander the 13th had ever had, was more frustrated than angry, but that made little difference to the lieutenant commanding Bravo Company. Jacobi merely had the misfortune of being assigned to the sector with the heaviest enemy resistance—and not being equal to the challenge.

"Third platoon is ready to go now," Jacobi said. He gave an order over his helmet radio and thirty men started forward by squads and fire teams while the rest of the company laid down covering fire.

Stossen turned to watch. The first relay of men had not gone ten meters before the sound of Schlinal wire rifles opened up. Third platoon hit the dirt. For several minutes, the firefight raged. The gunfire was continuous but largely ineffective. Stossen and Jacobi both eventually took cover. Some of the enemy fire had started coming uncomfortably close.

"That's what I've been telling you, Colonel," Jacobi said, forgetting the old army wisdom of not saying "I told you so" to a superior officer. "Every damn time. We've even tried *crawling* forward. Same result. 'Cept then they used grenades too."

Stossen turned away from the lieutenant and spoke into his helmet microphone, on a channel that Jacobi's helmet did not receive.

"Sit tight," Stossen said when he had finished. "Be ready to advance in five minutes—your whole company. You're going to get what they used to call a walking barrage."

Jacobi was uncertain what a walking barrage might be, but he suspected that it would be massive. He ordered his people to get as down as they could manage.

Helluva waste of ordnance, Stossen thought while he waited for the artillery. It was not the normal sort of fire mission that the Havoc crews trained for. Usually, the self-propelled howitzers were set against enemy armor and strongpoints, using ammunition sparingly, one shell to a target. With pin-point targeting, that was commonly all that was needed. This was something more primal, *primitive*. The 200mm rounds came in volleys over the front, the first salvo exploding sixty meters north of Bravo Company. Each subsequent volley landed another twenty meters out. The suspended plasma explosives erupted with devastating force, felling trees to a radius of fifteen meters and scorching the ground even farther away.

"Get moving, Lieutenant," Stossen ordered. "Nothing's going to stand up to that."

"Yes, sir," Jacobi replied, stunned by the din and by the visual impact of the barrage. Jacobi's men were well within the area where the first blasts had hit before they noticed that the bombardment had stopped. Dozens of small fires remained burning. Had the trees and grass been drier, the explosions would have set off a wildfire of considerable proportions.

Joe Baerclau closed his eyes, just for a moment, after the start of the artillery barrage. Neither the guns nor their targets were particularly close, but the Havocs made a terrific din even at a distance. There was the explosion of propellant and the high-pitched whine of shells being hurtled from the guns, followed by the broader sound of the exploding round.

I'll never get used to that racket, Joe thought, not for the first time. Back at base, when the 13th's howitzer battalion was on the firing range, the noise could be that intense. He took a deep breath, then opened his eyes in surprise.

"Cinnamon toast?" The words came out so softly that he could scarcely hear them himself. There was certainly no toast around. Even if there was fresh bread available, there were no cooking fires to brown it; and Joe had never come across cinnamon in the army. Joe rubbed a hand in the mossy ground cover near his face and the smell grew stronger . . . and gradually less familiar. But the first scent had triggered childhood memories of waking in the morning to that aroma, and hurrying out to the kitchen to get his toast while it was still hot. He almost never thought about his childhood anymore, not even in his dreams. When his memories did travel back that far, it was more like viewing someone else's past than his own. His years of military service, and most especially the combat he had seen, had drawn a wall between his notion of self and memories of how he had gotten to the present. Five years in uniform might as easily have been five decades. His life before the army seemed that far in the past. That was what made this so surprising.

"Something's sure getting the hell pasted out of it," Kam whispered next to Joe. Baerclau turned to look at him.

"Just as long as it's not us on the receiving line." Joe was uncertain how Goff would turn out. Joe had taken both new men into his fire team so that he would have an easier time keeping track of them. Al Bergon seemed absolutely steady. He took his secondary duties as squad medic seriously without neglecting his primary function as a rifleman. But Goff . . . Joe just could not make up his mind.

"Yeah." Kam laughed nervously. "Yeah."

"Just take it easy." Joe shifted around, trying to get comfortable. "We're here to draw attention."

"Those guns'll sure do that," Kam said.

Joe took a moment to scan the field of grass in front of their positions again, looking for any indication—visual or electronic—that Hegemony soldiers might be moving in for an attack on this section of the perimeter. There was a gentle breeze moving from left to right, bending the tops of the grass in an easy rhythm. *Anyone crawling through that grass ought to disturb that rhythm,* Joe told himself. There were no electronic signatures out there, but he was far from convinced that the instruments in his helmet would definitely pick up anything. They were *supposed* to, but in Joe's experience, they worked only slightly more than half of the time, even in training exercises. The electronics the Schlinal soldiers used in their helmets were shielded almost as well as those that the Accord used.

"Sarge, how bad will it get?"

Joe lifted his visor this time. He wanted Goff to see his face. "There's no way to know that up front, kid. However bad it gets, we'll do our job. We have to keep the Heggies here, keep them from going off to reinforce any of the other worlds in this sector." *Don't scramble your brains worrying about things you can't change,* he thought.

"Our people will come for us, won't they? They won't just abandon us here?"

"They'll come," Joe assured him. "We don't have so many troops that they can afford to write off an entire assault team."

"But if they *don't* come, then what?"

"Then we'll do the best we can for as long as we can." *Shut up and watch your fire lanes, kid.* "Just take it easy. We've only been here an hour. It'll be four days, maybe more, before our pickup shows. It takes time. They're not going to forget about us."

If they don't show up? Joe pulled his visor back into place and looked out at the grass again. If the main fleet failed to come, did not cover the evacuation, the 13th would be in deep trouble, and Joe knew it. The shuttles would be sitting ducks lifting off, easy targets for anyone with a shoulder-fire missile. And if there were enemy fighters in the air . . . They might be lucky if ten percent of the regiment made it back to the ships.

But that would not happen. At least, it had never happened before.

"Our orders are to hold until we're relieved or recalled," Joe said softly, talking only to himself now. He did not like to think about the price of failure.

He spotted movement behind the line and off to the side, and turned to look. He recognized Lieutenant Keye by the way he moved. One soldier in combat kit looked pretty much like any other. There were no bold badges of rank for an enemy to target.

Keye dropped to the ground at Joe's side and handed him a small pack.

"Take your squad out a klick," Keye said without preamble. "Plant a line of bugs across the company front. You know the drill."

Joe did know the drill. He gathered his men and split the pack of recon bugs among the squad. Once activated, the thumb-sized sensors would detect sound, electromagnetic emissions, and, at very close range, the body temperature of a large warm-blooded animal—or human. The bugs had transmitters with a three-kilometer range to send back their readings.

Using hand signs and soft commands over the squad frequency, Joe got the men moving forward in a skirmish line, with plenty of space between men. They walked slowly, rifles at the ready, stopping after almost every step to listen, and to look into the grass ahead of them. Grass, no matter how tall, would not stop a burst of wire. And it could hide an enemy or his mines.

Grass. The tallest patches reached five centimeters above Joe's web belt, but he was the shortest man in his squad. The tops of the stalks were brown and going to seed, but lower, the stems were still green, and moist. The night's dew had not been dried yet by the sun. Joe's boots were soon wet from wading through the grass.

Eighty meters out from the line, the squad crossed a dirt track through the field. It was scarcely wide enough to have been made or used by humans, but Joe held his men up until they had a chance to scan for booby traps or any indication that humans had used the path. Satisfied finally that the trace was animal, Joe ordered his men across. They crossed it quickly, then went prone in the grass on the other side, just in case.

"Okay, I guess we're clear," Joe whispered after a moment. There had been no clatter of gunfire, nor any other sounds from in front of them. "Let's get moving." He would not have routed his men *along* that trail even if it had been headed precisely in the right direction. The easy way could too easily be lethal.

Joe was the first on his feet, scanning the grass tops quickly but thoroughly, looking for any hint of unnatural movement. He had his carbine up and stared across the sights, ready to fire if he even *thought* that he might have a target. He could feel his hands sweating on the stock of his zipper. His hands sweated ferociously when he was nervous, and he was always nervous in combat. Joe's thumb reached for the carbine's fire-selector switch, to make certain that the safety was off.

He suddenly realized that he was hearing no firing at all, not rifles, not artillery or Wasp munitions, not even in the distance. *Somebody call the battle off and forget to tell us?* He didn't bother to laugh at his own joke.

In any case, the silence was short-lived. Joe had taken no more than three steps when he heard rifle fire, well off to the right. Still, he paused for a moment, and held the squad back until he could assure himself that the fire was getting no closer. Just as he started the squad forward again, a shadow passed overhead. Joe looked up and saw the familiar silhouette of a Wasp fighter going toward the source of the gunfire. The Wasp opened up with its cannons, two very short bursts. The rifle fire stopped.

Joe looked up again to see the Wasp bank left, climbing through a tight circle.

Then he saw a rocket trail climbing toward the Wasp.

"Down!" he barked over the squad channel. Joe dove forward, landing on forearms and legs in a fluid motion that brought his rifle to his shoulder even though he had nothing to shoot at. A wire carbine could never bring down a missile, even if a rifleman could hit something moving that fast.

The Wasp pilot hit his throttles and started maneuvering violently in an attempt to avoid the rocket. Joe leaned sideways to watch. His view was partially obstructed by the grass, but he did see light reflecting off of the silvery particles of chaff that the Wasp pilot dropped in an attempt to confuse the missile's guidance system.

For an instant, Joe thought that the Wasp was going to escape. The missile seemed to lose its lock. The Wasp pulled almost straight up, then spiraled back on itself, two-hundred meters above the missile and going in the opposite direction. Silently, Joe urged the pilot on with all the fervor he could muster.

Then the missile righted itself and streaked toward the Wasp again. The pilot continued trying to evade until the last second, but the rocket caught it dead center from below. On the ground, Joe could not tell if the pilot had ejected at the last instant before the missile hit, or if the explosion had blown the cockpit module clear of the rest of the fighter. The parasail opened, but that was automatic.

"Baerclau?"

"Yes, Lieutenant," Joe replied over the command channel. "I see it."

"How far are you from where that pod'll land?"

"Hard to say yet, sir. The way the wind's blowing, it could be a couple of klicks, over toward Delta Company, maybe past them."

The rest of the Wasp fell, scattering over an area more than a kilometer in diameter. There was little in the way of flames after the primary explosion. The warheads on the Wasp's rockets had exploded when the missile hit. Some of the shells for its cannons had also cooked off, but most of the fire was out before the wreckage hit the ground. A few chunks of superheated metal started grass smoldering for a moment, but there was little danger of a wildfire. The grass was too damp.

"Go for it," Keye said. "We don't want to leave him for the Heggies. Forget the bugs until you can tell if that pilot's alive. I'll clear with Delta so you don't get shot by our people."

"Roger." *I sure as hell hope you clear us*, Joe thought. The idea of being hit by friendly fire could send a chill down any man's spine.

There was no time to waste for long reflection. If there were Schlinal forces around, they would undoubtedly be hurrying toward the escape pod as well. It might be a close race.

"Ezra, we're going after the flyguy. Move your team out first. I want you on point for this. Anyone else, it might take too long."

"On my way," Ezra replied. He sounded calm.

The Wasp's escape pod did not stay in the sky for long, but every second that it was in the air, it traveled farther away from Joe and his men. It came down in the open grass, far from any of the isolated trees. For a couple of minutes after the module landed, the parasail continued to flap. Although Joe could not be certain, it appeared that the chute might be dragging the escape module. If the pilot was alive, he couldn't be in any condition to trip the release that would sever the lines.

Joe's squad moved in a loose wedge now. Ezra Frain was out in front. The two other men from his fire team trailed ten meters back and ten meters apart. The rest of the squad came in a third line. The spacing between the last two lines was the same as that between the first two, but Joe kept the lateral distance between his men closer to five meters. Although he knew that there might be enemy soldiers in the grass, or concealed by one of the isolated trees in the field, he did not expect to run across mines or other booby traps. The Schlinal garrison on Porter could not possibly have anticipated the landing—or that it might take place on the plateau—and there had been no time since the landing for enemy troops to devise traps or bring mines from barracks or armory.

But the 13th would not be able to count on that for long.

After five minutes of hurrying through the tall grass, Joe began to think that his initial estimate of the distance to the escape pod might have been grossly short. The parasail had finally quit flapping in the breeze. Now it lay like an immense target across the top of the grass.

"Keep your eyes open for Heggies," Joe reminded the squad. "If there are any around, they'd probably like nothing better than to nab a flyguy."

"I know," Ezra said. He was beginning to sound short of breath. Trying to maintain a rapid walk through thick grass carrying more than thirty kilograms of gear could do that to anyone. The men in the Accord's SATs had to be in good condition to start with, and their training regimen ensured that no one became flabby, but there were still limits.

A few minutes later, Ezra reported, "I have the pod in sight."

"Any sign of the pilot?" Joe asked.

"Negative. I'm looking at the bottom of the pod from about two-hundred meters. But at least there's no sign of hostiles."

"Set up your team on the far side of the pod. We'll take the near side. Al, you check on the pilot." Joe had little hope that there would be anything for Bergon to do. He assumed that the pilot must be dead. But they had to know for certain, one way or the other.

The shooting started just as Ezra and his men moved around the capsule, still some thirty meters away from it. The metallic whizzing sound came from farther away from the Accord perimeter, but it was well aimed. The sound of wire fragments hitting helmets and visors carried clearly, like hail striking aluminum siding. At any distance, there was little to hear when those tiny projectiles hit resilient body armor . . . or puncturable flesh.

Joe didn't bother to dive for cover this time. He started firing short bursts of wire over the side of the escape pod, toward where he thought the enemy shooters were. The rest of his fire team joined in. The men did move farther apart, but they kept advancing—more rapidly now. They went straight for the pod. That, at least, offered some cover—as long as they chose the correct side to shelter behind.

"Ezra, talk to me," Joe said.

There was a maddening delay before Ezra said, "It's kinda hard right now," through obviously clenched teeth. Joe had no doubt that Ezra was wounded. The voice was a sure giveaway.

"Tod, Wiz. What shape are you in?" Joe demanded.

"Tod's hurt, not too bad, I think," Wiz Mackey said. "His helmet's bust though."

"What about you?"

"I've felt better, but I'm not bleeding, and I don't think anything's broke."

"Can you get to Ezra?"

"I'll get him," Al volunteered.

"Check on that pilot first, Bergon," Joe said. "Wiz?"

"I'm already moving toward him."

"Stay put," Ezra said. "I'll come to you. I'm not dead."

While he talked on his helmet radio, Joe had reloaded his zipper, shucking the empty wire coil and inserting another twenty meter spool. The carbine's power cell was good for two hours of continuous firing, but twenty meters of wire lasted no more than ten seconds on automatic fire.

Al Bergon crawled around the Wasp pod, snaking on his belly to get to the canopy on the far side.

"Can't tell if he's alive or not," Bergon said after he got his first look inside the cockpit. "He's unconscious at least. How do you open these things?"

"Front end of the canopy, about twenty centimeters down, there's a panel that lifts out, and a handle underneath," Joe said. "Either side of the cockpit. If you can't reach the one on the low side, you'll have to try the one on top. Let us know. If you have to go for the exposed handle, we'll lay down covering fire."

A moment later the others heard a grunt over the radio. "Damn, it's going to be close," Bergon said. "I think . . ." There was a pause, and then, "I got the panel up. Now, if I can get my hand under there."

Joe waited, almost holding his breath. He heard the sound of the latch releasing before Bergon confirmed that he had it open.

"The whole canopy slides backward, if it isn't too badly damaged," Joe said.

"It's moving," Bergon said. Then, another "Damn!"

"Now what?" Joe demanded.

"Stuck. I don't know if I can wiggle in enough to . . . Yeah. I've got my head and arms in. Jeez, there's blood all over in here."

"Is he?" There was no need for Joe to finish the question.

"There's a pulse," Bergon said. "It's weak, but it's there."

"Can you get him out by yourself or do you need help?"

"I could use a hand," Al admitted.

"Hang tight. Mort, see if you can get around there without getting your ass shot off."

"I'll get there. I'm very attached to my ass. Never go anywhere without it."

Joe raised up and started spraying wire over the top of the capsule, more interested in suppressing enemy fire than in finding any targets. There would be time for that later, once the pilot—and his own casualties—had been recovered and treated.

Mort scooted around the capsule.

"See if you can drag the canopy back a little more," Al told him. "Maybe both of us together."

After a few grunts and curses, Al said, "There, I think that's enough. I'll open his harness. Be careful when we pull him out. He survived the rocket, I don't want to lose him to the rescue."

"Oh, crap." That was Mort. "He can't have much blood left inside him."

"Enough to raise a pulse," Bergon replied. "That's all we can ask for right now. Careful there. Let's slide him around . . . Hold on, his foot's caught on something. I'll have to get in there again."

"Hurry it up," Joe told them. "We've got company coming." He switched channels. "Lieutenant, we have hostiles moving our way, two hundred meters out on a bearing of 325 degrees from the capsule, at least ten men."

"You'll have help," Keye promised. "Hold one." When he returned to the channel, he said, "Two Wasps coming in right now."

Ezra's fire team moved closer to the rear end of the escape pod. Ezra was moving with difficulty, but he was moving on his own. Neither Tod Chorbek nor Wiz Mackey showed any lingering effects from being shot. The wire had come from too far away to penetrate, though the side of Tod's helmet was badly cracked.

Slee and Zel came in fast, wingtip to wingtip. They triggered their cannons as soon as they saw their targets, riding their guns harder than the shooting instructors recommended. Rules went out the canopy when Wasp pilots were protecting one of their own who had been shot down—or the mudders who were trying to save him.

"Come on, you bastards," Zel muttered under his breath. Out in the tall grass, the enemy soldiers were clearly visible. Even though they had dropped to the ground, they had nowhere to hide. The open patches where they had flattened the grass or pushed it aside marked them as clearly as spaceport beacons.

Blue three and four came in low, below fifty meters at the bottom of their strafing run. Then they pulled out and turned through a wide climbing loop to the right to come in again from a different angle. They could see the enemy, and the cockpit of the downed Wasp was there to remind them where the friendlies were.

The cannons of the two Wasps shredded the tall grass more efficiently than a scythe. Under concentrated fire, the Schlinal soldiers caught in the bursts were shredded almost as thoroughly. Body armor could not stand up to the deadly darts.

On the ground, Joe and his men instinctively ducked when the Wasps opened fire. The sound of the 25mm cannons was almost deafening, even under battle helmets. But Joe could not stay down. He lifted his head to watch as the strafing mowed a corridor thirty meters wide through the grass . . . and riddled the enemy soldiers.

"If there's anyone left alive out there, maybe we can get some prisoners," Joe told Lieutenant Keye after the second pass. "Interested?"

"Only if you can get to them in a hurry, after the Wasps pull out."

"Tell them it looks like they've done the job, sir."

Joe went around the capsule as the two Wasps climbed higher above the field. The downed pilot was lying on his back, still unconscious—but still alive. Al Bergon was kneeling over him, putting pressure sealers over several open wounds.

"He needs more help than I can give him, Sarge," Al said when he saw Baerclau standing over him. "Don't know though. Even carrying him back to the lines might be more than he can take."

"We've got to try. Do what you can for him. I'm going out to see if anyone survived in that lot out there." He nodded toward the grass that had been mowed down. "Mort, you and Kam come with me. The rest of you, start back to the lines with the pilot as soon as possible, even if we're not back."

CHAPTER
4

The three soldiers moved fast now. In full combat gear, none of them were likely to come anywhere near the standards of athletic competition for the two-hundred meter race, even without the tall, clinging grass, but they ran as fast as they could. Joe didn't want to give any surviving Hegemony soldiers time to recover their wits after the Wasp attack.

I'm getting too old for this, Joe thought. He couldn't have spoken the words out loud on a bet. Running through that grass in full gear took all of his air, and begged for more.

The two Wasps remained overhead, circling now, as the pilots watched over Joe and his companions. Kam Goff was the only one on the ground who really noticed the Wasps though. He was young, and considerably larger than his sergeant. He felt the effort of running with so much extra weight, but he was further from his limits than Joe Baerclau was.

If they spot anyone, I hope they let us know, Kam thought. That was better than occupying his mind with fear. He already had more than enough of that. Except while the shooting was going on. Kam had not realized that yet. While he was shooting, or being shot at, there had been no fear at all. He had simply done his job the way he had been trained.

The three men kept as much space between them as they could until they converged on the area where the enemy shooters had been. Goff, moving just a little faster than the others, was the first to spot bodies. He stopped short, still ten meters from the nearest. The body was barely recognizable as human. It had been mutilated badly, with both legs severed—one leg simply did not exist any longer. Only the man's head appeared untouched. His battle helmet had been blown off, but it *had* protected the head. The dead soldier's eyes were wide open. Kam fancied he saw a look of utter horror on the dead face.

That was when he started to vomit.

"Turn around and get down on your knees," Joe Baerclau said in his "command" voice. By this time he was standing right at Goff's side. He hauled in a difficult breath. "Don't present a target."

Joe and Mort Jaiffer conducted a quick search of the area around the section of grass that had been chopped apart by the strafing, looking for signs that any of the enemy had escaped—and might be lurking, waiting for a chance to ambush them. There were no obvious signs that anyone had crawled away from the carnage though, at least not far.

One Schlinal soldier had apparently survived for a minute or two. He had pulled himself nearly three meters from where he had been struck. But he was dead by the time Joe checked on him. There were twelve bodies. No survivors.

Joe reported that news to Lieutenant Keye. "We're heading back now," he added. "The rest of the men are already on the way in with the flyguy. Couple of my men may have some minor injuries too."

"The doc's already on link to your medic," Keye said. "Get back in here as quickly as you can. I'll get someone else to plant those bugs."

One small favor, Joe thought as he started back toward the lines with Kam and Mort.

Even with the sophisticated radio links available to everyone in the 13th, there were inevitable delays in communications. Colonel Stossen could hardly function if he received reports directly from each platoon or squad that did something, or did not do something. Only company commanders and the Wasp and Havoc squadron commanders reported directly to the colonel, except under extraordinary conditions. Even then there were often times when there was simply too much for the colonel to hear it all immediately. That was the purpose of having staff officers, to gather the reports and decide which the colonel needed to hear immediately.

The early stages of an invasion were like that. Too much happened too quickly for the commander to stay instantly on top of everything. Once combat was joined, even on a piece-meal basis, priorities could shift, again and again. Sometimes, even a top-notch officer simply had to sit down and try to figure out just what was going on.

Colonel Stossen was sitting with his back against one of the conelike mounds of dirt that surrounded every tree in the forest to the north and west of the LZs. He had his mapboard on his lap, and his executive and operations officers were kneeling across from him.

"Okay, just where the hell are we?" Stossen asked. The question was not completely rhetorical. It was only an hour and fifteen minutes after the first shuttle had touched down, and the colonel's voice was already hoarse. Like many officers in senior field commands, Stossen had already learned that he no longer really fought his battles, he *talked* them.

"Well, we finally got George Company back to the perimeter," Dezo Parks, the ops officer, said.

"What?" Stossen looked up. "Where were they?"

Parks shook his head. "I'm not quite sure. I don't think *they* know. Somehow, they got out of their landers and started out in the wrong direction—double time. They were nearly two klicks from the section of perimeter they were supposed to establish before Vickers figured out that something was screwy." Like nearly a quarter of the men in the 13th, Dezo was from Bancroft. He had recruited a good percentage of the men from his homeworld, and had transferred to the Accord Defense Force with them.

"Vickers, the new man." That was no question. Stossen might not know every enlisted man in the 13th, but he did know all of the officers, well enough to conjure up an image and a rough idea of their background.

"New to the 13th," Lieutenant Colonel Terrence Banyon, the executive officer, said. "He's had nearly five years of service, four-plus with his homeworld defense force and six months with the ADF training regiments before he came to us." Banyon was from Ceej, Tau Ceti IV, as were Stossen and about thirty other members of the 13th.

"Five years and still a lieutenant?" Stossen asked.

"He was a captain in his HDF," Banyon said quickly. "He took a voluntary reduction to escape a waiting list when he transferred to us. He's good, just a bit overanxious for his first action."

"We'll get back to him later," Stossen said. It would not do to get completely sidetracked with something nonessential just now. They had already wasted too much time, particularly since no harm had been done by the mistake.

"What about that flyer? He going to make it?"

"Too close to call," Banyon said. "They got him into a trauma tube in one piece, but it was a near thing. Doc *thinks* he'll pull through, but no guarantees."

Stossen nodded slowly. A trauma tube and its medical nanotech devices could work wonders, but there were still limits.

"What else is going on?"

Dezo Parks leaned closer to the mapboard. "We've consolidated our initial perimeter, more or less on schedule. Only scattered resistance, nothing very concerted. You know as much about that as I do." They had hoped for an unopposed landing, and had come closer to it than they had any right to expect. "Apparently, the Schlinal forces on-world don't maintain any combat aircraft on anything approaching ready alert. As of five minutes ago, there hadn't been a single report of enemy air activity—from our people down here or from the monitors back in CIC. That's a definite plus for us. We're a considerable distance from any Schlinal garrison, as we hoped we'd be. As far as we've been able to determine, the Hegemony has strictly an occupation force on Porter, and they stick close to the centers of population. Those we've come across must be part of the force used to control the people around Maison, the only real town here on the plateau."

"Our objective for tomorrow," Stossen commented. "Any word on enemy strength there yet?"

"Nothing substantive," Banyon said. "The latest estimate is that the maximum size of the garrison in and around Maison must be below two thousand."

"In other words, intelligence wants us to think that we at least outnumber the Heggies stationed up here on the plateau," Parks said.

"As if that matters," Banyon replied. "We came into this assuming a total enemy garrison of at least ten thousand on Porter, nearly five times what we have. They may have a lot more than that. Even if they were all stationed in Porter City, five-hundred klicks from us, they could probably move the whole circus to the plateau by midnight."

"They may not go that far, but there is enemy movement," Parks said. "Two convoys have started out from Porter City. They've got too much active anti-air with them for the Wasps to take them on, in daylight anyway. I ordered our planes out of range after a couple of preliminary strikes against the advance party for one of the columns. They'll continue to monitor the movement. The Wasps and CIC."

Stossen nodded. That was something that had been decided well in advance. It would be foolish to waste the Wasps in a daylight attempt to stop a major troop movement when the fighters made such easy targets. If it did become necessary to expose the Wasps to that level of danger, it had better be for a more critical advantage.

"If they're moving on the ground instead of in the air, it may mean that they don't have the transport. Or it might mean nothing more than a lack of any intelligence on our numbers yet," Stossen said. "As soon as we can tell which route up the escarpment they'll take, we'll dispatch a few Wasps and Havocs to contest the climb. Soon as it's full dark, we can sneak a couple of Wasps in for hit-and-run strikes as well."

"There aren't many decent routes up, for vehicles, at least," Parks observed. "We can pretty much deny them those without too much danger to our people."

"Only temporarily," Stossen said. "We'll slow them down, of course, maybe force them to use air transport instead of ground, but we *want* engagement, remember." *Limited* engagement, if possible. "And we want to be able to cover their approach without spreading ourselves all over ten thousand square kilometers of this plateau. If they decide we're isolated up here, their warlords might pull some of them off to back up the defense on Devon."

"We do need to be able to get down into the valley ourselves," Banyon added.

"We're not here to liberate Porter, Terry," Stossen said. "Just to give them some hope." *But how will they feel knowing that we've come and gone, abandoning them to the enemy again?* He didn't share that thought with the others.

"Tighten your straps, lads," Gunnery Sergeant Eustace Ponks told his crew. "We're finally going to get moving." As usual, Ponks spoke louder than he needed to. His hearing had been moderately affected by his years of work in Havocs. Broad across the shoulders, and with a bulky torso, Ponks had found a home in the Havoc self-propelled artillery. With short, bowlegged legs, he looked taller sitting down than he did standing up.

" 'Bout time," Simon Kilgore, his driver, said. "Hair's been standing on the back o' my neck since we landed."

"Course is zero-two-seven, Sy," Ponks said. "It looks like we'll get to see that patch we blasted the hell out of."

At a range of ten kilometers, the 200mm howitzer of a Havoc could drop a round within a shell's length of its aiming point, even if the Havoc was moving at its sixty-kilometer-per-hour maximum speed. Extend the range to twenty kilometers, and it could still be accurate to within three meters—ninety percent of the time. Since the suspended plasma of its munitions had a primary blast radius of ten meters, that was usually more than sufficient.

The Havoc was self-propelled artillery, not a tank. The barrel could be elevated or depressed, but the entire machine had to be pointed roughly at the target. To minimize the vehicle's height, the gun barrel could only be rotated six and one half degrees to either side of the center line. The Havoc was nine meters long, three wide, and (except for the muzzle of the barrel at full elevation) no more than two meters high. Its treads were powered by separate engines. The engines and the tanks and converters for the hydrogen fuel occupied most of the front half of the carriage. The gun commander and driver sat almost precisely at the midpoint of the vehicle's length, one on either side of the barrel, at the front of the low turret. The other two members of the crew, gunner and loader, had positions much closer to the rear, and lower. Above and behind them was the ammunition bay.

"When do we get something real to shoot at?" Karl Mennem, the gunner, asked. "I'd feel better knowing."

"I think we're just going out to plow a few hectares of prairie this time. Just be glad there's nothing close enough to shoot back," Ponks said as the Havoc rolled away from its support van. "We get this baby shot out from under us and we're *mudders* for the rest of the campaign, and if you were good enough to hit anything with a rifle, they wouldn't have you ridin' around on your ass."

Karl grumbled at the flagrant canard. He was a sharpshooter. It did not matter if he was firing a 200mm cannon or a slingshot. He quickly achieved deadly accuracy with any aimed weapon that he picked up.

It was not at all true that a ride in a Havoc could scramble an egg that the hen hadn't laid yet. The suspension in the gun carriage was almost perfect, especially for the gun itself, which was gyroscopically stabilized. To hit a target at a distance while the gun was moving at speed, that was essential. While the men did not rate the same level of accommodation, they were not jostled about so much that they could not do their jobs efficiently—and for long periods. There was even a certain amount of sound insulation between the men and the engines. A 200mm cannon could not be muffled, but the constant engine noise would have been harder on ears. The men still had to communicate through helmet radios, and after a time, more than two thirds of all men assigned to the big guns suffered some hearing loss, at least in certain frequencies.

The men who rode the guns preferred to be moving when there was any chance that an enemy might be shooting. Counterbattery fire would be at least as accurate as the fire the Havocs loosed. The guns had to keep on the move or become wasted hulks, like clamshells lying open on the sand.

Five other Havocs moved away from the staging area with Ponks's "Fat Turtle"—the name written on the side of the turret next to the commander's hatch. Within the defensive perimeter that the 13th had established, the six guns moved in single file, but as soon as they passed through the infantry line, the

Havocs fanned out, giving themselves as much maneuvering room as possible. The six gun commanders worked hard to avoid showing any sort of regular formation, any *pattern* to their spacing or movement. Pattern was the most deadly trap of all. Once they were well out from the rest of the 13th, the six Havocs put as much as a kilometer between themselves and their closest neighbors. There was no need for the guns of a battery to stay close together for fire missions.

"Talk to me, Control," Ponks muttered once they were beyond the perimeter. The Havoc was just a gun. Its targets were always out of sight of the crew. They needed others to provide target data, spotters on the ground or in Wasps, or information provided directly from the Combat Information Center on the flagship in orbit.

"You're doing fine, Basset two," the voice in his headset replied. The Havoc batteries all had the names of dog breeds, a pun that went back nearly three and a half millennia: "Cry Havoc and let slip the dogs of war."

"Nobody ever tells us nothin'," Ponks complained after switching off his transmitter link to CIC for a moment. When he got back on the channel, he asked, "Is there any sign at all of enemy artillery or armor on this plateau?"

"That's a negative, Basset two, no tube artillery or tanks. If they're around, they're staying under cover." He didn't need to add that a Havoc could fall victim to any infantryman with an antitank rocket. The Havoc carriages were only armored enough to stop small-arms fire. To try and put enough armor on them to stop anything more powerful, the Havocs' speed would have been compromised. They used speed as their first line of defense.

With luck, it would take time for the Schlinal garrison to draw antitank weapons from their armories. Rockets probably would not be in much demand in their normal routines as occupation force.

Joe Baerclau sucked on a peppermint-flavored stimtab and marveled at the smiling face of luck. None of his men had been injured badly enough to take them out of action, even temporarily. Ezra's wounds had been the most serious, and even he had nothing more than badly flayed skin on the back of his left hand and a dozen small, though admittedly painful, bruises and tiny cuts. The medics had even ruled out the possibility of cracked ribs, though they had feared initially that there might be several. Ezra had been dosed with a systemic analgesic and the bruises and abrasions had been smeared with a salve larded with medical nanobots to hurry along the healing process.

The pilot they had rescued was another matter, but he would live. Joe and his men had hung around the first aid station long enough to hear that. Now, the flyer was being evacuated to the hospital ward in one of the troop ships in orbit. The campaign was over for him—and perhaps his flying days as well.

Might be a bit of luck at that, Joe thought. He was under no delusion that this campaign would be easy. While it had not been bruited about that they were merely a diversion, Joe—and most of the other senior noncoms (and even some junior officers)—had guessed that they were considered expendable to assist the main action on some other world.

Joe sat hunched up on the ground, arms clasped around his knees. His helmet was on the ground at his side, upended so he would hear any call on the radio. He had stripped off his web belt and backpack. The loss of all of that weight made him feel almost as if he would float away. He had eaten a meal pack and drunk half a canteen of water. He felt rested now, at ease. He sat with his eyes closed, but he did not sleep. He already felt the exhaustion that combat always brought, but it was not an exhaustion that brought sleep. Not for Joe. Soon enough, it would be back to the lines and whatever might come next, but Lieutenant Keye had okayed a short break. Joe's squad had gone through some of the morning's heaviest action, and there was no immediate need for them to hurry back to the grind. For the moment, nearly the entire perimeter was quiet. The 13th had faced nothing but small unit actions so far, no enemy units larger than platoon strength.

"Sarge?"

Joe opened his eyes slowly and lifted his head. Kam Goff stood a meter away, helmet in hand, waiting to see if he would respond.

"What is it, kid?"

Kam squatted next to Joe before he spoke. "I was scared before."

"We were all scared. That's what combat is all about. The drill is to do your job anyhow. Don't freeze up and don't go berserk." Joe hardly had to think to spout a full load of clichés. Each phrase had become trite because it was accurate. And clichés were easier for a stressed-out mind to accept than novel ways of saying the same thing.

"I never saw anybody dead before today, and sure not all chopped to shit like that. I just ain't used to it."

"You ever *do* get used to it, it ever gets to where it *don't* bother you, you don't belong in my squad."

That seemed to stump Goff for a moment. His mouth opened, but he didn't speak for a moment. Then, slowly, he nodded. "I see. I get to like it, I wouldn't want me around either."

"Just keep on, keep up on yourself. It may get worse—probably will. This morning wasn't nothing. But the first time, well, you don't know what to expect. Now you do. More of the same. Maybe a lot more of the same, now and then."

Once more, Goff hesitated for a long time before he spoke. "I don't know if any of that makes me feel better or not, Sarge."

There was no humor in Joe's laugh. "Just don't think it to death. Come on. It's about time to be getting back. Maycroft'll be lookin' for us."

When Joe put his helmet on, the other members of the squad, all sitting around the grove, got the message. They stood and put their gear back on. It was time to go back to the war.

CHAPTER
5

The new spy satellites that the Accord fleet had deployed gave the Havoc gun commanders real-time video of their target, along with the hard data they needed to lay their rounds where they wanted them. The intelligence analysts of CIC had decided that they had identified the main barracks of the Hegemony troops in the town of Maison. The six guns of Basset Battery were scattered through heavy forest between eleven and sixteen kilometers from those buildings. Their support vehicles stayed farther away, but close enough to the guns to replenish ammunition stocks, just in case the battery should get that busy.

In Basset two, Eustace Ponks could see only one of the other guns, and it was a kilometer away, across one of the clearings that dotted the forest.

"Okay, Karl, give me an extra fifty meters this time," Ponks said after watching their first shot strike well short of the wall surrounding the target buildings.

"Jimmy says he'll goose it personal," Mennem replied. Jimmy was Jimmy Ysinde, the crew's loader.

"Jimmy'd goose anything that stood still for him," Ponks said. "Just get the round over that wall. You shot this bad on the range, the lieutenant would have you scrubbing latrines for a month."

"Must be the atmosphere, Sarge, or maybe the go-juice." Karl was cursing inwardly. He had never missed any target that badly. The Havoc's fire-control computers took everything into account, including atmospheric pressure and humidity, anything that might affect the flight of a round. And with exact positions being calculated through the assistance of target acquisition satellites, missing a target by fifty meters was inexcusable.

Before Ponks could answer, the second round had been fired. In the crew compartment, there was incredible noise, but little noticeable recoil. The gun's gyroscopic stabilizing system absorbed virtually all of the shock of firing.

With no enemy counterbattery fire to worry about yet, the Havocs were shooting from a halt. Still, the guns moved after every shot. It was that random movement that had brought Basset two within sight of another howitzer.

Simon Kilgore had Two moving almost before the round cleared the muzzle. He backed the Havoc away from its firing position and turned around a large tree, then started off at a 60-degree angle from the line of flight of the last round. Simon could drive his gun with the best. "Give me a millimeter clearance on either side, and I'll take it anywhere," he liked to brag. On better days, he got more extravagant. "I can make her dance around a dozen eggs without cracking a shell."

Ponks reserved one eye for his periscopes, the other for the damage assessment monitor. There was no way to actually *see* the shell coming down toward its target. The view that Ponks was watching was relayed from a satellite cruising three-hundred kilometers overhead. While he might be able to identify an object as a basket of corn, he would never be able to distinguish the individual ears.

This time it was impossible for Ponks to be absolutely certain that their shell had hit the exact point he wanted because three shells exploded almost simultaneously—apparently within a three-meter diameter. The stone wall along the near side of the barracks compound was gone when the smoke of the blasts settled, and so was the nearest of the buildings inside.

"On the money," Ponks announced. "New aiming point is thirty meters from the last, relative bearing three-zero-two." The actual calculations for the ranging were done by computer. The gun crew did not have to worry about calculating their own position and movement or coordinating that with the position of their target.

The gun had only moved four-hundred meters by the time Ysinde announced that he had the new round in the chamber.

"Simon, bring the gun around to the firing vector. Karl, put five quick ones in the same area. Work a twenty-meter grid on the aim," Ponks said. With the rest of the battery doing likewise, that would saturate the compound. Anyone not in a deep hole would have little chance of surviving a bombardment like that. There was not a man in the Havoc squadron who would want to attempt it, in any case.

"We get the last round out, start moving us south-southwest, Simon," Ponks said.

"Roger. Okay if I move us farther out from town at the same time?"

"You getting nervous?"

"I was born nervous."

"Okay, but don't put us *too* far out. You'll give Karl fits if you make him work at maximum range."

The quirks of six gun commanders maneuvering their vehicles at random brought three of them within an area little more than a half kilometer in diameter for a moment. The three howitzers were moving in different directions, and Ponks saw that neither of the others would come within a hundred meters of Basset two, but that was still too close for comfort.

It *did* mean that there were friendly witnesses to what happened to Basset five.

Basset five was the closer Havoc to Ponks's gun. Obviously, there was no warning. Five suddenly erupted in a ball of flame and shrapnel. Until the fire and smoke cleared, the other gunners could not tell for certain whether Five had exploded internally, perhaps from an accident with a shell, or had been hit by enemy fire. When the smoke cleared, though, it was obvious that the explosion had come from outside. The front end of Five had been crushed inward.

The mission became something much more than a drive through the countryside then.

• • •

The Hegemony's first coordinated counterstrike against the landing came from the air, and despite all of the spyeyes and pilots watching, it came virtually without warning. Two dozen Boem fighter-bombers converged on the Accord LZs. Another pair of enemy planes attacked the Havocs that were bombarding the Schlinal barracks compound in Maison. The enemy fighters proved to be as radar-neutral as the Wasp, and they appeared to match the Accord's premier fighter in speed and maneuverability as well. The Wasps were caught by surprise. The first hint that some of them had of enemy aircraft was when they found that their planes were on the wrong end of a target lock.

The aircraft fought at distances as great as eight kilometers. Still, the maneuvering as pilots sought to line up on an enemy—or tried to get free of a hostile target lock—was as frantic as any dogfight fought in the infancy of atmospheric flight, but at much greater speeds. Those Accord pilots who were running low on power for their antigrav drives had to move fast or risk being destroyed when they landed to replace batteries.

Two Wasps were dispatched to provide cover for the battery of Havocs that had come under attack. Four Schlinal Boem fighters pursued them. That spread the aerial battle over a lot more of Porter's sky.

Though the brunt of the initial Hegemony counterattack fell on the Havocs and Wasps, the infantry was not spared. Enemy fighters made strafing and bombing runs, cycling from one target to another. But the 13th fought back. The heavy weapons squads brought their Vrerch missiles into play almost instantly. The television-guided Vrerch could be used surface to surface, or surface to air. On the ground, the missiles were fitted with armor-piercing warheads to penetrate enemy armor. But there were also explosive warheads that were more than sufficient to blow a fighter out of the air.

This first air engagement did not last long. It was over, for all practical purposes, in less than five minutes. After making their strikes, the Schlinal fighters veered away. Accord Wasps followed in pursuit, for a time, then returned to the landing zones to replenish power and munitions while they could. Four Hegemony Boems were downed, either by Wasps or by ground-fired Vrerchs. But three Wasps were also lost in the encounter, bringing the 13th's total losses for the first three hours to four—out of twenty-four.

On the ground . . .

Joe Baerclau and his men had not reached their positions on the perimeter by the time the Schlinal air attack started. The squad's first warning of the enemy attack came over their helmet radios, an anonymously screamed alert over the "all-hands" channel, while they were crossing the densest part of the forest. The canopy overhead was so thick that they could see little more than an occasional hint of sky.

Even though they could neither see nor hear any approaching enemy planes, the seven men went down immediately, each of them sheltering next to the ground cone of a large tree. The basic problem with that tactic was that they had no sure way to know which side of the tree to hide behind, which direction the enemy might come from.

—Until they saw a pattern of bullets erupt through the trees and throw up spatters of moss and dirt. The sound of gunfire followed the bullets. There was no engine noise, not from an antigravity drive airplane. Leaves and small branches fell as the slugs raced from west to east. Those men who had taken cover on the wrong side of the cones scurried to correct their mistake. Several of them raised their rifles, looking for something to shoot at, but the forest canopy was too heavy. A zipper would not have brought down a fighter in any case, save by the wildest luck, and none of the men in Joe's squad were armed with Vrerch missile launchers.

What the hell do we do now? Joe asked himself. If they could not fight back, and hiding didn't look like much of an option, what *could* they do?

"Lieutenant?" he asked on his link to Keye.

"Where are you and what's your condition?" Keye replied.

"About two-hundred meters from you, I think. So far, nobody's been hit, but something strafed right on past us a few seconds ago."

"Get back as best you can. The Heggies finally came out."

"Mudders too?" Joe asked.

"Not yet."

Joe switched to his squad channel. "The good news is, the enemy knows we're here." He paused, but not long enough to give his men time to reply. "The bad news is, the enemy knows we're here." He wasn't looking for a laugh, and he didn't get one, but perhaps it did stop the others from wishing they were moles or other deep-burrowing animals for a moment.

"Okay, now," Joe said when he had everyone's attention. "We've got to get back to the rest of the platoon. They're lonely without us. But let's be careful. Don't figure 'cause that one plane came in from the west that the next one will as well. No traffic signs up there." He jerked a thumb skyward.

Joe was the first man on his feet. He stayed hunched over though, as if that might make him a significantly smaller target, or help him get to the ground faster if they had to dive for cover again. Joe looked around to make sure that all of his men got up, and he kept glancing up into the tree canopy, wondering if they would have enough warning the next time an enemy plane took a blind strafing pass.

Or was it blind? Joe asked himself. He had no idea what sensors the enemy pilots might have available.

Baerclau's squad raced along behind their own lines as if they were leading a charge into the heart of a fortified enemy position. Though no one in the squad had been hit by the strafing run, or even had bullets come within three meters of them, any illusion of safety under the trees was gone. They could still hear planes strafing, but they were no longer close. The sound was different, Dopplered, heading even farther away. Several of the men wondered what sort of ammunition the airborne automatic weapons had been spitting out—was it wire, fragmenting slugs similar to those used by their own Wasps, or something entirely different, perhaps large-caliber bullets that would bore deep and wide holes through them, body armor and all. No one was anxious to find out the hard way.

It hardly seemed to matter where the squad was. When the men returned to the platoon, the rest were doing no more than hunkering down behind the best cover they could find or manufacture. Those men who had been on the line the longest, while Joe's squad was off on its mission and getting the wounded taken care of afterward, had excavated decent slit trenches for themselves. Those holes could not stop a bullet coming out of the sky, but they made their residents a trifle less uncomfortable about the danger.

"Nice of you to drop by for a visit," Sergeant Maycroft told Joe, face-to-face. The platoon sergeant came to show Joe where he wanted his squad. Maycroft had been platoon sergeant since Joe first came to the company as a corporal. Maycroft had recommended Joe for his third stripe almost immediately.

"Well, we had nothing better to do, Max," Joe replied. "Thought we might keep you company." The two sergeants came from the same town on Bancroft, but they hadn't met until Joe came to the 13th. Max had been one of the first 'Crofters to join the Accord military. Now, their families back home had become friends, just as Max and Joe had.

"I heard that flyguy's gonna be okay," Max said.

"That's what the medic told me. Pretty soon, he'll be in a cushy hospital bed." There was just a hint of wistfulness in Joe's voice.

"Want to bet he'd trade places with you in a second?"

"You think he'd give all that up for a hole in the ground?"

"We've finally got 'em on the move, Van," Terrence Banyon told his boss. "The air strike was just to get our attention, I guess."

"And to cover their ground movements," Dezo Parks added.

Banyon shrugged. "There's one group coming our way from Maison, as expected. The looks our Wasps have gotten seem to indicate that the garrison there was considerably larger than we anticipated, perhaps as many as three thousand, maybe even thirty-five hundred."

"Hell, the *population* of Maison wasn't supposed to be more than eight thousand," Stossen said.

"Maybe not," Banyon said, "but the Heggies are coming, and they've got enough anti-air with them to keep our Wasps standing well off. And that armor they didn't have, they do have—tanks, if not SPs. There are still those two other columns working this way from Porter City. Major numbers. Can't pinpoint them yet. Also anti-air and armor with them."

Stossen nodded. "I never did trust the numbers. Anyway, they know we're here and they're coming after us. That was, more or less, the point. Can we keep their air cap away from us?"

"Now that we know they're around, yes," Parks said. "The

men have Vrerchs out and ready. And we only lost three Wasps in this attack."

"Don't say 'only,' " Stossen said harshly. "That's an eighth of our total. Twelve and a half percent is not 'only.' "

Parks didn't respond to the reprimand.

"We'll send 1st recon and Charley Company out to harass the troops heading our way from Maison," Stossen said, going right on with business. He had made his point. There was no need to dwell on it. "If Basset Battery can stay free of air attacks, we'll use them for whatever cover they can provide."

Parks made a couple of quick notes on his pocket compsole.

"We'll move George Company southeast, as if they might be headed for the number two route down off the plateau. We'll move Alpha just a little south, toward the number one route, but I don't want either company getting too close for now. We don't want to leave major gaps in the perimeter for this."

He stopped and looked around, and more importantly listened. For the moment there were no sounds of strafing planes, or of rockets. There was even very little rifle fire. Stossen nodded absently, to himself.

"For the sake of argument, let's assume that we're going to draw just about all of the Schlinal troops out of Maison. If that's the case, as soon as we have full dark tonight, we'll move 3rd recon and Echo Company around in a counterclockwise loop to come in from the east. Liberating Maison is the tactical objective, even if that liberation only lasts for as long as we're on Porter. Besides, if we manage to get our men in behind the Heggie force, we can cut them off from their base and pincer them between the two forces."

Charley and Echo companies, even reinforced by two of the 13th's four sixty-man recon "platoons," would still be outnumbered by more than four to one, but once those elements were in place, they would have help—all of the help that Stossen could get to them.

Charley Company and 1st recon moved out first. Shortly after their departure, the companies whose segments of the perimeter bordered Echo's moved to cover that wedge. The companies that were being moved toward the routes down the escarpment shifted at the same time. Echo Company moved back and northeast through the forest to rendezvous with 3rd recon, which had already moved beyond the lines of the main perimeter. They would all take what rest they could manage until sunset. Then they would start their long march to come into the town of Maison from the far side.

"Close to twenty klicks, in the dark," Joe whispered before telling his men to grab some dirt and try to sleep for a few hours. "And we need to cover it all before first light." He was only talking to himself. It would be a long march, even if there were no problems along the way—and there were always problems.

Night was the friend of the infantryman. The infrared detectors in their helmets meant that it was that much less likely that they would walk blindly into an ambush, and they would be able to see their targets no matter how well they were camouflaged. The night-vision systems the Accord used in its infantry helmets combined techniques to optimize seeing. Infrared technology was added to that for enhancing available visible light. Although the combination meant that the wearer required a certain amount of time to get accustomed to the double vision, the system provided better results than either technique used on its own. Even under a forest canopy beneath a moonless sky—Porter had no proper moon, only a pair of very small rocks, asteroids captured by the planet's gravity— the battle helmet allowed seventy percent of daylight vision, with relatively little loss of depth perception. There was also little loss of night vision after a sudden blare of light. Without augmentation, the eye's capability to see under night conditions could be seriously degraded for a half hour or more by even a modest light; with the helmet optics, it took less than thirty seconds for the system to readapt.

Joe took his own advice to get a little sleep. On his third campaign, Joe was an old hand. He had no difficulty at all dozing off. A soldier had to learn to take whatever opportunities for sleep came his way in the field. Once he had settled himself on the ground, close to the largest tree in his vicinity, Joe simply shut his eyes and took one long, slow breath. By the time it was out, so was he. There were no dreams to trouble his slumber, and no further air raids to interrupt it. He slept until a call from Max Maycroft told him it was time to get ready.

"On your feet," Joe said over the squad frequency, instantly alert. "Grab a meal and a drink. Do whatever else needs doing. We move out in fifteen minutes."

While he was talking, Joe pulled the heat strip on a meal pack. Ten seconds later, he tore off the lid and started in on his supper—his first meal since leaving the troop ship fifteen hours earlier.

CHAPTER
6

The troops formed up silently, without undue wasted motion. The major sound was of rifles being checked one last time for full magazines and charged power packs. Helmet radios picked up the softest of whispers, and visors kept soft voices from carrying other than through the radios. Earphones channeled transmissions directly to the ears, gently enough that the soldier could still hear any sounds in the environment around him. If hearing became more critical, it was possible to turn on a pass-through feature that would have microphones on the exterior of the helmet pick up sounds and run them through the earphones within. Once the force started out for their night march, the scouts and flankers would use those pickups routinely.

Twelve men of 3rd recon led the way, starting out ten minutes ahead of the main force. It was the recon squad's job to scout the route, to discover any enemy that might be lurking in wait, to neutralize them if possible, or to warn the main force. Behind the advance squad, the rest of 3rd recon took the point on three different columns. One platoon of Echo

Company would cover each flank. Another would bring up the rear. That left 2nd platoon in the center with the headquarters staff and the heavy weapons and counter-air sections of the company.

Captain Teu Ingels had made the choice to put 2nd platoon in the middle. "Baerclau's lot has had their rough duty for the day," he told Lieutenant Keye. "Of course, once we get there, things may change." Ingels was a popular commander because no matter how rough he had to be, in training or working his men, he was scrupulously fair, and in any dealings with outsiders, he always supported his men. His criticisms were never reckless, and he was even quicker to praise good work. He managed to seem friendly even while maintaining the degree of aloofness that any commander must have to lead men effectively.

Being in the center of the formation moving cross-country did not necessarily mean that Joe and the rest of the platoon were in the safest location. A well-placed, and well-led, ambush might easily wait for the center to come by before opening up. Any air or artillery attack would likely aim for the heaviest concentration of troops. But being in the middle did mean that they were farther from the audible clues that might be the first hint in the night that something was amiss. The sounds made by their comrades, soft and infrequent though those noises might be, would cover up any but the grossest sounds coming from farther away.

Echo Company kept a steady pace, moving forward fifty-five minutes out of each hour. There were few alarms, and none of those proved genuine. In one case, Joe and his men saw a small antelope bound away. Half of the company had moved past the animal before it took alarm and fled, giving dozens of men a fright they neither needed nor welcomed.

Near the end of the second hour of the advance, the recon squad out in front of the march did find humans, but not the enemy. They were the Jeomin family—father, mother, and three children, two of them almost full-grown. The Jeomins knew enough to freeze when commanded to, and they waited until three recon soldiers came close enough to identify them.

"You outta Maison?" a corporal named Nimz asked.

Oscar Jeomin shook his head slowly. "We're farmers. Our place is this side of Maison, about six kilometers. We heard about the landing. We had to come to you." Jeomin looked as if he were fit enough for the 13th. His two sons were both tall and broadly built. Only their faces showed that they were not yet men. All of the Jeomins were dressed well, if plainly. They did not look as if they had been through any real physical discomfort.

Nimz nodded slowly, as if the Jeomins' decision to come out at night, hike through a forest, and make contact with the new army made perfect sense to him. He detailed two men to escort the family back to his sergeant, who asked a few more questions and routed the family on to Captain Ingels.

It was almost time for a five-minute rest when the Jeomins arrived at the main body of the force. Captain Ingels did not hesitate to stop the company a few minutes early. A civilian family was a complication he had not anticipated, and did not relish.

"Sit down," he invited. He did so himself. Half of his headquarters staff was standing around, watching curiously. The men were not nearly as concerned over the complication that the Jeomins posed as they were curious about what they might have to say about the occupying Schlinal army.

"Have you eaten lately?" the captain asked next, casually, as if he had nothing better to do than spend the entire night chatting with these strangers met in a forest. Small talk gave him time to organize the more important questions he needed to ask.

Oscar Jeomin chuckled, but quietly, as if he fully understood the danger of noise. "We've eaten. That's not what made us set out. You can tell by looking at us that we haven't missed many meals. It's just that those bastards have taken over our farm, just this evening. We knew about the landing and figured you must be close, if not *this* close. Coupla times, Jason—he's my oldest—heard heavy shooting, artillery, he thought. When we saw the Heggie bastards coming, we hightailed it as quick as we could. But Jaiza threw together a picnic basket. We left that after we ate."

"How many soldiers?" Ingels asked. "At your farm."

"Thirty-six. I counted twice," Jeomin said. "Rifles, some heavier guns, and rockets. Nothing one man couldn't carry without getting a hernia though."

"What's it been like with them on Porter?"

Jeomin shrugged. "Hasn't been all that bad up here in the highlands, leastwise, not till lately, but we've heard stories about down in Porter City, and around there. We don't have much industry on the plateau, and industry seems to be mostly what the bastards are keen on. Brought in managers and so forth to take over, and posted soldiers everywhere to make sure the managers were obeyed. But it's just recently that we've really had a fair number of them soldiers on the plateau. They been moving up kinda regularlike for the last two, three months. And buildin' barracks for more of 'em. Making *us* build the barracks."

Ingels had dozens of questions he would have liked to ask, but there was no time. Echo Company had its mission to accomplish, and Lieutenant Colonel Banyon had sent orders to escort the Jeomins back to headquarters. Ingels did get Oscar to locate their farm on a mapboard, and to give a brief description of the buildings, and the vantages that an infantryman might use to set up an ambush.

"I know you mayn't be able to help it, but please try not to bust the place up any more'n you have to," Jaiza said. "It's been good for us."

"We'll do what we can," Ingels said. "I'll send a man along to guide you back to our headquarters. I'm sure the colonel has some questions, and the folks back there can probably find you bedrolls and a place to spread them."

A quick radio conference with Colonel Stossen brought a small change in plans for Echo Company and its recon detachment. Two of the recon platoon's twelve-man squads would detour to the Jeomin farm, along with two squads from 3rd platoon and two splat gun teams from Echo's heavy weapons squad. The splat gun was the lineal descendant of earlier machine guns. It fired heavy bursts of the same wire that the Armanoc zippers used, but the splat gun spat longer segments at a higher rate and velocity, and instead of twenty-meter spools, it loaded two-hundred meters of wire at a time. Up close—within fifty meters—it was as deadly as the cannons of a Wasp, able to saturate a target area.

Echo Company and its recon platoon did not start out until ten minutes after the Jeomins had been led back toward the LZs. Then, Ingels directed the raiding party that was going to the Jeomin farm off at an angle to the main advance. He told them to push their pace so they would be in position well before dawn. After that group was gone, the rest of Echo and 3rd recon angled more to the other side, rapidly putting distance between the two forces. No matter what happened at the farmhouse, there would be no reinforcements for the men sent to take it . . . at least not before morning saw the primary job finished.

Zel Paitcher had been sleeping in the narrow clearance under the cockpit of his Wasp. After spending ten hours cramped up in his fighter, he was exhausted. His entire body ached. Even for a small man, the cockpit of a Wasp was tight.

The Wasps were *almost* maintenance free; theoretically, they could be kept in the air as long as there was a pilot to sit in the cockpit. But, as valuable a weapon as each fighter was, there were limits, human limits, to the time it could spend in the air, whether in combat or not. There were no spare pilots. Pilots needed sleep. Ground crews needed sleep. In a sense, perhaps even the Wasps needed their share of "sleep," inactive time to allow circuits and weapons to cool, to give batteries longer to recharge, to permit more thorough maintenance inspections.

Beginning late in the afternoon, the colonel had started ordering a few Wasps down at a time, hoping to give all of the pilots as much rest as possible while keeping enough of them in the sky to fly a proper air cap and respond to any renewed Schlinal assault. At least there had been no second major air raid by the enemy. From time to time, two or four Schlinal Boems would shoot in a few rockets from extreme range, but they went to great pains to avoid engagement. They always veered away as soon as Wasps started toward them.

Zel was untroubled at having nothing more than hard ground under him and a slight thermal blanket to provide some cover. He slept through exhaustion in something scarcely less deep than coma. Though flying a Wasp was not particularly demanding physically, it did take intense concentration, and that could be even more draining than physical exercise. Zel had not even taken off his flight helmet when he crawled under his plane. At least the cushioning in the helmet gave his head some ease.

It seemed that he had only been asleep for minutes when Slee nudged Zel's foot with his own.

"Up an' at 'em, Zel." Slee's voice sounded as exhausted as it had when they had finally been relieved from flying. Slee was also slightly hoarse after breathing in chilly air for several hours. Even though the day had been scorching hot, the night was almost cold. The plateau was four-hundred meters above sea level.

For more than a minute, there was no sign of any response from Zel. Save for the snoring, he might almost have been dead.

"Come on, Zel," Slee said. "I'd like another six hours myself, but we've got to let the others have a turn."

Slee stretched his neck, flexing it as much as he could, back and front, side to side. There was a deep ache right at the back of his neck, as if he had taken a stiff jolt against the top of his spine. The ache had wakened him once, if not for long, and the pain was worse now.

Finally, Zel moaned, soft but long, and turned over. Slee nudged Zel's foot again, which brought a slightly louder moan, almost as if the touch had caused physical pain.

"I know it's hard, but they keep talkin' about sound discipline, Zel. You'll make folks think there's a lovesick heula around here." The heula was a thousand-kilo ruminant from Slee's homeworld. It liked to wallow in shallow water and wail through the night.

Zel pulled his knees up toward his chest, then wrapped his arms around them. He was awake now, barely, but far from alert. He was a flyer. His instincts did not jerk his mind to the ready instantly, the way a veteran infantryman's would.

"Let me die in peace," Zel mumbled.

"Come on. Get a stimtab in you. We're supposed to be in the air in five minutes."

Never make it, Zel thought, but his mind was beginning to function. Slee knelt at his side and forced a stimtab between Zel's lips. Zel resisted, but only for a moment. He sucked on the lozenge and slid out from under his fighter, pulling himself up to a sitting position.

Their crew chief was running a final check of the two Wasps. The planes had been replenished with ammunition and fresh batteries immediately upon landing, six hours earlier, in case they were needed in a hurry, sooner than planned. Now, the chief was simply double-checking everything. Roo Vernon, crew chief for these two Wasps, was a very cautious man.

"Any special orders for this trip?" Zel asked as the stimtab started its work.

"Mostly quiet work. Scouting. The colonel's trying to keep track of every warm body on the planet."

Zel stood and went through a series of stretches. That, and the stimtab, soon had him alert.

"She's all ready, sir," Roo told Zel.

"Thanks, Chief." Zel suppressed a yawn. "Two minutes, and I'll be ready." He wasn't exactly thrilled at the idea of getting back into the air, but as ready as he was likely to feel. There were times now when Zel could hardly recall that it had not been all that long before that he would have gladly forsworn sleep altogether to stay in the air a little longer.

Cruising in a Wasp at night was very like being a ghost, or even the shadow of a ghost, almost completely invisible. The light-absorbing skin of the fighter made it almost impossible for eyes to see the craft in the dark, save as it might occult some light source, and the plane was always invisible to radar. Cruising at minimal speed, it was also nearly silent, the whisper of its passage easy to miss, or to pass off as nothing more than a gentle zephyr. Most of the time, the loudest sound in the cockpit was the pilot's own breathing—and the cockpit was insulated well enough to prevent that sound from escaping.

Once Zel was in the cockpit of Blue four and going through his preflight checklist, all thought of exhaustion and aches vanished. As always, Zel felt himself becoming part of the Wasp rather than merely a rider in it. At night, the metamorphosis was even more convincing. Outside, there was the darkness, a cloak. Inside, there were only the soft green and red indicator lights and the muted colors of the video displays, contrast and brightness kept as low as possible. Every surface inside and out was designed not to reflect even those minimal levels of light; numbers and graphics seemed to float in the blackness.

Zel tightened his safety harness. The comforting pressure of the straps quickly faded from his awareness. He could reach everything he needed to within the cockpit. There was so little room for the pilot in a Wasp that Zel could almost have reached all of the controls with his elbows.

"Clear on the ground," Roo Vernon reported over his radio link.

"Roger," Zel replied automatically. "Slee?"

"Let's do it," Slee said.

Not fifteen meters from Slee's Wasp, Zel could scarcely mark the outline of the other fighter's canopy. At night, the flyers would depend on instruments to maintain station on each other. Encrypted electronic beacons let them fly in close formation—wingtips as little as fifty centimeters apart—even when they could not see each other. The encryption kept the system safe from enemy interference, or even detection. The Wasps also had anticollision systems that would automatically veer them away from each other if they came closer than fifty centimeters.

Blue three and four lifted silently out of the LZ. As soon as they were clear of the surrounding treetops, Slee turned north. Their first assignment was to check on the progress of the Schlinal troop moving in from the town of Maison. Paradoxically, flying at night, the pilots had a much clearer view of what lay below them than they did in full daylight. Radar painted all the picture they needed of natural terrain. Large animals, or humans, could be seen easily in infrared, even beneath the canopy of leaves. Good insulating battle dress should have muted the infrared signature, but that appeared to be one point where Hegemony technology fell short of the Accord's.

Night was also great for removing distractions. Zel kept his attention inside the cockpit of Blue four. A navigation screen kept him located over a real-time photographic map of Porter. The heads-up display on his canopy provided everything else.

"There's the Heggie column," Slee announced no more than four minutes after takeoff.

Zel increased the magnification on his display. The heat of trucks provided beacons in the night on infrared, and the soldiers were a speckling of pale green dots on the screen. Given a little time and a pair of passes along the length of the column, the sensors built into the Wasp could have provided a virtually precise headcount. But that was not on the agenda.

"Do we give them something to remember us by?" Zel asked after they had flown the length of the Heggie formation. The enemy certainly was not marching down a road, but even the pattern of dispersal had an almost regular look to it. Zel had a fleeting thought that these were *garrison* soldiers, not experienced front line troops.

"One pass," Slee replied after checking with CIC—which sought Colonel Stossen's input. "We don't want to scare them off. The colonel wants them out in the open, not heading back to Maison." Away from the civilians. A major battle inside Maison would tie the hands of the Accord troops.

"How do you want to handle it?" Zel asked.

"Concentrate on the trucks. We'll come at them from the front, get right in their faces. Then we peel off. You go right. I'll go left. Rendezvous at ten-K meters twenty klicks east." That would be well out of the range of any shoulder-operated SAM missiles the Schlinal force might be carrying.

They circled around to approach the enemy troops from in front again. Zel set his weapons selector and waited for Slee to make his move. First rockets, then cannon: go for the trucks first, then strafe the least-dispersed groups of men on foot. Slee targeted the first two trucks. As soon as his missiles were away, he switched to cannon, weaving no more than a few centimeters from side to side to scatter the needlelike projectiles over as wide an area as possible. Zel fired rockets at the next two trucks before the first two erupted. Then he too started to strafe, side-slipping to the right. There was no time for more than two seconds of gunfire before the last elements in the enemy force flashed by beneath his Wasp. The four trucks were all afire now. Zel pulled hard to the right and shoved his boost control to maximum, soaring up to ten-thousand meters in little more than twenty seconds.

One Schlinal missile did climb into the sky, but it was a blind shot, and the missile's target acquisition circuits never achieved a lock on either of the invisible Wasps. Zel smiled as he turned toward the rendezvous.

It was a silent night until the Wasp raid on the Schlinal troops. Even the nervous soldiers on the Accord perimeter had rarely found any reason to let off a burst of wire. The soldiers of Echo Company, a dozen kilometers from the nearest enemy, heard the explosions as missiles hit their targets. The subsequent sound of strafing was almost inaudible at that distance.

Who's gettin' hit, us or them? Joe wondered. Several minutes elapsed before Max Maycroft relayed that information, during another of the company's brief halts. This one was somewhat longer than most had been, but Joe knew that they had made good time on the night march. There had been no interruptions, save for the encounter with the Jeomin family. Most particularly, there had been no firefights to slow them down and disclose their presence. Echo Company could afford to take ten or fifteen minutes this time.

"Max, how 'bout getting the captain to let us cycle out to the perimeter for a bit," Joe asked. "We need a change to keep these guys from falling asleep."

Joe felt his own alertness pick up once they started marching again. Second platoon was on the right flank now, and Joe's squad had the point—an inevitable assignment after Joe asked to get out on the edge. Every breath sounded loud in his ears now. His surroundings seemed to take on a new intensity, more than he could account for simply because he had turned on his exterior microphones to give him that extra hearing edge. Out on the flank, that was where any action was most likely to start.

Starting out, Joe had his fire team in front. Mort Jaiffer walked point, thirty meters ahead of anyone else. Kam Goff was behind Mort, and Joe was in the third position, the usual spot for the squad leader. Al Bergon was close behind Joe—too close. Joe had to caution him several times to hold his interval. Ezra's fire team was another thirty meters back. If the point walked into an ambush, it would be up to Ezra's team to come to their rescue, or provide covering fire until the rest of the platoon, or company, could get into the act.

Like many men who manage to survive—even thrive—in combat, Joe Baerclau had developed the ability to focus completely on his surroundings. On patrol, he sometimes fancied that he could even hear an insect breathing ten meters away. At other times, in garrison, where there was no danger—and mostly after he had drunk a cup or two—he might recall that when he was a child his mother had read him Bible stories, and used to tell him that not even a sparrow could fall in the forest without God knowing it. When he was stuck for an explanation of the way he tried to pay attention to every

detail around him in the field, he sometimes fell back on that
story for an analogy.

"I ain't sayin' I'm God," he would always hasten to add.
He was not particularly religious, but he did not *disbelieve.* If
there was a God, Joe did not want to offend Him . . . not as
long as he was a soldier who might need divine help to get
through the next campaign, or the next minute. "But I don't
know no other way to put it. You got to hear the slightest
sound, see the least little movement. That is, if you want the
best chance to come out of it alive and in one piece." *You do
what you can, knowing that the time might come when even
that won't be enough.*

Second platoon had been on the flank for an hour and a
half—past one break and halfway through the next leg of
the march—when Mort called for a stop. "I heard something,
Sarge," he reported over the radio, his voice little more than
a whisper.

"What kind of something?" Joe asked. He started forward
again, very slowly, watching the ground to make certain that
he did not step on anything that might prove noisy.

"I'm not sure. It didn't sound like an animal though. I don't
see anything on IR or visual, but I know I heard *something.*"

"Hang easy, Prof. I'm on my way."

It was unlike Mort to get so excited. "The Professor," as
nearly everyone in the company called him, was usually the
calmest man around. *Heggies? More civilians? Or just an
overactive imagination?* Joe wondered as he moved through
the trees. He hardly paid attention to those thoughts though. It
was more important to assume that Mort had heard a Heggie,
and to concentrate on anything that the night might tell him.

The trees were no longer the bulky shapes with cones of
dirt around their bases that had predominated around the LZs.
Most of these trees were thinner and taller, angular rather than
full. The leaves were much smaller as well, also long and thin.
These trees would provide less cover in a firefight. That was
the important consideration.

Mort was prone on the ground, taking what little cover one
of those thin trees might offer—any cover was better than
none. His rifle barrel extended out on the right, the muzzle no
more than twenty centimeters off of the ground. Mort had his
finger over the trigger guard though, not on the trigger itself.

"Hear any more?" Joe asked as he got down on the ground at Mort's left. To preserve the silence, they whispered over the radio even though their shoulders were almost touching. Joe settled in behind his rifle as well, just in case there *was* something to shoot at in front of them.

"Not a thing," Mort admitted. "But I know there's something, or some*one,* out there, Sarge. I've been through this before. I'm not dreaming. You know me better than that."

"Can you pinpoint the location any?"

"As close as I can tell, the direction is right down the barrel of my zipper. I can't tell about distance. Not too far, maybe." His rifle was pointed at an angle of 45 degrees to the line of march.

Joe did hesitate for a moment, but they dared not just lie there all night. They could ill afford even a short delay.

"We'll have to go out and take a look," he said. "You and I might as well get on with it." That was far from doctrine. The squad leader had no business going out on this sort of prowl. By the book, Joe should have stayed put and sent privates out. Privates were, by definition, more expendable than noncommissioned officers, but . . .

"You go right. I'll go left," Joe said. "Slow and easy."

Joe held his breath as he got to his feet, listening as much for any noises that he or Mort might make as for a repetition of whatever Mort had heard before. The night was almost too silent. Joe realized, with some surprise, that he had not heard any insect sounds even. Porter did have insects. He had seen plenty of them during the day. But they did not chatter or chirp, or make any of the other sounds that he expected from bugs.

"Go," Joe whispered when he saw that Mort was in position.

Joe took his first step with exaggerated caution, angling just a little to the left. It would not do for him to get too far from Mort. The object was for them to be able to pincer anyone between them, and to be close enough to do something about it in concert, quickly. Mutual support. If there was someone lurking, they would try to take care of him, or them, silently. If possible.

Although they moved steadily, each step felt as if it took minutes. Joe would look at the ground where he intended to put his foot, then slide it forward, only slowly transferring his weight, ready to pull back if he felt anything brittle under his boot. Then he would wait, straining for any hint of noise or movement in the area that Mort had indicated. Then it was time for another wary step forward. It seemed more protracted than it actually was. There *was* some urgency about this. A few meters away, Mort was moving just as cautiously. He might have moved a little faster on his own—not impatiently, but with somewhat less patience than Joe. He held back though, knowing that he had to stay even with his sergeant.

Ten steps. Then Joe's foot came down on something that was *too* smooth to be natural. Though he realized that something was wrong almost instantly, he felt as if considerable time passed before he was able to react—before he was forced to react.

He stopped and brought the muzzle of his rifle down quickly, just as his foot was jerked out from under him. Joe's movements were instinctive, but that instinct came from years of training. Subconsciously, he realized that he had stepped on a blanket or tarpaulin, and that there was someone under it, someone who had jerked on the fabric, coming out from underneath, coming to his feet.

Joe fell but managed to land on his ass without tumbling. The figure who emerged from under the tarp had a long knife in his hand. Joe had no time to get his rifle pointed at his attacker. He could do nothing more than swing the barrel toward the knife, using his zipper as a club while he got back to his feet.

The Heggie jerked his knife to the side, out of the way, and dove at Joe's middle. Joe dropped his rifle as the two men went to the ground together. Joe had to have both hands free, had to get to the Heggie's knife. Net armor might stop a bullet or wire, but it would do little to stop a knife thrust.

Neither man spoke, or did more than grunt from effort or impact. But the disturbance was an outrageous din compared to the total silence that had preceded it. Joe did manage to say "Mort" into his microphone.

Joe's assailant was considerably larger than him, perhaps by as much as ten centimeters in height and fifteen kilos in weight. Joe let the Heggie's momentum carry them backward and over, and he put his knees into the man, sending him over his head. But the Heggie kept his grip. Together, the two men rolled in the dirt, with the Schlinal trooper's weight and size beginning to tell.

Joe did not see the end of the fight coming. He heard a dull thud and then a sharp crack as his foe's neck snapped, and then he felt the Heggie shudder in his grasp and go limp.

"You okay, Sarge?" Mort asked.

Joe took a moment to consider that while he hauled in deep breaths. "Yeah. I'm okay."

"He had something like a splat gun hidden under that tarp with him," Mort explained. "I tripped over it trying to get to you."

Joe got to his feet slowly, helped up by Mort, and then he bent over again to retrieve his rifle. As well as he could in the dark, he checked to make sure that nothing had fouled the barrel.

"That tarp," Joe said, after signaling the rest of the platoon to start moving again. Ezra's team would take over the point now—with even greater caution than before, in case this man was just part of a larger force. *What would one man be doing out here alone with a splat gun?* Joe asked himself. "Check it out, will you?"

"Must be some sort of thermal shield," Mort said after a quick look. "That's why we couldn't see any IR signature."

"Bring it along. Intelligence might like a look at it," Joe said.

The other fire team moved on by. Joe and Mort fell in behind, with the rest of their team. No one paid any attention to the dead Heggie. He no longer mattered.

CHAPTER
7

Four men lay under cover of a thicket that blanketed the side of a hill overlooking the town of Maison. Members of the special intelligence detachment assigned to the 13th SAT, they had been on Porter for ten days, one of two teams that had been infiltrated ahead of the invasion. Their shuttle had never landed. The teams had jumped at twenty five hundred meters, free-falling most of that distance before deploying black parasails. Those chutes were jettisoned before they reached the ground. The men released their harnesses and landed on personal antigrav packs. That technology was so new that it had never before been used in combat.

One man from the team targeted against the Schlinal forces in Maison had died in the landing. He had misjudged his timing, releasing his chute too soon. The personal antigrav packs were only good for thirty seconds of power before their batteries failed. He had fallen the last thirty meters and died on impact. His companions had buried him, leaving not a trace of the grave visible. The parasails had been equipped with nanotech systems to self-destruct once released. Not so much as a clasp survived of them.

Ten days. The teams had jumped and landed separately, hundreds of kilometers apart. The Maison team—it had no other identifier—had hiked sixty kilometers before their first dawn on Porter, then spent two days hiding, well away from Maison or any other settlement. Seventy-two hours after landing, the Maison team had come out of hiding to move toward their target, slowly and carefully. Stealth was a way of life for these men. Their passage was scarcely noted even by the animals of the plateau. They wanted no contact at all with the world's humans, certainly not the Hegemony's occupying force, but not even with the longtime residents. They were prepared to go to the most extreme lengths to avoid capture, and if that appeared to be insufficient, each was prepared to commit suicide—with a chemical that would insure the rapid destruction of brain cells, so that even dead they could not be milked of their secrets.

The hundred-hectare thicket on the slope above Maison made a perfect refuge. The slope was gentle. The Accord observers crawled under and through the maze. In all that expanse, there was no place where a man could stand upright. The thicket was like a stunted forest, dense but short. Wrist-thick trunks supported the bushes. Their canopy of glossy leaves, with thorns only on the upper branches, was thoroughly interlaced and much too thick to allow any passage to walking men or large animals. But beneath that canopy, the four men had little difficulty moving around. Like ants in a crystal-sided ant farm, they had scores of meter-high passages available to them, concealment without the sense of complete enclosure that tunnels might have engendered.

Gene Abru was the leader of the Maison team. Stocky and a little below average height, Gene had made a fetish out of physical fitness. His interests ranged from lifting weights to the most arcane of martial arts. The discipline he had forced on himself was mental as well. He had entered the army of his native world, Ceej—Tau Ceti IV—at the age of seventeen, and he had served there long enough to qualify for minimal retirement. But when he retired from that army, it was only to enlist in the Accord Defense Force. He had been invited into military intelligence, and had proven himself over and over in that capacity.

Alone of the more than two thousand men in the 13th, Gene Abru had been on one of the core worlds of the Schlinal Hegemony since the start of the new Schlinal drive into Accord space. Past forty years of age, he was the oldest man attached to the 13th, save for a few of the senior headquarters officers and the regimental sergeant major. Nominally only a platoon sergeant, there was no company-grade officer in the 13th (outside of Special Intelligence, that is: Abru was of a type, not unique) who would have dared try to enforce their orders on him. Like the other senior noncoms in Special Intelligence, he had entrée to the highest command levels in the assault team. Even Colonel Stossen found himself fascinated by Abru . . . and perhaps, though he would never admit it, even a little frightened of him.

A week of idleness, doing nothing but watching Maison, was starting to tell on the entire team, but they maintained their silence. They had uttered scarcely a word in all of the time they had lain in wait in the thicket, and then only in the softest whispers, face-to-face. Though they had helmets, and helmet radios, they had not used the radios, not wanting to take the slightest chance of giving away their presence on the world. In a week, not a man of them had even been able to stand and stretch. But that was over now, or would be soon. In radio contact with the CIC aboard the flagship, Gene and his men knew that the 13th was on the ground, and that they had started to move on Maison. The team had witnessed the artillery barrage that had leveled the Hegemony compound at the edge of town. They had seen the column of enemy troops move out toward the Accord LZs.

"I guess we'll find out now if our legs still work," Gene told his companions as they prepared to move out. They had marked the route they would take their first day in the thicket, and each man had studied it at length. Gene was certain that he could find his way along it blind. There was a long draw leading down and at an angle to the right. Even after they left the cover of the tangled thicket, they would be out of the line of sight of anyone in Maison until they were nearly down to the level of the town's streets and no more than a kilometer from the outlying houses.

They were armed no differently from line infantrymen. Each man carried an Armanoc zipper and a belt knife. They carried no explosives or incendiary devices. But they did carry small transmitters—radio beacons that could be placed to mark important targets for Wasp or Havoc attention.

Single file, the four men worked their way down off of the hill, through the angled draw past a formation of rocks that blocked the bottom of the cut. Despite the fact that all four men were as fit as rigorous daily training regimens could make them, the week's forced inactivity told on them. Legs were stiff and knees ached. They pressed on without complaint. At the bottom of the draw, they paused for a rest. Gene got back on the radio to CIC for a final confirmation that the attack was on time, that the forces were moving on schedule.

"It's a go," Gene told the others. Each of them nodded at him. "We've all got our work to do. See you in the morning."

Though no one in Echo Company knew it, the hill they moved around in the last hour of their night march was the one that had sheltered the intelligence team. No one outside Colonel Stossen's headquarters even knew that those teams had been dropped onto Porter well before the invasion. When Captain Ingels received the radio call on his command channel, he was surprised . . . and suspicious.

"Captain Ingels, this is Gene Abru, of Special Intelligence. We met three months ago at the Accord Day ceremony. You remember?"

For a moment Ingels was completely at a loss. The last thing on his mind was some garrison doings months back. It was difficult to take his mind away from where he was now. But, finally, he nodded to himself, and said, "I remember. Major Parks introduced us."

"There was a reason for that, sir," Abru said. "It was so's you'd know me now."

I didn't even know there was going to be this now then, Ingels thought.

"All dressed up and nowhere to go," Abru said next. That phrase startled the captain. Abru had used it twice during the few minutes they had talked at the Accord Day party in the officers' mess.

"I take it that that's some sort of password?" Ingels said.

"You could call it that, sir. Now, my men and I are inside Maison. The town is wide open, not a Heggie in it. Not alive, anyway. They took all but a few guards with them. The guards didn't get a chance to call for help before we got 'em."

"You're certain that there are none of them left?"

"Certain as I can be without searching every building in town. Most there could be is a few isolated individuals, and they wouldn't be good for much 'cept snipin'. We've made contact with the locals. They're plum delighted that the Accord's finally come for them."

Until we leave again, Ingels thought, but there was no need to mention that. He assumed that Abru knew about that as well. Special Intelligence: they would damn well know, even if they weren't supposed to.

"Ingels, this is Stossen." The captain was also unprepared for the sudden addition to the radio conference. "Yes, sir," he managed, not quite stuttering.

"Don't knock the free ride," the colonel said. "Get your men into Maison and set up your positions on the west and south to keep the Schlinal forces from getting back inside."

"Yes, sir." Ingels did not waste time with excuses about not knowing that SI had people on the ground inside Maison, or about not having *proper* authentification procedures. It *was* possible for the enemy to tap into what were supposed to be secure channels—highly improbable, but possible.

Despite Abru's assurances, and the fact that Colonel Stossen had confirmed the man's identity, Ingels still did not simply march his company into Maison. The recon platoon was sent ahead, to take up positions around the town and to set up listening posts on the approaches. Then Echo went in as cautiously as if they *knew* that every building concealed an enemy sniper. The men had been warned that Maison was apparently empty of enemies, but to be on the alert anyway.

Although there was still an hour left before dawn, more than half the people of Maison came out to greet their liberators, or simply to watch from windows and doorways, making sure that they were clearly visible—and seen as no threat. There were a few cheers, but most of the people were content simply to wave or say a few words to whichever troops came nearest them.

Maison was the second largest town on Porter, but it was
no metropolis. There was not one building in town more than
two stories high, and most were only a single story, particularly
the residences. Porter clung to a common colonial style—large,
rambling single-story homes, most commonly built around a
central courtyard, completely enclosed on every side. In some
cases, the original homes had been expanded one or more
times, spreading to include two or three courtyards. On a
primitive world, such designs were often literally a matter of
life and death. And, on many worlds, such as Porter, later generations never quite escaped this sort of architectural common
memory.

After centuries of settlement, Maison was a far cry from
the one real city on the planet. The vast bulk of the world's
population still lived in Porter City, or in a belt of suburbs
that had grown up around, and gradually more distant from it.
Maison's population had never topped ten thousand. Now, it
was somewhat below that figure. More than a thousand people
had left Maison to open a new settlement farther to the north,
just months before the Schlinal invasion.

"Glad to see you lads," one elderly man called out, his voice
sounding uncomfortably loud to the soldiers.

Joe looked at the man. He was dressed in soft clothes, what
might have been pajamas on a world like Porter. Joe could not
tell at a glance, and there was no time for more than that.

"About bloody time," another voice called, more softly.

Five streets went through Maison from east to west. Two
went north to south. The streets were broad, except right in
the center of town. Later additions had marred the symmetry
there. Also except in the center of town, the buildings were
generally spaced well apart, or in small, tight clusters separated from other neighbors. Although only a small fraction
of the populace still farmed extensively, almost every family
appeared to have a small garden near their house, some right
out in front, between house and street. It made Maison seem
more rural than it actually was.

"You need a hand, we're here."

Joe turned his head to look again. *That* voice had belonged
to a woman, but he could not decide which one. There were
several women, or girls, in a cluster. It might have been any of
them. Joe glanced around at the men of his squad, wondering

how long it would be before one of them broke discipline
to say something back to one of the locals, particularly the
women. The robes they wore against the night chill might
not have been particularly becoming, but a soldier didn't need
much to excite his imagination.

"Don't worry, Sarge," Tod Chorbek said over the radio.
"They ain't gonna attack us."

"That's not what I'm worried about," Joe replied tightly.
"Just mind what you're supposed to be doing. There's still a
lot of Heggies between us and home."

Echo Company moved completely through Maison. Only the
headquarters detachment and the heavy weapons squad would
wait for the enemy's return in town, or on its edge. The rest
of Echo, and the recon platoon, would be out in front of the
town, between the civilians and the Hegemony garrison that
might soon be retreating toward it.

"Dig in fast," Joe told his men when they were in position
southwest of town. They were in farmland now, but there
were occasional groves of native trees, and orchards—various
sorts of fruit and nut that the settlers had brought to Porter
with them. Second platoon was lucky. They found themselves
posted in an orchard of apple and pear trees. Though the pears
were far from ripe, some of the apples were close enough to
be tempting.

The sun was up before Joe had his men dug in as well as
he wanted. Then, there was time for a meal, several drinks of
water, and a chance to rest.

"The Heggies are still an hour away," Joe told his men after
he got the word from the first sergeant. "Use the time. Long
as I don't hear any snoring, I'm satis."

Joe stuck a hand inside his tunic and scratched at his chest.
He had been inside his clothes for more than twenty-four hours,
and he felt filthy. There was no way to guess how much longer
he might spend in those clothes, quite possibly until the 13th
returned to its ships. It would take a week of frequent scrubbing
before he would feel really *clean* again.

After Joe had eaten, he pulled off his boots and spent a few
minutes taking care of his feet. He wiped them dry, powdered
them, and put on fresh socks. When he zipped his boots back
on, he felt marginally better. For an infantryman, feet were as
important as his rifle. He could get nowhere without them.

Joe closed his eyes then. He could hardly have kept them open unless there was shooting. Twenty-four hours—Porter's day was very close to Earth standard, just a few minutes short of twenty-four hours long—but ninety minutes shorter than the day on his native world of Bancroft. Exhaustion was hardly the word for the way Joe felt. At times like this, he sometimes fantasized, usually about being Rip Van Winkle and sleeping for twenty years. *Long enough to retire.*

Joe woke with a start. There was a scream in his ear: "Watch your front. They'll be in sight in a few minutes."

It was Max Maycroft's voice, the alert. And he had not screamed. It had merely sounded like it to Joe's sleeping mind. He shook his head and blinked rapidly several times, feeling himself come alert as adrenaline poured into his system. *They're coming!*

This won't be like yesterday, Joe thought, and then he repeated it for his men. "Couple thousand men, running from one fight into another," he added. "They're gonna be downright desperate. Mind yourselves."

He checked his rifle. The indicator showed full power and a full magazine. Spare spools of wire were in pouches on his belt, and two were on the ground next to him, where he could get to them even faster. Deep breaths: two, three. Joe took his hands off of his rifle and flexed them several times, so that there would be no stiffness to distract him from what was about to come.

What was about to come. This was an ambush on a massive scale. A lot depended on how quickly the Heggies recovered from the shock of finding enemies waiting for them. If the ambush *was* a surprise, if Echo Company had not been spotted, what was to come could be brutal. If they had been spotted, if the Heggies knew what they were facing, things might get dicey for Echo Company. The Heggies did have overwhelming numbers on their side.

The Schlinal force retreating toward Maison was still a coherent unit. Their discipline had not evaporated under the harassing tactics of Charley Company and the Wasps and Havocs. Although they were retreating, making a "tactical withdrawal," they outnumbered their attackers by a much larger margin than they could know, and they were moving under orders, paying attention to the fundamentals. Most of their trucks had been abandoned, or destroyed, but most of these garrison troops were infantry anyway. They might be out of practice, but they did have training to fall back on.

If the Heggies were not expecting to walk into an ambush close to Maison, they did react swiftly when the shooting started. Few of the Schlinal soldiers waited to see where the firing was coming from. Most immediately dove for cover, protecting themselves before they worried about countering the attack.

Echo Company had the surprise, however briefly, and they used it to good effect. A single word of command from Captain Ingels brought every weapon into use. The first short bursts from wire carbines and splat guns raked over the nearest sections of the Hegemony force. Some few of those bursts actually managed to evade or penetrate the body armor of the Hegemony soldiers, though the range was too great for maximum effectiveness.

The Schlinal troop was caught in the open, with little real cover available. With Echo Company in front of them and dug in, and Charley Company pursuing, the much greater numbers that the Hegemony enjoyed were of little use. Within a minute after Echo Company sprang its ambush, the guns of Basset Battery started pouring in on the Heggies. Four Wasps flew in to add their cannons and rockets to the commotion.

It took the Schlinal commander less than ten minutes to decide that he had only one way to avoid the wholesale slaughter of his entire command.

"Cease fire!" Joe repeated the command on his squad channel even though Captain Ingels had used the all-hands frequency for the original order.

Silence returned quickly, except for the moans and cries of the wounded. For several minutes, there was little movement on either side while Ingels and the Schlinal commander discussed the methodology of surrender. The soldiers of Echo and Charley companies and the recon platoons watched, their guns still at the ready, fingers near triggers. The four Wasps circled high overhead, ready to return to strafing if the discussions broke down.

Then the Hegemony's soldiers started to stand up. They left their weapons and battle helmets on the ground. With raised hands, they started marching toward Maison again, gradually forming into four columns. The 1st and 3rd platoons of Echo Company were detailed to guard the prisoners, and to search them. Some of the prisoners had neglected to leave all of their weapons on the ground. Some still had knives. A few had pistols concealed on them, or radios.

Max Maycroft walked along the line of 2nd platoon, calling the squad leaders forward.

"We've got the cleanup detail," he told the other noncoms. "Have the men collect all of the weapons and helmets the Heggies left out there. We'll have most of Charley Company helping."

"What do we do with them?" Joe asked.

Maycroft gave him a sour chuckle. "We turn the rifles and ammo over to the good people of Maison. Maybe the prisoners as well. We're sure not equipped to deal with a couple of thousand POWs."

CHAPTER
8

The campaign on Porter did not end with the capture of the plateau town of Maison, but the defeat of the town's garrison and the simultaneous destruction of the platoon that had taken over the Jeomin farm did slow the pace of fighting considerably. The columns that had started out from Porter City, heading toward the plateau, turned around and went back to their barracks. Only a token force, no more than five or six hundred men, was dispatched to continuing harassing the 13th. There were occasional air strikes against the Freebies (as the Accord military was known among the forces of the Schlinal Hegemony), but those were more a nuisance than a serious threat to significantly degrade the capabilities of the 13th. The air raids came primarily at night. During the day, the skies over the plateau were too dangerous for Schlinal aircraft. The local commander did not have an unlimited supply. There supposedly had been no reason to give him a strong air arm. His duties were occupation, and an army that controls the population base of a conquered world should not need many attack aircraft.

Colonel Stossen was cautiously pleased with the state of things . . . but nervous.

"They can't just sit down there and do *nothing* about us," he told his staff early in the morning of day four. "No Hegemony warlord would dare sit on his ass and ignore the sort of threat we represent, especially not after losing more than three thousand men killed or captured. He'd get his head lopped off as soon as his superiors found out."

"Why borrow trouble?" Terry Banyon asked. "Another day or so and it won't matter. Our people should be here to cover our evacuation." More quietly, he added, "After that, it will be up to the locals to give him troubled nights." Twenty-eight hundred rifles, and a considerable stock of ammunition should make for a lot of troubled nights. The executive officer had heard the early stories about what the Heggies had done to the civilians of Porter. Although the forced labor gangs had only recently started in Maison, they had been busy since the beginning in and around Porter City, where most of the world's industry was located, and news of what happened in the capital had reached Maison and the other outlying settlements. Old factories had been converted to provide materiel for the occupying army. Some had been enlarged. Two new factories were under construction, all with forced labor. The able-bodied people of Porter City were being worked twelve to fourteen hours a day, seven days a week, to supply the conquerors.

"The only thing we can reasonably do now is turn the Wasps loose on Porter City," Dezo Parks said, speaking up before the colonel could jump all over his executive officer, "even though they won't have much time over the target. They'll have to get in and out or run their batteries dry. The capital is too far away to hope to get troops there and back before pickup—unless we use the shuttles, and that poses more risks than anything else. We can't even use the Havocs for a raid. They wouldn't be able to cover that distance and get back either. Even if they could, they'd be sitting ducks without infantry support. We might lose more than half of them before they got within range."

Stossen paced away from the others and stood looking off across one of the LZ clearings for a moment. When he turned to face his executive and operations officers again, his voice was calm.

"I know. I just don't like it. I don't like sitting here and not being able to do anything constructive. I'm not all that crazy about leaving the Porters to the mercies of the Heggies. Or a dozen other things. I do have half a mind to use the shuttles. That would certainly give the Heggies something to think about."

"What about using shuttles to take one company," Banyon suggested. "Not all the way to Porter City, but close enough that they can make it the rest of the way on foot. Give the shuttles plenty of air cover. We can bring the men back the same way then, if we have to get ready to leave in a hurry."

Stossen turned the idea over in his mind for a moment. "Tempting," he admitted, "but we can't risk a company. They might be outnumbered a hundred to one, and if they got into trouble, we'd have to risk the rest of the regiment on a rescue. That could lead to disaster. There might not be time to pull it off before pickup."

"We *are* accomplishing our primary objective," Parks pointed out. "There won't be any reinforcements leaving Porter to mess up the main invasion on Devon." He laughed. "They wouldn't dare leave with three thousand of their men in the bag."

"We hope," Stossen said. "Don't make the mistake of thinking that the Hegemony will consider those men the way we would. They might just write them off."

Joe Baerclau stood within a meter of the scarp, looking across the rift valley with power binoculars. The nearest portions of the valley were littered with rockfall that had accumulated over millennia. Out to a distance of ten or twelve kilometers, there appeared to be very little greenery, just those grasses and scrub brushes that could find niches among the rocks. Even beyond that limit, the valley seemed to green only gradually, as if much of the flora of Porter had given up trying to establish itself near the sheer rock wall, or the detritus that had collected at its base.

There were now three companies of the 13th at or near the scarp, ready to cover the two nearest access routes from the valley floor. The sun was low in the west—it looked as if it were below the level of the plateau. Joe forced himself to look straight down, and wished he had not. Where he was standing, the drop was almost sheer all of the way to the bottom, three hundred meters down. Instinctively, he moved back a step and took the binoculars from his eyes. Looking down through the glasses had strengthened the feeling of vertigo. He looked around to see if any of his men had noticed what he had done. As far as Joe could tell, though, no one had. The men who were close enough to have noticed were looking out over the valley, the same as he had been. Too far away to be seen directly, Porter City sat, guarded by its thousands of Schlinal soldiers.

They can't get at us, and we can't get at them, Joe thought. That did not make him feel as good as he thought it should. Hundreds of kilometers.

"What good are we doing here?" Joe whispered. His visor was tilted up to let him use the binoculars. That put his microphone far enough away that his words did not carry to his men. "We came here to fight, not to stand around with our thumbs up it."

"Hey, Sarge."

Joe took another step back from the escarpment before he turned to see what Mort Jaiffer wanted. Mort hadn't bothered with his helmet radio. The platoon was, more or less, off duty now. The only attack they had to fear in this location was from the air, and there had been virtually no enemy air during the daylight hours since the first day of the campaign.

"What is it?" Joe asked.

"How come they didn't let us stay in Maison? It would have been nice to sleep with a roof over our heads."

"We want to keep the locals on our side," Joe said, grinning. Mort worked hard to make the rest of the men in the platoon forget that he had been an egghead in civilian life, a professor. "Captain said we had to keep the likes of you away from the pretty girls, 'specially now that their papas have all those Heggie rifles." The rumor within the platoon was that Jaiffer's decision to leave the university and join the ADF had something to do with the daughter of a chancellor, or dean, or department chairperson. The details varied from telling to telling. The story was, however, totally unconfirmed.

"Hell, I'd need a bath and twelve hours sleep before I could even think about the ladies," Mort said. "They would have been safe."

"You'd have found a way." Joe shook his head. "You couldn't have got your mind off 'em anyway. This way, maybe we can get you to give the job at least *some* thought."

"Why? Nothing's going to happen now. This time tomorrow, we'll be back on ship, heading for home and a chance to feel human again before the next time. Besides, it's not me I'm concerned about. It's Tod. He got the big eyes over somebody he saw when we went through Maison."

"All the more reason to stay clear. How d'ya figure those folks are gonna feel about us when we pack up and leave, with all those Heggies still down in the valley?"

That took the smile off of Mort's face. "Why *are* we doing that, Sarge? Why not bring in enough men to finish the job while we're here?"

"Because we don't *have* enough men to finish the job on all of the worlds we're hitting. We're just here to let 'em take Devon back for good. Porter's just a diversion, remember?"

Mort's "I remember" was a mumble too soft for Joe to really hear it, but he did understand what Mort said.

"Maybe next time it'll be Porter's turn," Joe suggested. "We've got a lot of worlds to take back from the Heggies."

"I got no argument with that," Mort conceded. "We've let them get away with crap too long as it is." *That's why I'm here.*

"Two, three years from now, maybe we'll have enough ships and trained men to get the job done right. For now, it's do what we can. Keep 'em off guard. Keep 'em too busy to even think about taking more of the Free Worlds." It was never just repeated propaganda for Joe. He believed every word of it.

"Besides," he added, "you're no conscript. You volunteered for this just like the rest of us."

Mort shrugged and walked back to where his gear was piled, next to the latest of his slit trenches. He had lost count. He was no longer sure if this was the fourth or fifth hole he had dug since coming to Porter. When he was digging, he sometimes thought that that was all he did in the army. But digging couldn't shut off his mind, or his addiction to second-guessing the way the war was being waged.

Joe turned his attention back to the expanse of the rift valley. He had seen many kinds of terrain before, on more than a half-dozen worlds, but he had never seen anything quite like this. He could see what he thought was a line of peaks in the distance, far beyond the ranging capability of the binoculars, but even so, those peaks were just bumps on the horizon. Across most of the valley, he could see no proper end to it at all. The valley extended on beyond the horizon. He knew that, off to his left, almost two hundred kilometers beyond Porter City, there was an ocean that extended over more than two thirds of the surface of the world, interrupted only by a few score large islands until it lapped the western shore of the world's only true continent. To his right, the rift continued for another thousand kilometers or more. At the end of it, the mountain range he thought he could see in the distance actually met the plateau, and climbed to peaks as high as nine thousand meters. He would have liked to see those high mountains.

"Wonder how long it's been since they had a proper quake 'round here?" he asked himself as he looked at the scarp again. That was enough to move him farther from the edge. The escarpment on a rift valley, the edge of a tectonic plate. Maybe the zone was inactive now. Joe seemed to recall that it was—had been for perhaps a million years. Someone had asked during one of the mission briefings. But still . . .

"That's really all we'd need."

The efficiency of the huge tarpaulins had never really been tested under actual combat conditions. According to the data from the acceptance trials, the thermal shields would block the heat of Havoc engines, and even the heat of a barrel that had been used intensively for three hours. But heat signature was not the only way that a Havoc could be spotted from the air at night or in conditions of reduced visibility. That much ferrous metal (even though sophisticated composites were used extensively in the Havoc, there was still a considerable amount of steel and steel alloys in it) made for a strong magnetic signature, one that could be localized, if not always positively identified by sensitive instruments.

It was because of their uncertainty about the quality of their shielding that Eustace Ponks and his crew didn't set up their bedrolls on the engine deck of Basset two, under the thermal shield. The night would have been a little warmer, and the metal deck of the gun carriage would have been only marginally harder than the ground they did sleep on. The crew was tired enough that they would have been able to sleep soundly strapped into their seats inside the Havoc. But a Havoc would always be a prime target for any enemy, so they set up their bedrolls under the trees, some twenty meters from the gun.

"What the hell," Karl Mennem said as he lowered himself to his blanket. "I can put up with this one more night."

"Yeah," Jimmy Ysinde pitched in quickly. "Tomorrow night we should be back on the ship, showered and between fresh sheets." The sigh he let loose might almost have signaled sexual gratification.

"I wonder how much time we'll have in camp before they ship us out again," Simon Kilgore said. He was already wrapped up in his blanket, eyes closed. He did not worry about chatter. Soon, he would be asleep. Used to the sounds of a 200mm cannon going off next to him, a little subdued talk would never matter.

"Don't sniff the sheets till you see 'em," Eustace advised. That was a typical comment from him. He made a habit of it.

The quiet lasted almost until dawn.

The Schlinal Hegemony's Nova tank was not in the same league as the Accord's Havoc self-propelled howitzer. Though more heavily armored, the Nova's main weapon was a 135mm cannon, with a range only half of the Havoc's 200mm gun. The Nova was also smaller and carried only a two-man crew. In top speed, however, they were about equal.

The two weapons platforms served different functions, a distinction as old as the earliest examples of the two types of weapon. The Havoc carried a long-range howitzer, intended to stand back from the front lines and bombard the enemy from a distance. With less than half the maximum range of the Havoc's gun, the Nova was an in-your-face weapon, meant to lead infantry into battle, or to seek out and destroy enemy heavy weapons and strongpoints. The Nova also carried three machine guns, two that fired wire, and one supplied with 20mm ammunition of a variety of types. The Nova also found use as an instrument of civil control, and not just on worlds that had been newly conquered by the Hegemony. The Nova, now in its fourteenth variant, had been designed and was built primarily on Schline, the capital world of the empire. It had even found use there, and on other Schlinal worlds, often enough. The populace of the Hegemony was not always placid.

In the last minutes before dawn, six Novas came out of the east in a broad wedge, driving straight into the Accord perimeter. Infantry came behind the tanks, and alongside them. In a separate foray, Schlinal foot soldiers attacked the Accord line farther to the north, without armored assistance. The Novas opened up with all of their guns, cannon and machine guns. Until that moment, they had not been spotted, or even heard. For the first time in the war, Accord soldiers learned just how silently the Nova could move. In that, the Hegemony was far ahead of the Accord.

Howard Company was spread thin, covering what had been considered a "low risk" section of the perimeter. Almost before the men of Howard knew what had happened, the spearhead of the Schlinal attack was through their line. The six Novas broke through and kept going, speeding up once they had passed the initial line of resistance. Their target was the group of Wasps on the ground near the center of the Accord's position, and their support services. Getting rid of the support vans, with their spare batteries, chargers, as well as maintenance and ammunition stores, would be nearly as crushing a blow as destroying the fighters themselves. Without that support gear, the fighters would quickly become useless.

Perhaps the fact that all of the Schlinal satellites above Porter had been destroyed in the first hour of the Accord incursion made the difference. If the Nova crews had known precisely where those Wasps and support vans were, the destruction might have been nearly complete. Only two Wasps were in the air when the attack started, but all but one of the 13th's remaining fighters managed to gct airborne before the Novas came within range. The last of the Wasps, Red four, was destroyed by a single shot from the lead Nova. Its pilot and crew chief were both killed.

The Nova formation broke up. With enemy fighters in the air, each of the tank drivers headed for cover, and separation. The Nova's weapons were poorly suited for anti-aircraft use.

The men assigned to the 13th's headquarters detachment found themselves fighting for the first time on Porter. Mostly, they took cover, simply trying to stay alive until men from the line companies could come to their aid. Headquarters detachment had no Vrerch missiles, and their wire carbines had no chance of even worrying tank crews.

Terry Banyon made a valiant attempt to stop one of the Novas. Staying in his slit trench until the tank rolled next to it, he jumped up onto the rear deck with nothing but his carbine and a smoke grenade. He emptied his zipper on the driver's porthole, hoping to smash that so he could lob his smoke grenade inside. That, he figured, would make the crew open up, and once a hatch was open, someone else could do the honors with a fragmentation grenade—or even a carbine, if he had no time to reload his own.

It was a futile attempt. The "glass" of the Nova viewports was nanofactured diamond, and the uranium wire spit out by an Armanoc zipper could hardly scratch it. The crew of the Nova would have ignored their unwanted passenger, knowing that he could do them no harm, but when the tank's left tread ran over a large rock, Banyon was thrown from the rear deck. As soon as the tank commander saw that, he threw both treads into reverse. He could not miss a "gift" of that sort.

Terry Banyon had no chance to escape.

"Saddle up," Joe told his men, breaking into the sleep of half of them. His was the second call. Max Maycroft had already broadcast to the entire platoon. The noise of the fighting was too far away to wake heavily sleeping soldiers, but once they started to come awake, they could hear the commotion in the distance. The cannon fire of the Novas had subsided, to be replaced by the occasional blast of a rocket from a Wasp, or from soldiers on the ground. But the small-arms fire was heavy—too heavy, Joe thought, for anything less than full-scale involvement by several companies.

The rest of the perimeter was not abandoned to meet the raid. Though Echo Company moved out of the line, there were still enough others nearby to fill the gap. There was almost no chance that an attack would come along the escarpment. There was no way that the enemy could approach unseen.

Morning twilight was moving toward sunrise as Echo Company started moving toward the center of the 13th's foothold on Porter. That was where the tanks had headed following their breakthrough. Before Echo got that far, they were redirected toward the line to help there. Howard Company was keeping the Schlinal infantry busy, even though it had been unable to slow down the tanks.

By the time Echo reached the fighting, the situation had stabilized. There was still shooting going on, on both sides, and the line was no longer solid. Some of the enemy infantry had broken through. Joe's platoon was put to work trying to ferret out all of the enemy who had gotten behind the lines while the rest of Echo reinforced Howard to keep more from penetrating.

The men of 2nd platoon were spread out, five to ten meters apart, close enough to cover each other and make certain that no one slipped through this net. They moved slowly. Each man kept his head and eyes moving, looking for any hint of movement in the long shadows of early morning. There was no good cover, no place to hide. That worked more for 2nd platoon than against it. The Heggies were the ones looking for places to hide. Tree trunks without any stands of bushes or tall grass would give them little help. Visibility was too good. Those Heggies cut off inside the lines had few choices after their tanks deserted them for the other hunt. Some dropped their weapons, raised their arms, and surrendered. Others decided to obey their orders and went down fighting. There were not many of the latter.

Chal Tomer in third squad was killed by one of the Heggies who would not surrender. Two men in second squad were wounded by a grenade. None of the Heggies involved in those incidents survived.

The breakthrough on Howard Company's front and the subsequent death of Terry Banyon was not the worst news of the morning for Colonel Stossen. Only minutes after the death of his executive officer, Stossen had a call from CIC on the flagship. The 13th's relief was not in-system. Only a message drone had come.

"Hold until relieved or recalled. Covering force for your evacuation has been delayed."

CHAPTER
9

Van Stossen refused to let himself feel grief, even though he had served with Terry Banyon for years. Their association, their *friendship*, went back long before the founding of the Accord's fifteen Spaceborne Assault Teams. They had been close, professionally and personally. They were friends and their wives were friends. Their children had played together since infancy. But Van and Terry were both professional soldiers, and death was part of their profession.

"We'll have to get a burial detail," Stossen told Dezo Parks when they stood together next to Banyon's mangled body. The last of the Schlinal tanks had been accounted for, finally. Van turned away. He could not look at his dead friend past that first glance.

"I'll take care of it," Parks said. He called for men to help.

Stossen moved away, back toward the command post. He had more urgent worries now. His two thousand men depended on him for leadership. Later, when the campaign was over and the 13th was back in garrison, or perhaps just in transit to the next battle, there would be time for reflection. If the 13th went back to garrison—as they would almost certainly do, at least long enough to replenish supplies and train replacements—Van would raise a toast to his friend. He would take the news to Terry's widow personally. There could be no thought of just making a compsole call or sending the official letter of notification. That his own wife would accompany him would not make it easier, but he would never even think of evading that final obligation to his friend.

"We've knocked out all six of the enemy tanks," Major Parks reported softly after a detail of enlisted men had started digging a grave for the executive officer.

"Sorry about Terry." Parks had seen Terry Banyon killed. He had directed a medical orderly to him before it was clear that Banyon was beyond any possible field repairs. Dezo's visor was up now, and his face was grimy. He watched the colonel closely. He knew how close Stossen and Banyon had been.

Stossen shrugged. *It happens*. "You're exec now, Dezo." If his voice was less firm than usual, neither he nor Parks gave any sign. It was something that would never be mentioned.

"I don't think this raid was just a throwaway," Parks said after a moment. He was operations officer for the 13th, but intelligence analysis was always part of that job. "It wasn't strong enough to be a serious attempt to dislodge us, but it was too strong to be just something to keep us occupied."

"A diversion?" Stossen asked.

"Has to be. It seems fairly clear that the Heggies have been moving large numbers of troops out of Porter City at night. And they're moving them *away* from us, as near as we've been able to tell. Out of range of our Wasps. How they've routed them from there is anybody's guess, but mine is that they're staging for a major attempt on us. I don't see it simply as a retreat, keeping out of our way. That would mean that they knew—beyond a doubt—that we're here merely to keep them in place. Without that knowledge, no Schlinal warlord would dare retreat and ignore us. Even without the overwhelming advantage in numbers they have, that would be a capital offense in the Schlinal military. So they *must* be staging for an attack."

"How long do you think we have?"

"Unless their concealment measures are a lot better than we think they are, they must still be more than a hundred klicks away from the perimeter, most likely a *lot* farther. Our observation out to a hundred klicks is simply too tight to miss significant numbers. We're patrolling that much area with regularity, and that's also the primary focus for the sensing from the fleet and the spyeyes we launched. But if the Heggies have shuttles ready to move their men, that still might not give us a lot of warning before the attack comes." Even if the enemy launched a fleet of shuttles three-hundred kilometers away from the perimeter, the men on the ground might be lucky to receive ten minutes warning.

"Come at us from somewhere up on the plateau, not up either of the access roads to the valley?" Stossen had his own opinion, but he wanted to hear what Parks had to say.

Parks shook his head. "I don't think they'd dare try to come up from below, not in any real force. They have to know that we can hold either of those routes against anything they can throw at us. Easier than the three-hundred Spartans." Even after nearly six thousand years, that stand was recalled by career military officers. It was studied in nearly every military academy in the Terran Cluster.

Stossen pulled out his mapboard and clicked it back to a broader view of the entire plateau region.

"Most of the area within three hundred klicks is heavily forested. For that matter, most of the plateau is. Trees and occasional regions of prairie." And most of it was unsettled, even after centuries of human presence on the world. The staff had gone over maps of all of the regions of Porter that might have any bearing on their planned operations. Stossen was a careful thinker though, and he preferred to have his maps open and in front of him at a time like this. It helped him to keep his thinking straight if he went over everything as if it were completely new to him.

"The clearings here, more around Maison." Stossen pointed to areas north and northwest of the town. "Rocky areas here." He pointed off to the east and northeast.

"Too open," Parks offered. "No cover, visual or IR, and too much chance of the movement being spotted by someone in Maison. The Heggies have to figure that we left people there, spotters, or at least radios for the locals to call us." A number of radios *had* been left in the town, and instructions on how to report anything of interest. The Special Intelligence men from the Maison team were also still in the town, undercover now.

"Maybe the Heggies could hide a few hundred men for a time in the crevices and gullies in the rocky areas, but not for any significant amount of time. And you can't throw a heat shield over several thousand men and all their equipment in either area. You'd get leakage no matter what." Parks had no hard data to back up that assertion, but he had no doubt about it, and Stossen merely nodded agreement. That many men, there would be *some* sign.

"If they're going to stage on the plateau, I'd suggest that either of these places is more likely." Parks pointed out two other areas, both farther away from the 13th and from Maison. Both areas offered thick forest with small clearings that were large enough for VTOL shuttles to get in and out quickly.

"We can get a look at them," Stossen conceded. "Of course, there's nothing that says there's any limit on the places they *might* be. Or even that they have to stage on the plateau. Assuming they have sufficient lift capability, they could pick just about any place they like, anywhere on the continent." Porter's sole continent stretched from the north polar zone to latitude 60 south, as much as nine-thousand kilometers wide in places.

"We can't watch the whole continent that closely," Parks said. "We can get coverage—do get coverage—but not the intensive sort we'd need to find them. Not without launching a lot more spyeyes, and it would take a day or two to get them all in position, assuming that the ships are carrying enough to do the job. We could increase the diameter of the inner zones . . ."

Photo and video surveillance of the planet was based on distance from the regiment's landing zones. Out to a radius of one-hundred kilometers, the coverage was most intense, virtually continuous. From one hundred to two hundred kilometers out, there was at least hourly observation of each section, though at somewhat lower resolution. From two-hundred to five-hundred kilometers, the frequency of coverage was still less, as little as once in four hours for some areas. Farther out than that, an area might be eyeballed from orbit as infrequently as once a day.

Stossen shook his head. "Even that would take more satellites, and we can't tell if we have time for it." He took a deep breath.

"You know," he said more softly, "there's no way to know how long we'll be here now. Pickup delayed. Hold until relieved or recalled. No matter how long it is, we'll have to make do with what we have, here and aboard the ships." He didn't want to think about what might have caused the delay. Once he started doing that, it would be far too easy to let his imagination run away with him, dreaming up all sorts of disasters.

"Food and ammunition." Parks nodded. "Food may be less of a problem. We can always do a little foraging. There is game around here, and nothing native is supposed to be toxic to humans. No reported problems anyway. Porter's been settled long enough for any incompatibilities to show up. We can check with some of the locals about edible plants."

"Game means cooking fires." Stossen shrugged. "Well, they know we're here. The men will have to be careful about it though. Just in daylight, early enough so the ashes are cold before sunset. That sort of thing."

"But ammunition," Parks said. "What do we do, pull in and stick with strictly defensive fire? Maybe collect some of the weapons and ammo we left in Maison?"

Stossen was quiet for a minute before he replied. He thought of the Havoc barrage he had loosed the first morning, just to ease the way for one company that was having a little too much difficulty reaching their objective. There was no helping that prodigality now. Those rounds were gone. "No, we won't go back to Maison unless it becomes absolutely necessary. Hunker down and wait?" He shook his head. "I don't think so. The Heggies get the idea that something's wrong, they'll really be all over us. Or ignore us and send part of the garrison off to Devon, and that's what we're here to prevent."

"Continue with our original harassment?"

Stossen let a smile spread across his face. He did not spend a lot of time mulling over the idea that had just come to him. It *felt* right. "No. Let's really go for it."

"You mean take Porter back all by ourselves?" Parks returned the smile.

"Maybe not, but maybe we can make the Heggies rethink their own plans. When our pickup does come, it will be easier if we don't have Heggies stacked up around our perimeter here."

"Head for Porter City?"

"There's no other suitable target, is there?" Stossen asked, his voice mild, with a touch of humor. He continued to turn the idea over in his mind. There were risks, serious risks, but that was true of any possible course. They were on their own. For how long, neither of them could even guess. Doing everything possible to keep the Schlinal garrison reacting instead of acting had to help. He hoped.

"How strong an effort?" Parks asked, his mind switching over to tactics.

Stossen took time to consider that. "We want the effort to be strong enough for the Heggies to take notice, but not so strong that we're a pushover here. Say, the same sort of effort we directed at Maison—two line companies, two recon platoons, one Havoc battery. We'll give them as much Wasp cover as we can, as needed."

"The Havocs could range about a bit," Parks said. "We can't hold them back to the speed of men on foot."

"But Havocs need infantry support. You saw how long the Novas lasted once they got away from their support."

Parks nodded, conceding the point.

"You think we can afford to use shuttles to put the strike force closer to their target?" Parks asked. "Going full out, it would take six days for them to walk the whole distance to Porter City. That gives the Heggies too much time to chop them up. And we don't know how many days we've got."

"That'll take six landers, five with a little overcrowding." Stossen didn't hesitate now. If this move was going to have any effect at all, it would have to be done quickly, with panache, before the Schlinal forces could mount whatever attack they were preparing. Stossen grinned, then nodded.

"Get them into five shuttles. Set it up so the landers are down fifteen minutes before sunset. We'll load up and get them moving as soon as it's dark. The Havocs and their support vehicles will have to go on their own. They can catch up, rendezvous near Porter City."

"How close do we set the infantry down?"

"Let's look at the map and see what we've got," Stossen said.

"Why us again?" Wiz Mackey asked as Echo Company gathered at the LZ. "We had our fun. Shouldn't one of the other companies draw this gig?"

"We shouldn't have done such a good job," Mort Jaiffer said. "They must think we're the experts, the aces. We're going to get all the impossible jobs now."

Joe let the men talk. He stayed out of the general grousing though.

"They're not just going to leave us here, are they, Sarge?" Kam Goff asked.

"No, they're not going to leave us here," Joe replied. It had not taken long for word to spread that they were not going to be picked up on schedule, and that there was no definite new rendezvous time. Whatever was going on, it did not sound good. But Joe had to believe that the Accord would not abandon an entire assault team. That would be—if nothing else—a public relations disaster.

Joe was uncertain how to feel about this new mission. It did seem unfair that Echo Company would get chosen again. Most of the companies in the 13th had done nothing but lay around along the established perimeter since the first day of the fight. Echo had been in on everything.

The mission briefing had been pitifully short on details, and the whole idea seemed a little less than sane to Joe. In one breath the first sergeant had told them that they would have to start conserving food and ammunition, especially ammunition. With the next breath he had told them that they were going on a long-distance raid against the Heggie forces in the capital, with the possibility that they would face odds of more than fifty to one. Perhaps a lot more. And that they were expected to keep all of those Heggies busy, possibly for several days.

"How the hell can we conserve ammo and do that?" Joe had asked the first sergeant, face-to-face, not over the radio.

"I know how it sounds. Just tell your men not to get trigger-happy on this lark," First Sergeant Iz Walker replied, very softly. "We do what we can, Joe. I don't make the orders."

"Yeah, well." Joe just shook his head and walked away. He had made his point. All he could do then was obey those orders, the best he could.

Now, he was shepherding his men back into one of the shuttles, but not to return to the ship for a ride home. Realizing that made Joe feel uncomfortable. *Home.* Maybe home was nothing more than a private room in a barracks full of soldiers, but it was a definite place to Joe Baerclau.

"Just going to be a nuisance to the enemy, buzz around and keep them busy," Joe told the squad when they were in their seats in the shuttle. "In and out, back and forth. Play keep away if we have to. We did so good up at Maison, the colonel thinks we can lick the whole Heggie garrison."

No one responded to Joe's light assessment of the mission. The platoon had already lost three men killed and two more seriously wounded and evacuated to the hospital ship. The fight had gotten personal. Everyone had lost buddies, but more than that, the news that the exec had been crushed by a tank had really sobered the men. *Brass* never got killed. They stayed back where it was safe. Most of the men continued to think that, despite evidence to the contrary.

As soon as he strapped himself in, Joe leaned back and closed his eyes. It was no surprise that he was two days short on sleep and ready to go another night not only without sleep but marching across hostile territory toward a morning attack. Joe did not sleep in the shuttle, not really. He was not certain whether or not he even dozed. Afterward, he figured that he might have napped for three or four minutes. It could not have been longer than that. As soon as the shuttle lifted off, Joe was awake, eyes open, looking around.

How long will my luck run? he asked himself. That was especially disturbing. He had never gone into combat asking himself that question before.

Originally considered to be "merely" a refinement to the latest reconciliation of general relativity and quantum mechanics, the Loughlin-Runninghorse equations were first sketched out in the twenty-first century AD. Even then, full expansion of the basic system of seventeen equations required nearly fifty hours of concentrated attention from a network of the six most powerful academic supercomputers on Earth. Under-standing the equations and their most "obvious" implications took physicists and mathematicians most of the next century. It was recognized that if correct, the theories implicit in the equations required the objective reality of a paradimensional aspect to space—*hyperspace* (though the scientific community struggled heroically for years to find an acceptable alternative to that term, the general public, conditioned by two centu-ries of the term's use in fiction, refused every offering)—and the potential for the development of what was immediately (though somewhat imprecisely) dubbed antigravity because that was the use most readily imagined for the promised tech-nology. More properly termed a projectable artificial gravity generator, it becomes *anti*gravity only when its field is used to nullify local natural gravity. The field can also be projected so that its effect is *added* to local natural gravity, or directed at any angle to the natural field. For a time, considerable amounts of research money and thought were devoted to exploring the possibility of using projectable artificial gravity generators as offensive weapons, but eventually those efforts limped into oblivion.

The Loughlin-Runninghorse equations also pointed the way to the development of the first hyperspace drive, a technol-ogy that proved to be surprisingly close to that for artificial gravity—a superset of the artificial gravity technology. In the words of one less-than-original contemporary academic wag, "You can't have one without the other."

Perhaps the greatest measure of the significance of the theo-retical work can be gauged from the fact that the year of the original publication of the Loughlin-Runninghorse equations was chosen as Year One, SA.

The five shuttles lifted off from the LZ together, then quick-ly moved apart. The only noise made by the drives that pow-ered them was an almost subsonic whine, more felt than heard. Within the shuttles, there was the inevitable slight vibration, a product more of being in an atmosphere than just of being under AG drive. The shuttles headed west-southwest, barely clearing the highest treetops on the plateau. As soon as they passed the escarpment, the pilots of all five shuttles reduced power long enough to drop them nearly to the level of the rift valley below. The effect, for their passengers, was rather like being in an out-of-control lift cage as it hurtled three-hundred meters downward. Near the end of the drop, as the throttles were edged forward to provide more power, apparent gravity within the shuttles increased briefly to more than two and a half times normal. Once the descent had been checked, the feeling of weight returned to normal.

"Another hot landing drill," Joe cautioned his men once he had recovered from the sensation of falling three-hundred meters. "We go out as if the entire Heggie army might be waiting for us." *They might be,* he warned himself. Supposedly, the Heggies were unable to spot and track the shuttles in the kind of maneuvers they were making. Perhaps they had spotted the landers coming in over the LZ earlier. It had still been daylight then, and the black craft would have been visible to the naked eye. But, according to Captain Ingels, the Heggies had no spyeyes in orbit over Porter any longer. Those had all been wiped out the morning of the initial landing, and there were no Schlinal ships around to replace them.

But who really knows? Joe asked himself.

"Get out in proper order and find a good piece of ground to hug," he continued, speaking slowly over the squad frequency. "According to CIC. there won't be any Heggies right there, but assume they're wrong. It wouldn't be the first time." That was more for effect than accurate. CIC might occasionally miss something, but rarely by much. They were good. The 13th could not survive without good eyes, and better brains, watching over them. That meant, at present, that even if there were Heggies around where they landed, the force would probably be no larger than—perhaps—platoon size. A patrol that large might slip past the spyeyes.

"Just tell me this isn't as crazy as it sounds," Mort said over his private channel to Joe.

"Colonel's always been pretty savvy, Mort," Joe replied. It was the most positive comment he could come up with at the moment.

Most of the men tried to get what rest they could during the short hop in the landers. Soldiers got like that. Sleep when you can, even if only for a few seconds. It might be days before you get anything longer. Joe looked around. He saw closed eyes. Perhaps not many of the men were actually sleeping, but they looked the part. Of the privates in his squad, only Kam Goff had his eyes open—wide open, staring blankly ahead of him.

Gonna have to watch him closer than ever, Joe thought. Goff looked as if he had gone beyond fear, and Joe couldn't guess which way the rookie would tumble. He might come out of it on his own, but he also might freeze up or become foolhardy. In any case, there was no way that Joe could cut Goff out of the action now. He might still work out, with a little luck, and the right nudge at the right time, but Joe hoped that he wouldn't have to bet his life on it. Still, that was why Joe had taken both new men into his own fire team, so he could give them as much personal attention as possible. At least Al Bergon was cool. He had shown from the start that he could handle whatever combat threw at him. That was far from unusual among men who volunteered for additional duties as medics. Joe shook his head, an almost-invisible gesture within his helmet. *Where do they come from?*

"Thirty seconds," the pilot warned, and time for reflection was gone. Eyes opened. Men looked around, as if they might see something new within the troop bay. The monitors on the bulkheads showed an infrared image of the ground they were approaching, overlaid on a photographic map. The shuttle was flying low, so the cameras didn't show much, and the view moved by too rapidly for the men to see any detail. But there were no telltale hot spots showing up, nothing too bright to be natural in IR.

The dim red lights that had been the only illumination in the troop bay were extinguished before the shuttle landed. Equally dim green lights came on over the exits. Shielded inside long cylinders, and hitting only nonreflective surfaces, the lights would not show through to anyone on the outside. The men all had their visors down and night-sight gear activated. They didn't need additional lights. Before the four doors were fully open, the men were all on their feet moving toward their assigned exits, safeties off on their rifles, ready for action the instant they went through the doorway and had a field of fire open in front of them.

"Stay close to me, kid," Joe whispered to Goff as they went through the doorway. "I mean *close.*"

"Yes, Sarge," Kam replied. His voice sounded distant, as if he were not truly inside his head.

The terrain where the shuttles landed was much different from up on the plateau. Around the main LZs, the ground had been flat, except for the cones of dirt around the trunks of that one species of tree. Only up near Maison had the land been at all uneven, and there it was a matter of a few small hills. In this part of the rift valley though, the ground was extremely broken up, uneven and rocky. There were thickets and small stands of trees, narrow valleys with thin, shallow streams running through them, large stone protrusions and occasional dry clefts in the ground, ravines, or gullies. It was topological confusion, an excellent arena for soldiers who preferred not to have their presence detected.

The shuttles had been forced to separate to find spaces to land. There was no single flat area around where all five of them could have landed together. There was scarcely a place where two would fit, even with exceptionally talented pilots.

That meant that a certain amount of time was wasted after debarkation as the separated units joined up and commanders made sure that no one had been lost in the initial confusion. By the time the strike force had reorganized itself for the march toward Porter City, the shuttles had lifted off and disappeared into the night, flying farther west before lifting toward orbit and a rendezvous with their mother ships. It was too dangerous to hold the shuttles on-world where they would be tempting targets for the enemy. If the 13th had to make a hasty exit from Porter, under fire, they would need every shuttle the fleet carried.

"I knew we had a long march ahead of us," Mort told Joe once the force had started moving, "but I didn't realize it was mountain goat country."

"Good cover," Joe said. He kept his head turning. The platoon was in two columns, one on either side of a creek running along the bottom of the gully they were in.

"Good cover for the enemy too," Mort replied.

"I know, so cut the chatter and keep your eyes open." Men got too used to the privacy of communicating over their helmet radios. Sound discipline was an enduring problem.

The enemy has no business being close enough to set up an ambush. Joe repeated that to himself. The strike force had landed in the most deserted sector to be found within fifty kilometers of Porter City. There weren't even any farms within twenty kilometers, no sign at all of human habitation. It *might* be just the sort of area a military commander would choose for field exercises, but the Heggies were unlikely to be out on training maneuvers with the 13th sitting on the plateau. At a time like this, everything would be for real, not training.

But Joe remained nervous. That was the only way to go into combat.

Eustace Ponks had his hatch open as Basset two raced across the rift valley. Every few minutes—when the ride seemed smooth enough—he would reach up, grab the rim of the hatchway, and lift his head out into the open air. The Havoc was making a steady sixty kilometers per hour, very close to its top speed. Eustace was unaware of the discussions that had taken place between the 13th's commanding and operations officers. All he knew was what was in the final orders that had come down. Basset Battery was to race full tilt toward Porter City. They had to cover five-hundred kilometers in less than ten hours in order to be in position to support the infantry raid against the city. The sooner they could get within range of the strike force, the sooner they would be able to bring their guns to bear, in case Echo and George companies and the two recon platoons were discovered and attacked before they reached their target.

The Havoc was far from a racer, but there was the same sort of feel to it. Eustace loved racing, of any sort. He didn't even need to have a bet down on the outcome. People, animals, wheeled or winged vehicles, boats—anything that could be pitted one against the other in a contest of speed and talent—Eustace loved to watch, loved to cheer on a personal favorite.

His favorite in this race was his all-time personal favorite, himself. With fewer responsibilities, he might have chosen to boost himself up to keep his head out in the wind constantly, but he couldn't permit himself that foolish indulgence. His controls and warning systems were all inside the turret. He had the vehicle's radar and IR screens to watch as well as the real-time relay of data being sent down from the spyeye satellites and the ships of the fleet. There weren't enough men in a Havoc crew to let the commander dope off.

"Put antigrav drives on this baby and she'd *really* fly," Simon said, looking across the gun barrel at Ponks. Simon Kilgore knew how much his sergeant enjoyed racing, both as participant and spectator.

"Be a mean mother, all right," Ponks conceded with a grin. It was an old topic. The possibility of an antigrav gun platform was a perennial in the artillery. But the size power plant that would be needed would make the platform much too easy a target.

Maybe someday.

According to the latest satellite intelligence, updated since the battery of Havocs had descended to the floor of the valley, there was no enemy armor anywhere between the escarpment and the capital. There were also no known concentrations of enemy foot soldiers, though that information was far less certain than the other. There were enough spyeyes overhead to cover the entire area between the scarp and Porter City every twenty minutes, at the best resolution of the imaging computers. It took about three additional minutes for CIC to process the data and transmit the necessary information and coded map overlays to the forces on the surface. Worst case, the information Ponks and the other Havoc commanders were looking at should never be more than twenty-three minutes old, generally less than half of that. That was still long enough for a lot to happen.

"This mission strike you as just a little bit crazy?" Simon asked a few minutes later.

Eustace laughed, loud and long. "Just a little," he conceded. "That's what makes it so exciting."

"Brother, you and I have different ideas about excitement," Kilgore said. "Ranging off five-hundred klicks from the rest of the team, heading straight for maybe twenty or thirty thousand enemy soldiers and God only knows how much armor and air, and how many thousands of rockets. *And* not knowing how much longer we're even going to *be* here before we get some help, or a ticket off."

"You want certainty, you're in the wrong business," Ponks said. "You should have been a preacher or something."

"We don't have preachers, we have rabbis," Kilgore said. "And they don't have all that much certainty either. I know. My father is one."

"No kiddin'? Hey, I didn't know that, and how long we been together?"

"Too long, I think. You keepin' your eyes on our TA?"

Ponks took a quick look at the target acquisition monitor, then nodded. "I'm keeping my eyes where they belong. Just don't run us into something we can't get out of."

CHAPTER
10

Captain Teu Ingels of Echo Company was in overall tactical command of the strike force. Lieutenant Vic Vickers, the commanding officer of George, was second in command even though there were two lieutenants in Echo who were senior to him in rank. Ingels was the senior company commander within the 13th. Within six to nine months, perhaps sooner, he would be promoted to major and a job on Colonel Stossen's staff. With the death of Lieutenant Colonel Banyon, that promotion and reassignment were perhaps more imminent, though it would not come until after the 13th finished its job on Porter—if the 13th ever got off-planet.

The recon platoons ranged out ahead and to either side of Echo and George. It was their job to find a quick, safe route to the objective as well as to scout for any enemy positions or telltales that might lie across that route. The men who made it into the recon platoons were chosen specifically for their abilities. The fifteen Spaceborne Assault Teams were seen as an elite within the Accord Defense Forces, and the recon platoons were an elite within the SATs.

There was little chat among the men on the march this night. The pace that the companies had to maintain made spare wind for even whispered asides scarce. Joe Baerclau smiled at the thought. It took a lot to drive any comment at all from his men. At least, if they didn't talk, he didn't have to waste his own breath telling them not to.

Joe stepped out of the line for a moment and turned to watch as his men filed past. At the moment, 2nd platoon was in the middle of the line of march, in the left-hand column. George Company was a couple of hundred meters to the right, following the next indentation in the landscape.

Hardly a level spot around, Joe thought. He shook his head. He had paid little attention before to the description of this valley as a *rift* valley. The word simply had slid past without sinking in. Joe had heard the term before, but had never given it much thought. Mort had filled him in during their time along the escarpment, giving him a quick briefing on tectonics, an explanation of why the ground was so uneven, so rocky. "It's not old enough for erosion to have smoothed it all out yet," Mort had concluded, but it had taken this closer experience for Joe to really feel the meaning of that explanation.

This night march was little longer than the one Echo had made to Maison, but it was much more draining because of the terrain. Good boots eased the load on feet, but there was still the constant pull at leg muscles strained first one way and then the other. After five hours, Joe wondered if he could possibly keep going. The calves of his legs felt as if they had been bound in piano wire, and the wire was contracting, cutting into skin and muscle.

He was walking on a modest side slope, a layer of shale tilted by less than twenty degrees and strewn with igneous rocks that had fallen from another stratum, when his left foot slid out from under him. Joe's right foot caught against a rock for an instant, and he nearly tumbled headfirst down a three-meter embankment. His right ankle twisted as that foot came free, and he went down on his hip. After sliding halfway to the bottom of the gully, he managed to stop himself. For a moment, he could do no more than that. He let his head drop back against the rock and sucked in air.

His foot. No, not the foot. The ankle.

"You hurt, Sarge?" Al Bergon asked, sliding more carefully down the slope to come to a stop next to Joe.

"Right ankle," Joe replied. "I don't think it's sprained. I just twisted it."

"Better let me have a look."

"No time."

"No time is what it'll take," Al said. "You aggravate it and it's more than you think, *then* we have trouble."

Bergon didn't wait for his sergeant to agree. In his function as squad medic, he did have a certain amount of authority, authority that Platoon Sergeant Maycroft and Lieutenant Keye would support in an instant. While Al talked, he started taking off Joe's boot and sock. His hands moved around the ankle and along the muscles above it.

"Just a little swelling," Al said. "That may be just from the walk, not from the twist. I'll wrap a soaker around it and you should be fine."

He was already peeling the wrapper from the medicated bandage, and he got it secured around Baerclau's ankle in seconds. The analgesic in the soak started to work instantly, though the nanobots that would do any real repair work would take somewhat longer to do their job. Joe could feel the hot tingle of the bandage. He closed his eyes for a moment. The ankle had pained him more than he had really been aware, judging from the relief he felt as the pain started to abate. By the time his sock and boot were back on, the ache was scarcely a dull throb—bearable.

"I'll be able to walk on that," Joe said. He flexed the ankle several times. Despite an initial stab of renewed pain, that actually seemed to make the ankle feel better.

"And the soak'll take care of any muscle pulls or such," Al said. "But be careful the next hour or so. If there's more wrong there than I think you'll know that soon." *Probably within the first ten minutes*, Al thought. In the field like this, he was limited to what he could see and feel for his diagnosis.

"You okay down there?"

Joe looked up, even though the voice had come over his radio. Max Maycroft was standing at the top of the gully, looking down at him. Joe clicked his transmitter over to the noncoms' channel.

"I will be, Max. Slight twist. My own damn fault. Careless. But it's all taken care of now."

To demonstrate that, Joe got to his feet and started to scramble up the slope. Before he could object, Al Bergon was at his side, one hand half supporting him. Joe felt an irrational flush of anger, but squelched it before it could show in his face, or in the way he moved.

"Thanks, Al," he said when they were both off of the slope.

"Don't feel bad," Maycroft said, standing with his feet braced wide even though he was on nearly level ground. "We've had twenty people do that, that I know of. Some of them were hurt worse than you are. Best boot treads in the galaxy, and they're still not secure on a slippery bit of shale."

"I just got too careless, Max," Joe said, feeling more embarrassed than hurt at the moment. "Five, six hours of this shit. It was just getting to me, and it shouldn't have."

"I know what you mean. But now that you're back on your feet, you might as well get off them again. Fifteen minutes, maybe twenty. Captain's decided that we all need a breather. Our orders have been changed, in any case. Once we get to our positions, the idea now is we sit doggo until sunset, unless we're discovered. Hide. Recon lads will do a little work of their own. And the Havocs, but not us. Now, grab a quick bite, a little water." He paused a second before he added, "Maybe a stimtab as well. That'll help clear your mind."

Joe nodded slowly. "I should have thought of that myself, Max. Gotta watch it. I get a little tired, and I'm getting careless. That can get people killed, and not just me."

"Don't read anything into what I said but what I said," Max told him. "That wasn't a chewing out. It was just a suggestion."

Joe shrugged. "Whatever you say, Max." He didn't see the humor in his words. When Maycroft laughed, Joe looked up quickly, caught completely unaware.

"That's the spirit," Max said. "Now, on your butt. Give that soaker a chance to do its work."

Zel Paitcher stood behind his Wasp and watched Tech Sergeant Roo Vernon work. Zel was cold, despite the flight suit that was supposed to be adequate protection against any temperature down to minus twenty degrees Celsius. There was a decidedly chilly breeze blowing across the plateau, close to 25 kilometers per hour, but the temperature was closer to 20 above than 20 below.

All in your head, Zel told himself. The breeze could only touch his face and hands. He wouldn't feel so irrationally cold if he were in the cockpit, where he belonged. He wouldn't feel so cold if he weren't worrying that there might be something seriously wrong with Blue four, something that might keep him out of the air. As tiring as the long hours in the sky were getting to be, Zel knew that he preferred that to sitting on the ground and being nothing more than a spectator.

Zel had his arms folded tightly against his chest. He moved around a lot, stamping first one foot and then the other. The sense of cold was no less real merely because he knew that it was an illusion, a trick of his mind.

Roo worked in silence, his head up in the portside drive compartment of Blue four. Warnings had flashed on every monitor in the cockpit when Zel tried to power on. The Wasp's self-diagnostic routines were thorough, but they were almost instantaneous. Each of the computers that minded the circuits in the aircraft was dedicated to servicing just a small portion of the works. The system had shut itself down before Zel could get his hand to the switch.

Zel never even considered going over to Roo to offer his help. Though he had a basic understanding of the theoretical workings of the antigrav drives, he had virtually no mechanical competence—not with those drives. Even if he had been relatively competent, Roo would have turned down the offer. Blue three and four were *his* Wasps. He knew them better than their designer, or so he would claim. He knew the idiosyncrasies of each one. He knew what they could do, what they would do. And he had *The Touch* with them.

Slee was sitting in the cockpit of Blue three, waiting. The squadron commander had vetoed the idea of Slee going off without a backup, or with a wingman he was unused to, unless that became urgently necessary. Instead, the next pair of flyers in the rotation had been wakened and sent aloft.

Roo finally came out from under the Wasp. "She should be all right now, sir," he said. "Heat problem. Somehow got some dust caked in where it oughtn't to have been, and that like to baked a coupla circuits." He looked around. "Small wonder, I guess. But she's fine now."

"We're ready to go?"

"Two minutes. We'll put a new battery in on that side, just to make sure." The Wasps that had gone up in place of Slee and Zel were almost due to land again anyway. The rotation would, probably, remain changed.

"Thanks, Chief," Zel said. "Put another beer on the tab I owe you when we get back to base."

Roo grinned. "I think this is a two-beer tally, sir. I really do."

"Okay, two beers."

"Just bring her back in one piece, sir."

"I'll do my best."

Climbing into the cockpit and strapping himself in felt strangely liberating to Zel. The cold was instantly forgotten. Getting into his Wasp was almost like coming home. Soon, he would be back in the air, where he belonged. He took a deep breath and let it out slowly.

"Just about ready, Slee," he said over the radio. "Soon as they button in a new battery."

"About time," Slee replied. "I was about to fall asleep." Then he regretted the statement as a gaping yawn forced its way out. Sleep. *What's that?* he wondered.

The last half hour of the night march was sheer misery for Joe Baerclau. It wasn't that his ankle continued to bother him. Indeed, his right ankle felt fairly good. But he had been trying to ease the burden on it, and *that* had put more strain on the rest of that leg, and the other, and walking unnaturally had caused his knees to stiffen up and brought a growing ache to his lower back. But Echo and George companies had finally reached the bivouac areas that the recon platoons had found for them, scattered through two deep gullies and a patch of thick scrub forest where the two gullies met. There was water, and there was cover, all that an infantryman could ask for. Back near the head of the longer ditch—it averaged about nine meters deep—there were several small caves. Captain Ingels had moved into one of them. It would be his headquarters through the day. Another was turned into a dispensary for the soldiers who had been injured on the march. At least the caves were dry and unoccupied. No local beasties had come charging out to voice their displeasure at company.

"Come on, Sarge," Al said once the squad was in position. "I want the doc to have a look at that ankle of yours. You been limping something awful the last couple of klicks."

"Don't mind me," Joe replied. "The ankle doesn't hurt. A couple hours of rest and I'll be good as new."

"I hope so, Sarge, but I'll feel better knowing for sure, and so will you."

Though his mind instinctively rebelled at the suggestion, Joe didn't resist. After two steps, he no longer even tried to shrug off Al's help in moving. It was not very far from where Joe's squad had settled in to the cave that was being used as a dispensary.

"Doc" Eddles, Echo Company's senior medtech, wasn't really a doctor, but his training had gone far beyond that of the medics in the various platoons. The Accord Defense Force had provided him with eighteen months of medical training, enough to qualify him as a licensed medtech in civilian life once he completed his contractual three years of service following training. The 13th only had two physicians, both surgeons, although there were additional medical personnel assigned to the fleet ships that carried the 13th. But Eddles was qualified to handle anything short of invasive surgery, and with the availability of portable trauma tubes, that was rarely needed.

There were three men ahead of Joe, men whose injuries appeared to be worse than his. Doc Eddles was working on another, a private from the heavy weapons squad whose knee had been injured in a fall. Al had a quick word with Eddles, then came back to where Baerclau was sitting, propped up against the rocks outside the cave.

"It'll be a few minutes, Sarge, but wait it out."

Joe nodded. By this time, he ached enough that he would wait, if only to get something to ease the pain in his legs and back. "Tell Ezra he's in charge till I get back," he said. Then he switched over to his noncoms' frequency and told Ezra the same thing directly. "Get everyone settled in. Tell them to get what sleep they can. One man alert at all times to pass on anything we need to know."

●   ●   ●

Colonel Stossen palmed the stimtab almost as skillfully as a magician, and used the excuse of covering a yawn to pop the lozenge in his mouth. Major Parks noticed but showed no reaction. Seeing Stossen take another reminded him of his own exhaustion. He had been sucking stimulants at least as often as his boss. Neither of them had managed twelve hours sleep total in the last hundred. Parks thought of taking another stimtab himself but decided to wait . . . for a few minutes at least. He was well beyond safe dosage already, and an extreme overdose could produce quite unpleasant side effects—physical and mental—though nothing critically dangerous to the body.

"I don't know whether I'm coming or going, Dezo," Stossen said after nearly a minute of silence. Exhaustion pressed on him like a weight, making even the simplest action more difficult. The two men were sitting facing each other, Stossen leaning back against a tree cone with his legs stretched out in front of him, Parks cross-legged, leaning forward just a little. "I know I need sleep, but . . ."

"We both do, and so do probably ninety percent of our men," Dezo said. "Well, maybe it's not quite that high now. Things have been quiet long enough to let a lot of them catch up." Somewhat. No one really found much rest in a combat zone, even when they had the time and the quiet. Minds simply refused to let go enough to allow deep sleep. "Why don't you take four hours now? I can hold on that long, and then maybe I can get a little shut-eye after you've rested."

Stossen hesitated for quite a time before he shook his head slowly. He was having trouble thinking through even the simplest statement.

"Not yet. I want to make sure that George and Echo aren't hit at dawn." As if he might be able to do anything if they were. Stossen looked up at the sky. The east was beginning to show a little light, even to bleary eyes. The strike force was farther west. Dawn would be nearly thirty minutes later for them than it would for the rest of the 13th. "And the Havocs. What's the latest from them?" Stossen grimaced mentally. He had completely forgotten the artillery that he had sent to rendezvous with George and Echo.

"They've all gone to cover for the day. According to Lieutenant Ritchey, they're in a wooded area, cover not as good as he'd like it, but probably adequate." No gunnery officer was ever satisfied with the available cover. "The guns are under heat tarps. No mechanical breakdowns, no sign that the guns were spotted at any time during their run."

"How far are they from Echo and George?" Stossen knew that he should remember that bit of data, but it just wouldn't come to mind.

"About twenty klicks," Parks said quickly. "Close enough to bring their guns to bear in a hurry in case the strike force is attacked."

"What are we missing, Dezo?"

Parks took a deep breath. "We still haven't located the troops that the Heggies moved out of Porter City. At least five thousand, maybe twice that number. They've gone to ground somewhere, but the spyeyes haven't been able to find them yet. Either they're somewhere we haven't looked, or they've got cover too good for the eyes to penetrate."

"In other words, they could hit us with almost no warning."

"It's possible. That's always been possible. But it's also possible that they're waiting to see what we do, just making sure that they don't have all their eggs in the same basket. If they haven't spotted either element of the strike force, they might keep on waiting. That could be either good news or bad."

"What's your best guess?"

Dezo shook his head. "I don't know that I have one. Just no data to build an intelligent guess on. Worst case, those troops could be sitting somewhere waiting for us to attack Porter City, waiting to pincer our strike force the way we did the Heggies from Maison. I think that's what I would do under the circumstances."

"Are we ready for that?"

It was Parks's turn to shrug. "With everything we have. Whether or not that will be enough is another question. It depends on how hard they hit and how much warning they give us. We get the Wasps in as quickly as possible. If it's just the infantry spotted, we also have the Havocs chime in. Then, if necessary, we can move another company or two of infantry down as quickly as we can get shuttles in and loaded—say, eighty minutes with a little luck." That was an overly optimistic estimate, depending on the ships being in perfect position for immediate deployment of the shuttles, but Colonel Stossen would know that as well as Parks did.

Stossen rubbed at his cheeks with both hands. He needed a shave. From the feel of it, it must have been two full days since his last one. He could not remember. For a moment, the idea of appearing less than ready for a parade distracted him, worried him. *Too many years as a garrison soldier,* he told himself.

"It's no good, Dezo," he said finally. "I have to have some sleep or I'll drop. Not knowing about our relief . . ." He never finished that thought. Even with a partially dissolved stimtab in his mouth, Van Stossen fell asleep. Parks propped a pack next to the colonel to keep him from falling over, then moved away. If only he could guarantee Stossen all the sleep he needed.

By four o'clock that afternoon, Joe Baerclau could almost forget that he had hurt his ankle the night before. There was no pain left, not even when he flexed the ankle as vigorously as he could. He even felt rested, for the first time since landing on Porter. Doc Eddles had hit him with a sleep patch, without telling Joe what it was. That sleep had lasted for four hours, but Joe had slept on naturally, for two more hours. He hadn't even remonstrated with Ezra very strongly for not being wakened sooner.

"I guess I did need the sleep," he conceded. "How about the others? And you?"

"We've all had our share," Ezra assured him. "Captain put us all on one man on duty from each fire team. I guess we're all in better shape than we've been since the first morning here."

Joe nodded, still not fully alert. "We'll probably need that before this night's over."

He got up and stretched, then sat back down and ate a meal pack. When he was finished with that, he walked farther along the gully to where Max Maycroft was sitting.

"How's the ankle?" Max asked.

"Good as new. I miss anything important while I was out?"

Max shook his head. "We'll be moving shortly after sunset. I don't think we're going to wait for full dark. Have a seat and pull out your mapboard, and I'll show you the current plan."

Joe sat and pulled the map computer from the long pocket
on the right leg of his uniform. Max took it out and unfolded
it. He dialed up their current coordinates a little more quickly
than Joe would have been able to. Max had done it several
times already.

"This is all assuming that the Heggies don't find out where
we are and attack before we can get moving," Max said while
he was adjusting the field of view on Joe's mapboard.

"First recon is out on their own. They left three hours
ago. Just about full dark, they're supposed to hit the power-
collecting station here." Max pointed at a spot near the west-
ernmost reaches of Porter City. Recon types claimed that they
did not need darkness to cover their movements.

"Their objective is to cause just enough damage to put
the center off-line. Can't really tell about them though. They
might get too eager. We don't want to bash it so bad as to
inconvenience the legal residents for any great length of time.
I suppose that means that the Heggies will have it working
again in a few hours." He made a gesture of dismissal with
one hand. The strikes that the Wasps had made against the
capital's power stations the morning of the landing had not
kept those stations off-line very long.

"Not our concern. The idea is to get the Heggies looking
that way. As soon as we get word that the reccers have done
their job, we'll attack these barracks here. Supposed to be no
more than six-hundred Heggies left in that kaserne. The rest
were part of the force that they moved out of the city. At the
same time, the Havocs are going to target these buildings here,
fairly close to the center of Porter City. CIC estimates that
those buildings contain the Heggie headquarters for the entire
planet. Maybe that's so. Maybe it isn't. And maybe there'll
actually be a few brass hats around their headquarters late at
night. The Wasps are going to hit several locations as well, hit
and run."

"Sounds as if you're not real thrilled about this," Joe
observed.

"Between you and me?"

Joe nodded.

"I'm not. There may still be twenty thousand or more Heggies
in and around Porter City, and we don't know when we're going
to get any relief. The rest of the regiment is up on the plateau,

too far away to do us any good if we need help. We could find ourselves in one hell of a bind before morning, with no more ammo and supplies than we've carried with us."

"I almost wish you hadn't told me all that," Joe said softly. He looked at the ground between his feet for a moment. When he looked up at Max again, he said, "Well, they never told us it would be easy."

"We *do* get in and out in any kind of order, we move west, back into this miserable country," Max said. "From the maps, it looks as if what we walked through last night was easy compared to some of the rest. We draw off Heggies, fine. We're supposed to keep them busy, even if we have to run our asses off to do it."

"How long?"

"Far as I can tell, until our relief shows up to cover our evacuation from Porter. That's the only real provision the captain talked about. We have to keep an eye out for potential LZs in case we get the word to pull out in a hurry."

There were five buildings in the kaserne, all two stories high. Three were of stone or brick construction, the others had wood siding and appeared to be new, most likely built since the Schlinal takeover of Porter. With one building at the far end of the compound, and two buildings on either side, the remaining side of the rectangular compound, facing west, was open. The entire area was surrounded by razor wire, and there was only a single gate through the perimeter, on the north side of the kaserne.

The Schlinal occupying force appeared to be extremely lax in their security measures. There were no guard towers along the fence. Apparently, the wire was the only real defensive addition to the compound. There were no alarm systems planted on the approaches to the kaserne. A recon squad went over the area with their detectors and without finding a single bug that could give the garrison warning. Nor were there mines planted to wreak their own brand of havoc on intruders. There were only three guards posted to cover the two exposed flanks of the compound, with two more guards stationed at the gate. None of the guards seemed to be particularly alert. Joe watched with his power binoculars as the guards were taken out by specialists from the recon detachment, just as the Havoc bombardment started to hit other parts of Porter City.

Two minutes after the first Havoc rounds exploded, and ninety seconds after the Wasps started to hit their targets, Echo and George companies moved forward to attack the barracks. George Company had the direct assault. Three platoons raced across the last two-hundred meters of open ground toward the five buildings surrounded by razor wire. The heavy weapons squads of both companies were in position to pour covering fire into the buildings—Vrerch rockets and wire from their splat guns. Those marksmen armed with Dupuy rocket rifles, commonly known as cough guns, were posted where they would do the most good. The Dupuy fired a 12.5mm rocket-assisted round that could travel level for ranges of up to five kilometers—though it was rare indeed for a target to remain visible and stationary at that distance long enough for the sniper rifle to be truly effective. Like most infantry weapons, the Dupuy was normally used at much less than its maximum accurate range.

The rest of George Company, and the first two platoons of Echo, moved around to the sides of the compound, ready to come in from those directions, or to intercept anyone trying to retreat from (or move to) the kaserne.

The men of Echo and George were sparing of wire during the first minutes of their advance. The leading elements managed to get most of the way across the two-hundred-meter open field before they were spotted, and even after that, most of the Accord firing came from Vrerchs and splat guns behind them. The wire carbines were ready for use, but over and over the men had been cautioned that they weren't to shoot until they had clear targets, or until they started taking Heggie fire.

It seemed to take forever before the Heggies did start returning fire in any organized fashion. The delay may have been no more than two minutes, but that allowed much of the attacking force to get nearly to the buildings. Sappers blew holes in the perimeter fence. Three Vrerch rockets had taken out the gate house, the gate, and nearly ten meters of the barrier on either side. That was the hole that the lead elements of George Company poured through.

Finally, though, the men in the barracks did start to defend themselves, with wire, grenades, and rockets. The fire started out light, ragged, but it built steadily.

What'd they have to do, find the key to the armory? Joe asked himself, shocked more than relieved by the slow response.

Around on the south side of the compound, 2nd platoon had not come directly under fire yet. The early Heggie response was all directed toward the main part of George Company, advancing through the gap where the main gate had been. Second platoon was no longer running. The men moved forward by squads now, one covering the other. Mostly, the men walked in a crouch, ready to dive for cover when the enemy finally noticed them.

Joe no longer thought of the danger. He focused completely on each move, and on keeping track of his men and their situations. There was simply no room left for personal fear. He did remain mindful of all the urgings to be sparing of ammunition, but Joe Baerclau was always somewhat stingy of wire. His bursts were generally little more than a quarter second in duration, a light touch. Years of practice had given him an excellent feel for that, and he tried to restrain himself to shooting at visible targets. Wire carbines showed no muzzle flashes for an enemy to aim at. Joe had to look for people, or for their heat signatures in infrared. With rockets and grenades exploding on both sides, that became more difficult as the firefight progressed.

Part of the facade of the building that 2nd platoon was moving toward exploded outward. Bricks flew dozens of meters. Smaller bits of debris showered down on the approach soldiers. Then the rest of the wall seemed to bend outward, warping slowly. It finally twisted with a loud wrenching noise before it came down in apparent slow motion. Flames were rising inside the building, soaring from ground level through the roof. The Schlinal soldiers who had been inside were starkly illuminated, silhouettes against the dull orange and red flames. More than a few of the men were on fire. Those who could, jumped. The building was only two stories high. A soldier would know that he stood a better chance of surviving jumping from a height of seven or eight meters than staying inside to be roasted.

Weapons were dropped. Few of the men tried to jump clutching their rifles. The ones who were on fire obviously had other things on their minds, but even those who jumped before the flames reached them tended to jettison their rifles first, to give them both hands free for their landing.

"Come on, let's go!" Max Maycroft shouted in his helmet, which gave an almost deafening volume to the men of 2nd platoon.

Joe gestured the rest of his squad on.

The shouting intensified, almost at that moment. There was a fusillade from the largest building in the barracks compound, returned by 2nd platoon and the other Accord men with line of sight to that building. Men fell, on both sides.

Several Schlinal rocket grenades exploded nearly at once in the open. Joe happened to be looking past Max Maycroft when the platoon sergeant was hit by one of the rockets, right about on his left collarbone. The grenade exploded.

And so, in effect, did the platoon sergeant.

CHAPTER
11

The five remaining Havocs of Basset Battery had all refueled before dawn. Their support vehicles—normally, one unarmored truck carried supplies, principally ammunition and fuel, for two guns, as well as mechanics and their tools—had moved with them. Now, the support vehicles, and the security detachment who rode with them, were all concealed at some distance from the Havocs, farther from Porter City, ready to either move forward to replenish the guns again, or to cut and run if that became necessary. The trucks, unburdened by armor or the weight of the large guns, were capable of speeds nearly double those of the Havocs.

Naturally, the maintenance vehicles were on the same radio net as the Havocs. Most of the crews listened primarily to "their" two guns. Familiarity made that an almost unconscious process of selection. The technical support crews came to recognize the voices of the men in their Havocs, even under the most extreme conditions. Once the shelling of Porter City started, engines were left running in the vans. The crews were in place, and the troops whose job it was to defend them were close enough to hop aboard in case a hasty move became necessary—in either direction.

They had a lot to listen to.

"Get us out of here. Quick!" Gunnery Sergeant Ponks shouted. "Course two-six-five."

Simon Kilgore didn't wait for an explanation. Basset two veered sharply left, accelerating before the turn was complete. Two saplings were crushed by the right tread. Inside the gun carriage, the trees went unnoticed. Basset two was too far from Porter City to be in range of any enemy Nova tanks, but there *was* incoming fire.

"Must be a fighter," Ponks said, still shouting into his microphone. "Two rockets."

No one questioned how they had managed to escape being hit by one, let alone two missiles. If they had truly been spotted by an enemy plane, only the wildest luck could have saved them. No one counted on that luck holding through the next launch of rockets.

"Why ain't it on the scope?" Simon demanded. "Not a hint." Up close, within easy missile range, the stealth capabilities of a fighter—Accord or Hegemony—wouldn't be enough to hide the plane completely.

"What was the angle?" Karl Mennem asked, shouting as loudly as the others. "Maybe it was a mudder."

"Looked high, but I'm not positive," Ponks admitted. "Mudder, that'd explain the misses, maybe." Even a wire-controlled rocket could be aimed badly. Ponks hit the scan control on the outside cameras, wishing that there were more eyes. Something in the air, or someone on the ground? On the ground, a man with a rocket tube would need to be a lot closer to have a good shot. In the air . . .

"Incoming!" Kilgore shouted as he reversed direction on one tread to slew the tank around to the right.

There could have been no more than one and a half seconds warning, but it was long enough for each man in the Havoc to note several distinct events—the jerk of the vehicle as it continued to twist around, the sharp *tink, tink, tink* of a small piece of metal bouncing around in the forward compartment, and then the realization of what was about to happen—before the crushing sounds of metal and explosives erupted as the wire-guided rocket slammed into the thin fender over the sprocketed drive wheel on the rear right of the Havoc. The Havoc tilted up, away from the blast. The noise inside the crew compartments was beyond deafening. For an instant stretching toward infinity by echoes, the din was paralytic.

Eustace screeched, "Bail out!" but none of the others could hear him. He couldn't hear himself even. It would be a long while before any of them would hear normally again, if they survived.

No one really needed the order in any case. As soon as the crewmen found some return of coordination, their hands reached for the latches that would give them an escape route. Though rational thought was nearly impossible, their training had been thorough enough for each man to know what to do. If they could get out of the Havoc quickly, they *might* have a chance. The rocket had exploded low, but near the ammunition stores. The wall between ammunition and crew was armored better than any other part of the Havoc, and the compartment was designed so that the bulk of any explosion there would vent up and back, away from the crew. But if the gun's ammunition rack did explode, there still might be a fireball within the compartments, and if that happened, none of them would escape, or leave remains that could be identified.

Simon did think to kill the engines. That too was reflex, honed by hundreds of hours of drill.

The four men scrambled out of the hatches. Luckily, and because of exemplary engineering and construction, none of the hatches had been jammed by the blast. The men scarcely breathed as they scurried to escape. Each mind held an image of the fireball it expected. A second, two seconds: there might be no more time than that. The men jumped from the deck of the Havoc and ran straight away from it, not taking any thought to where the others might be headed, ready to dive forward at the first hint of light from the next explosion.

That second explosion did not come.

Forty meters from Basset two, Eustace finally collapsed, too out of breath to go another step. He fell forward, gasping for air. There was a delay before his mind was able to start thinking rationally. There had been no secondary explosion. The ammunition rack had not gone up. But somewhere, perhaps

very close, there was at least one Schlinal soldier, perhaps
many of them.

Ponks forced his mouth shut and worked to keep his labored
breath muted. The danger was far from over. It might only be
beginning. He rolled to the side, anxious to move from where
he had been. He started looking for cover, or for any hint of
an enemy approaching to finish him off.

He could see very little. Havoc crewmen didn't wear the
same battle helmets that their infantry comrades did, helmets
with built-in night-vision systems. The Havocs' optics took
care of that. Nestled inside their metal and composite compartments, the crew used periscopes and video cameras to do their
seeing for them, with greater acuity in any light than mere eyes
could ever know. The helmet that the crewmen wore was more
for sound insulation than for protection or for data readouts. It
had radios, but no fancy optics at all.

Eustace lifted his head slowly, a few millimeters at a time,
scanning as far as he could to either side, looking for any
hint of movement. There was little residual fire to aid vision.
The Havoc itself scarcely looked damaged in the starlight. The
crumpled rear fender was all that Ponks could see from his
position.

"Simon? Karl? Jimmy?" Ponks whispered the names, hoping
that his helmet radio still worked.

One by one, and quite slowly, each of the others replied. At
first, each spoke on a single word, his own name, just to let
the chief know he was alive. Besides, no one had spare breath
left for anything beyond a single word. At least, the responses
sounded like whispers to Eustace, almost lost amid the ringing
he felt in his ears.

Ponks crawled farther away from where he had first dropped,
moving very cautiously, concerned more to keep his silence
than to make any great distance. He went only a couple
of body lengths before he stopped and whispered into his
microphone again.

"Stay quiet, and stay down. There's got to be Heggies
around." He paused, trying to hear something in the night
besides the ringing in his ears. That was less severe than it
had been before, but he knew that it would be impossible for
him to hear very small sounds around him—for an indefinite
time. Too long. "Anyone hurt bad?"

There was no answer, no claim of injuries.

"Anyone see any Heggies, any sign at all?" Ponks asked next. "That must have been a shoulder-fired rocket that got us."

"I don't see anything," Kilgore said. His whisper sounded particularly raspy. "Don't hear anything that sounds like people either."

The others added their own negatives, more tersely.

"Don't look like the old girl's hurt too bad," Simon said a moment later.

"No time to worry about that now," Ponks replied. "We might still have company. Everybody stay put until we get help in."

With hardly a pause, Ponks said, "Rosey? You copying any of this?" Rosey—Technical Sergeant Rositto Bianco—was the chief of their support crew.

"We've got a lock on your position, Gunny," Rosey replied. "We're already highballin' it your way."

"Be careful, bogeys around," Ponks said.

"So I gathered. Just don't get your butts shot off till we get there. We've got six zippers and a splat gun. We'll take care of anything we find. And if we can't, there's a pair of Wasps almost on top of you now. You see anything 'fore we get there, give the sky-guys a shout."

"Looks like the gun might be salvageable," Ponks said, a little doubtful. He couldn't see enough of Basset two to say that with any confidence. Still, it hadn't been destroyed outright, and under garrison conditions it might easily be repairable . . . but in the field, far from most of the 13th? He doubted that they would have time to do much work. The damage under the bent skirt might be too extensive for anything less than a full shop.

"I'll eyeball it when we get there," Rosey said. "Just remember, a gun can be replaced a lot easier than a head. So keep it down."

Damn right, I'll keep it down, Ponks thought. He reached down along his side and slid his pistol from its holster. There was no room for Armanoc zippers in a Havoc. The only personal weapon that a gun bunny carried was a Depliht Mark VII RA semiautomatic pistol. The RA stood for rocket-assisted. The Mark VII fired a 7mm projectile on a 12.5mm base, a shorter version of the round that the Dupuy cough gun used. As soon as the slug cleared the barrel, the rocket ignited and burned long enough to double the muzzle velocity—about the time it took to travel ten meters. Since most pistol work took place at less than ten meters, the explosive, needle-nosed projectile would usually still be accelerating when it hit its target. That close, body armor did not prevent deep penetration. Any torso hit had a good chance of being lethal.

Ponks looked around with different objectives now, trying to estimate where the rocket that had stopped the Fat Turtle had come from. After a moment he had to concede that he had absolutely no idea. The way that Simon had slewed the Havoc around in his futile attempt to avoid the rocket, and the way Eustace had run and rolled escaping, made it impossible for him to even hazard a guess. The enemy who had stopped Basset two might be anywhere.

An itch started on the back of Ponks's neck. He resisted the urge to make a sudden move, but he *had* to look behind him. He slid slowly, crabbing around to look all of the way behind him, pausing after every move, scanning the night with eyes and ears. He kept his head down, the chin strap of his helmet touching the ground. With his eyes no more than fifteen centimeters off of the dirt, his view was extremely limited, and there was still a slight sense of a hollow ringing in his ears, uncomfortable, and enough to blanket all but the most blatant of sounds.

Where are you? he asked silently. *I want you before you get me or any of my men.*

For the moment the only shooting was coming from the Accord forces surrounding the barracks buildings. Joe looked around quickly, surprised. *They can't all be dead in there,* he told himself. *No ammunition? Or are they just waiting to sucker us in?*

"Cease fire!" The order came directly from Captain Ingels, over the all-hands circuit. "Save your wire until you can see a target."

The silence that came was not complete. The fires started by the rockets were making crackling noises. Part of the one building was still afire. Something inside—most likely a rocket, or a crate of them—cooked off with a noisy bang. There was still no shooting from inside any of the buildings.

Joe looked over toward where Max Maycroft had died. He didn't go to him. Even from a distance, it seemed clear that there would be nothing recognizable left—nothing Joe wanted to see. Max was gone. Joe's jaw worked, as if by its own volition. Max gone? It was impossible, yet, to think of life without Max.

Joe blinked several times, then took a deep breath and looked toward the building again, at the hole where the wall had exploded outward. Even after that, there had been shooting coming from the upper story. That had stopped quickly enough though as the men in there had jumped for whatever chance of safety they saw. The next building over, a mate to the one that had burned, had a smaller hole in the wall. There still had to be enemy soldiers in that barracks.

"Baerclau."

"Yes, Lieutenant?" Joe replied over the same channel.

"You're platoon sergeant now," Lieutenant Keye said.

Joe hesitated before he said, "Yes, sir." He hadn't progressed to thinking about that yet. He was the senior squad leader in 2nd platoon, so the shift in duties was automatic. But the job might not last for long. Keye didn't have the authority to make a permanent promotion, and Captain Ingels might decide to shuffle someone in from one of the other platoons, but even if he did, that would not happen in the middle of a fight, probably not until they got back to the rest of the 13th, up on the plateau—or even back on the ships.

"Lieutenant?" Joe said after another pause.

"What?"

"There are still Heggies in those buildings."

"I know. Captain hasn't decided how we're going to handle this yet."

"A few Vrerchs to tidy things up?" Joe suggested.

"I doubt it, but then, it's not my call," Keye said. After a short pause, he said, "Spooky, isn't it?"

"Maybe they're trying to find a channel to surrender over."

"Or they're hoping for reinforcements. Keep your eyes peeled. I've got to talk to the captain."

Tanks or infantry? Joe wondered. *Or air? The Schlinal garrison ought to have plenty of all three available, and not very far away,* Joe thought. He didn't have long to ponder the possibilities. Keye was back on the channel too quickly.

"Let's move, Joe," Keye said. "We get up and start forward again, for the building on the right. See what kind of reaction we get."

"You mean see if we get our asses shot off?" Joe said as he stuck a full spool of wire into his carbine. He saved the old spool. There were still a few meters of wire on that, and every centimeter of wire might be important before this campaign ended.

"Better not be your *ass* they get," Keye said.

Joe switched to the platoon command channel and ordered the men up. More from habit than anything else, Joe led the way with first squad. Lieutenant Keye had joined them by that time. He did not suggest any different alignment, and he stayed with the squad.

Hilo Keye was old for a lieutenant. In garrison, he often drew stares from officers and men who did not know his history. Past thirty when he joined the Accord Defense Force as an enlisted man, he had served in the ranks for nearly three years before being tapped for officer candidate school. He knew the work from both ends. He would not stay a junior lieutenant for long. It was an open secret in the 13th that Hilo Keye was slated for the fast track. He had the rare combination of extreme intelligence, a remarkable knack for the work, and well-placed relatives. He would rise at least as far as major before his lack of a military academy degree might slow his progress. If he lived that long. The doubt there had nothing to do with his age, just with the fact of the war. Away from the risks of combat, a man could look forward to reaching, or surpassing, the age of 140.

Second platoon advanced nearly half the remaining distance to the building next to the burned-out shell before the Schlinal forces started firing again. This time, the gunfire was sporadic, uncoordinated.

"Get to the wall," Keye ordered. "That'll give us *some* cover."

Joe's instinct was to run as fast as he could for the partial shelter of the building's wall, and the rubble—most of that from the neighboring barracks—that was scattered in front of it, but he checked his speed enough to look around to see how the men of his squad, and the rest of the platoon, were faring.

There was little sense of interval now. Everyone was anxious to get out of the open as fast as humanly possible. Speed was more of an ally than spacing now.

The chaos was less complete than it appeared. Second platoon was not simply running blindly into enemy fire. They were getting covering fire from behind them, and even from across the compound, from those troops of George Company who could bring their weapons to bear. And 2nd platoon did move by squads, if with less precision than in other circumstances.

Getting inside one building of the compound appeared to be the key to clearing up the entire kaserne. They could work from one building to another, limiting their exposure to outside fire. Of course, that kind of fighting—a room-by-room hunt for the enemy—could be the most deadly sort. There was a moment of truth entering each room, a moment of total exposure to whoever or whatever might be inside, an instant of vulnerability that could be minimized, but never eliminated. The platoon's grenades would not last forever, and even the explosion of a grenade or two inside a room did not always guarantee the elimination of all enemies within.

Lieutenant Keye kept his pace even slower than Joe's. He let nearly all of the platoon move past him while he kept his head up and turning to watch for any threat to them. Keye also kept his rifle up, and he fired short bursts, trying to do as much good as he could with the weapon. He was an expert marksman when he took the time to aim, but there were still few *visible* targets. Hilo Keye was not fearless. He had written his will long ago, and before every battle, he gave his soul over to the God he prayed to regularly. When his time came, he believed that he would be prepared. In the meantime, he had sworn an oath, and he meant to keep it as honestly as he could.

The panes had long since been shattered or blown out of all of the windows in the barracks buildings. When Joe reached the wall, he tossed a grenade through the nearest opening, then ducked to the side. As soon as the grenade exploded, he twisted around with his carbine's muzzle moving into the opening. He did not fire though. Even through the blue-gray smoke, he could see that there were no living enemies in the room.

"Inside," he ordered first squad. "Lieutenant!"

"Go for it," Keye ordered over their circuit. "Cover the hallway inside and I'll funnel the rest of the platoon through to you."

Joe backed off two steps, then ran forward and went through the window headfirst, grabbing the sill with one hand in an attempt to right himself. It was a far from perfect stunt. He landed off balance and went forward onto his knees with considerably more force than he had intended. The first fire team came in the window behind him, quickly but with more care. While the men were coming in, Joe did a quick check of the three bodies in the room to make certain that they were out of action. Then he went to the interior doorway. The door was missing. He pressed himself against the wall next to the opening, carefully edging around the doorpost to look down the hallway. Once he was certain that there were no Heggies in sight, he got ready to jump to the other side of the doorway, to look back in the other direction, but Mort Jaiffer moved into position there first.

"I'll do it, Sarge," Mort said.

Mort was as careful as Joe had been, but there were no enemy soldiers visible in that direction either.

"Secure the corridor," Joe said, waving the rest of the squad through. "See if you can find an outside door, or a bigger hole than that window. Should be down to the left," he told Ezra as the second fire team got ready to move out into the corridor. "It'll take all night to get the platoon in through one window."

He heard the shrill yipping of wire guns being fired somewhere inside the building, off to the left, he thought, where he expected the outside door to be. He took a quick look that way. Mort and Al were at the end of the corridor, their rifles aimed upward, apparently at something or someone up a flight of stairs.

The platoon's second squad was coming through the window finally, so Joe moved down the hall toward Mort and Al. They noted his approach but kept their eyes on the highest steps they could see from their positions. There was a landing, nine steps up, and the men at the bottom couldn't see around the corner.

"I saw someone, going up," Mort said. "Didn't get him."

"He shoot back?" Joe asked.

"He shot, but nothing came near us," Al said. "I don't think he was expecting us."

Joe called the rest of first squad to him. "We'll do this right," he told the two who were there already.

"We got to go up there?" Al asked.

"Yes," Joe said. *Be easier to just blow the building up, but I guess we can't do that now,* he thought.

"Mort, Kam. You're up first." Switching to a private channel, Joe added, "Just like a drill, Kam, except this is for real. Be careful. I'll stay close."

Goff looked at him and nodded. Joe couldn't see the rookie's eyes through his visor, but he pictured them wide open, halfway between shock and wonder.

Mort moved up the stairs first. Kam stayed two steps below him, his rifle pointed at the highest point he could find. If an enemy gun showed at the landing, Kam would have only a fraction of a second, with luck, to get his own zipper into action first. If a grenade came bouncing down the steps, there would be little either of them could do but go flat and hope for a miracle.

Joe waited for Mort and Kam to get to the landing and look around the corner. Then he and Al followed them up, keeping the interval. They waited at the landing until the first pair got to the top of the stairs. Ezra and the second fire team waited at the bottom of the stairs until Joe and Al reached the landing, then they hurried up to that point. Joe and Al went halfway up the second section of the stairway.

Just like a drill. An enemy might get one or two men on the point, but there would always be someone else close enough to return the compliment, and then some.

By the time the rest of the squad got into position, Mort and Kam were at the top of the stairwell, at the door leading out into the main corridor on that level. There was still a door in place. Behind the two men, part of the exterior wall was missing. The stairwell was right at the edge of an area that had been opened up by an RPG.

"This is the tough part," Mort whispered over the link to Joe.

"Wait up," Joe said. "Wait till we're all in position."

Mort and Kam were both lying on the top stairs, only their heads and shoulders and rifles above the level of the second-story floor. Mort was on the left. The muzzle of his rifle was within a couple of centimeters of the closed door.

The second we open that door, all hell is going to break loose, Joe thought, knowing that there was still no other way. Closed door. It looked to be a fire door, heavy—almost as if there were a layer of tank armor there. Joe guessed that the door would stop anything short of a Vrerch rocket. The door opened outward, toward the stairs. Joe went up onto the landing and stood behind the door, his back against the wall at its side.

Trusting more to hand signs than even the secure radio links they shared, Joe showed the others what he wanted to do.

"No use waiting for sunrise," Joe muttered finally. He sucked in a deep breath. "Now!"

Joe yanked the door open and used it to shelter his body, hoping that he was right about the strength of its construction. As soon as there was an opening, Mort started shooting out into the corridor, Kam tossed out a grenade, aiming it in the other direction, then pulled back. Joe pushed against the door, putting his weight against the power of the hydraulic rod that was intended to close the door slowly.

When the grenade exploded, the shock pushed the door back against Joe, but not with enough force to do any harm. He yanked on the knob again, opening it wide this time. Mort moved forward, dropping to his hands and knees as he threw himself out into the corridor. He dropped and rolled across the floor and came into a prone firing position as if that were the most natural maneuver in the galaxy.

Kam was more awkward going out to cover the corridor in the other direction. He slipped and fell forward hard, but he caught himself on his forearms and hands and was only a fraction of a second slower than Mort in getting his rifle up into firing position. Both men sprayed short bursts toward their respective ends of the hallway, and while they were firing, Joe and Al moved out into the corridor with them, going only to their knees. Joe was behind Kam, and Al was behind Mort. With four rifles, they could hope to meet any weapon that might come out of any of the doorways that lined the hall in both directions.

Ezra brought his men up and out then. Joe assigned one fire team to move in each direction. There were eight doorways, other than the one that led to the stairs, on that level. They had to check every room, *clear* every room.

CHAPTER
12

Eustace Ponks was beginning to feel almost comfortable slithering along on his belly. He was nearly able to forget that this was a deadly serious affair. Almost. Nearly. A continuing pressure against his temples and the hollow ringing in his ears helped to isolate his thoughts. Childhood memories touched at the edge of his awareness, games played with his two brothers and with the other children who lived in the neighborhood—neighborhood: an area perhaps as much as three kilometers in radius; homesteads had been somewhat isolated where Eustace grew up. Eustace and his friends and brothers had played at soldier quite frequently. Both brothers were also in the Accord Defense Forces. Ellis was a navigator aboard a transport. Ekko was an electronics technician, maintaining computers at one of the home ports of the fleet. Playing soldier as kids, the greatest triumph of all had been to sneak up on one of his mates and "count coup," get close enough to be able to claim a "kill," or just to scare the daylights out of the victim. Everyone—everyone *else*—would get a tremendous laugh out of that.

Now, he couldn't just yell "Boo!" or go "Zap! Zap! You're dead." This was real. The winner would live. The loser would die.

It must be just one Heggie, Ponks told himself. It made no sense, but he hoped there was only one, some luckless sap who somehow had managed to get separated from his unit. A man who could do that might get careless at the wrong time, like now. Although Eustace was looking for reassurance, he didn't take his own thoughts too seriously. He would not close off options, would not assume that it *had* to be merely one man. There might be a dozen of them. But no matter how farfetched it sounded, or how many times he warned himself to expect the worse, he came back to thinking that there must only be one man—two at the most. If there were more Heggies, they would be bolder, he thought. They would be on the prowl, looking to finish the job they had started when they disabled Basset two.

Eustace stopped moving and lay in what was as close to absolute silence as he could get. He held his breath for as long as he could, and even closed his eyes for a moment, as if that might sharpen his hearing. The ringing in his ears was no longer a strident blanket over all other sound, but there was still . . . almost a hollowness, a void that might conceal the minimal sounds he might need in order to find the enemy— before they found him. Eustace had no night-vision visor to his helmet. Seeing: that advantage would belong to the Heggie. Eustace had to look for *his* edge with the other extended sense, hearing . . . and his hearing remained questionable. Eustace's hearing was far from perfect under the best of conditions. In certain frequencies, he was more than half deaf from his years in the artillery. Background noise would blank those frequencies out completely. Against silence, it was never that bad. Still, after that explosion . . . he couldn't be sure yet what additional damage his hearing had suffered. The sounds he was listening for might be there, and he might not be able to hear them.

He strained against the moment when he would finally have to suck in air, hoping to get some clue to the position of his enemy first. Now that he had had some time to think, Eustace did have some idea where his own crewmen had to be. Though he had no helmet display to draw on, he thought that he had worked out approximately where they would be found. He could see the outline of the Fat Turtle in his mind. He knew where the other hatches were, and the most likely angle for each man to run as he got down. They had done quite a few evacuation drills in training, and everyone got into habits, patterns.

Finally, Eustace could hold his breath no longer. It was almost impossible to take a breath quietly after holding it for so long, but he did the best he could. Then he took two more breaths, less frantic. Then he held it again. Maybe this time he would hear something. With every minute that passed, his hearing *should* be improving, recovering from the transitory effects of the blast.

At first, he still heard nothing that was not obviously natural. Then, almost at the point when he would have to take another breath, there was just the lightest rustle. If he had been concentrating any less, Eustace might not even have noticed it, or might have written it off without thought as a normal background noise. But there was that slight rustle, not of grass or leaves in the wind, but more of cloth against cloth.

And he had the direction, or thought he did. The sound had come from farther away from the Havoc, far from where any of his own men might be.

I guess I've got some hearing left after all, Eustace thought.

He started crawling again, more slowly than ever. He stopped to listen after each twenty or thirty centimeters, waiting for a repeat of the sound. After creeping a total of about three meters, he went absolutely still again, looking in the direction of the slight noise he had heard—perhaps ten minutes before.

This time, the wait was shorter. Again, he heard no more than the slightest noise—a breath this time, too much air sucked in at once, close enough that Eustace was able to tell almost precisely where it had come from, distance as well as direction. There was a lump on the low horizon, just in front of him. The soldier lying there—not five meters away—was looking off toward Eustace's right, at an angle.

Now, is it an enemy or one of my own men? Eustace asked himself. Though he thought that the figure had to be a Heggie, the question was inescapable. A mistake was unthinkable.

The helmet? Eustace stared, trying to determine if the figure on the ground in front of him wore an Accord gunner's helmet

or an infantry helmet. The only sure way to tell that in the dark
would be to spot a visor—which artillery helmets did not have
in the ADF—and that would be difficult if Schlinal helmets
were as nonreflective as those the Accord infantry used.

Move, you bastard! Eustace thought, trying to force the
figure to move by sheer willpower. But the figure on the
ground did not lift his head or turn it enough to give Eustace
a better view of the front of the helmet.

Eustace was too near to risk calling his crew over his helmet
radio. This near a potential enemy, even a whisper would give
him away. A millimeter at a time, he brought his pistol into
position, ready for a shot the instant he was certain of his
target. The matte-black finish of the gun would not reflect
anything. There would be no way anyone would see the gun
until the flash of a shot.

How's your patience? Eustace only thought the question he
directed toward the figure lying on the ground in front of him.
I bet I can outwait you.

He had to.

It might have taken another ten minutes. Eustace could not
check the time and he did not trust the estimates his mind waf-
fled over. Something just short of eternity. There was simply
no way to be objective about that under the circumstances.

But the head did move eventually. It raised up, no more than
five centimeters. That was enough. The silhouette Eustace saw
was a helmet with a face visor, and that meant that it was not
Simon, Karl, or Jimmy. Anyone else had to be an enemy.

Eustace fired once, at the line where the helmet met the
body. The noise of the shot startled Eustace, even though he
was expecting it. But the shot was accurate. The figure in the
dark jerked back and up as the RA projectile hit bone and
exploded. Eustace had already fired again by then. The figure
jerked once more, twisting halfway to its left. The entire head
seemed to fly off of the shoulders. Then the body fell flat again
and was still.

"Eustace?"

"Yeah, Simon," Ponks replied. "I got one. I think that's all
there is, but there's no way to be sure. Karl? Jimmy? You both
there?"

He was relieved to hear both men reply.

"You see the gun flash?" Eustace asked next. "Move toward

it. Be careful though, just in case there's more of 'em. I'll double-check the Heggie I got and make sure he's really done for." There was little question about that. Without a head, the man had to be dead.

Kam Goff was in a corner of the room, puking again. He had started retching so hard that he was unable to stay on his feet even. He was down on his knees, the top of his head pressed against the corner. There was no longer anything to come out, but he couldn't control the heaving spasms. Joe Baerclau stood by the door, not looking at Goff, but staying close. The rest of the squad was elsewhere on the second floor of the building, away from this scene. The room Joe and Kam were in was on the far side of the building from the continuing action. Joe was not particularly concerned with stray fire. That would have a lot of concrete and stone to go through to get to them.

I don't think you're gonna last in this business, kid, Joe thought. The shake of his head was almost unnoticeable. He could picture a variety of sequels. Goff might make a foolish move and get himself killed. He might simply go to pieces and have to be invalided out for mental problems. Or he might swallow his zipper—kill himself.

Until Goff could be moved back up to the ships, Joe knew that he would have to continue to pay special attention to the rookie, just to keep him alive until he could get help. The therapists that the ADF had were supposed to be good.

The building was secure. The rest of the buildings in the kaserne would soon be taken or destroyed. The heavy weapons squads of the two companies were pouring rocket and grenade fire into the three remaining buildings now. There would be no more room-to-room hunts. Twenty prisoners had been taken in this one building, and another thirty Heggies killed, in a barracks that appeared to have been home to more than three hundred. Prisoners were a problem on a mission like this one. They could not simply be killed out of hand, but they would be an impossible handicap once the strike force left the city and tried to remain undercover, intact, in the broken country west of town.

Joe thought that he could guess what Captain Ingels would do. The prisoners had all been disarmed and had their radios and body armor removed already. Once George and Echo companies got far enough away from the city, the prisoners would be turned loose to make their way back to their own people the best they could. The captain might even be creative enough to have their boots taken from them to slow them down. With any luck, that would keep them out of action for several days—finding their way home, and then recovering from a long hike with little water and no food.

It might be stretching decency, but it was more humane than shooting them.

"Take it easy, Kam," Joe said when Goff's retching eased off for a minute. "Take a couple of deep breaths, then wash your mouth out. It's over for now."

"Won't nothin' take the taste of this away, Sarge," Goff said, his voice weak. He did not turn to look at Joe, but he did lift his head up off of the wall. Joe watched while Goff followed his instructions. Kam rinsed his mouth out and spat the water on the floor. Twice. Then he took a short swallow.

"Time to get up and get a move on," Joe said. "Sounds like the fight's over outside. We'll be moving out soon." There was no harshness in his voice. This was too serious for drill instructor tactics. Joe rather liked Goff. It was too bad that the rookie seemed to be totally unfit for this work—too bad for Goff as well as for the squad, the platoon. But some people simply had no business being soldiers.

Goff got to his feet slowly, using his carbine as a crutch.

"I've turned out to be a total waste," Goff said when he finally turned around. His face was so pale that Joe wondered, briefly, if he might pass out. Kam did not lift his eyes to meet Baerclau's gaze. He bent over to reach for his helmet. It had rolled away from him, and away from the pool of thin vomit in the corner.

"I just can't hack it, Sarge. I try, but . . ."

"Some people can't," Joe said. He couldn't lie, not about that. "There's no shame in it. Let's just get through this mission, kid. You'll be okay then. They got folks to help people, back up on the ship."

"I should live so long." Now, finally, Goff raised his head so he was looking straight at the sergeant.

"Don't give up on yourself. You'll make it if you just hang in there. Remember, it's never until *after* the shit is over that you react. Not until it's *over*. That's all that's important."

It was important. Joe knew that, but he was far from sure that he could find a way to convince a mixed-up rookie. That could be even more important, vital.

Before either man found anything else to say, there was an explosion that they could not ignore, a blast so massive that it shook the building and precluded any immediate possibility of conversation.

"Secondary explosion," Joe said, knowing that it was unlikely that Goff would hear. "Fire must have reached the arsenal."

After the echoes started to fade, he said, "Put your helmet on. Let's go see what's happened."

Fires had spread beyond the barracks compound, blown by a strengthening west wind. There were a few dozen civilians running about in the distance, trying to organize the local fire brigade to contain the flames before they could get completely out of hand. There seemed to be only a small area of buildings clustered close enough together beyond the kaserne fence for the flames to spread to. Porter City was, for the most part, a sprawling city with plenty of open spaces. Where the homes of local citizens were, starting perhaps a half kilometer from the east side of the kaserne, the homes were set off in the middle of large walled-in grounds. The walls surrounding those haciendas were of stone or pseudo-adobe for the most part. They would never burn, and the distance between perimeter walls and houses was generally enough to isolate the residences from the flames, even in a moderate breeze.

By the time Joe Baerclau led his men out of the building they had taken, the two nearest of the other barracks had been almost completely consumed by flames. What had not been leveled by the initial explosions was fully engulfed in flames. The rest of the buildings in the compound were all on fire. And over a space of a hundred meters, two buildings beyond the fence had also started to burn. Those buildings were wood frame, a style primarily found on the less populous colony worlds.

On the parade field in the center of the kaserne, the men of George and Echo companies had marshaled their prisoners

and relieved them of weapons and radios. The recon platoons
were set out around the area to provide early warning of any
new enemy movement. Captain Ingels could not lose sight of
the fact that his men were outnumbered by a hopeless factor if
the Schlinal garrison brought all of its local resources to bear
against them. This kaserne was one of many in Porter City,
and not the largest.

Ingels and Lieutenant Vickers of George Company took
time for a face-to-face meeting with their first sergeants and
executive officers.

"We've done what we came for," Ingels said. "It's time to
get the hell out of here before the enemy regroups and comes
after us in force."

"Back into the boonies?" Vickers asked.

Ingels nodded. "It would be nice to simply head back the
way we came—we'd know that we had good cover and all
the rest—but the Heggies might figure that out too easily. So
we head south, then turn west once we've put a few klicks
behind us."

"That puts us farther from Wasp cover, sir," First Sergeant
Iz Walker said. "Even here, those Wasps don't have much time
to give the Heggies hell before they have to head back to the
plateau for fresh batteries. Much farther off and they won't be
able to help us at all."

"The Schlinal commander has probably calculated exactly
how much time the Wasps can spend here by now," Vickers
said. "He'll probably expect us to head toward the plateau to
take advantage of our air cover. He might even decide to slip
troops in west or northwest of here to ambush us." Vickers
looked to Ingels to make sure that his evaluation was the same
as the captain's.

Ingels nodded again. "He could put us in the middle that
way, cut us off completely . . . *if* we were going that way." He
shrugged. "Or he might actually guess our plans. It's a gamble
either way. Once we've put a little distance behind us, we may
be able to bend around to the north." He shrugged again; the
gesture came too easily. "Or we may get instructions to go
even farther in the other direction to spread the Heggies out
more. Or in case we get our recall."

"I have a suggestion, sir," Walker said.

Ingels faced him squarely. He was too good a commander

not to listen seriously to the suggestions of his first sergeant.

"The weapons and wire we've taken off the Heggies. I think we should cart it all off with us. This safari takes much longer, we could run completely dry of ammo for our zippers. The Schlinal wire won't fit the Armanocs, so we'd need their rifles as well."

"Our people going to have any trouble using the enemy rifles?" Ingels asked.

"Very little," Walker said. "Their aim might be off a tad, but the Schlinal weapons aren't so very much different from ours—not to operate, at least."

"Okay, good idea. We'll do that. Too bad we couldn't liberate some food as well."

"It appears that their food stores went up in that blast," Walker said. "I had men look in the one building we captured more or less intact."

"What are our casualties?" Ingels asked.

"Too heavy," Walker said, looking to Vickers before he looked at his own commander again. "The count isn't final yet. I haven't heard from either of the recon platoons, and there are still a few of our own platoons, in both companies, that haven't given us their figures. But, so far, the count is seventeen dead and thirty wounded. Maybe a half dozen of the wounded aren't going to be able to walk out on their own. They'll have to be carried. We gonna be able to get in medevac for 'em, sir?"

"We're going to try, if the Heggies give us a little breathing space. But it may be morning before we can get a shuttle in. Maybe late morning. Anybody hurt too bad to hold on that long?"

"Not that I know of, sir," Walker said.

"We have a count on prisoners?" was Ingels's next question.

"Roughly 130," Walker said. "Call it twenty less if we leave behind the ones that are wounded badly enough that they won't be any use to the enemy for the next few days."

"We leave them behind, all enemy wounded," Ingels said without hesitation. "We're not equipped to deal with our own casualties, let alone theirs. We'll leave them here where the Heggies can find them. Give them what first aid we can, of course."

"Medics've been workin' on 'em right along, sir. You know that."

"I know." Ingels turned through a complete circle, looking around. "I want to move away from here as soon as possible, Izzy. We've been here too long now."

"Aye, sir. Looks like we're about ready."

"Form them up. The recon platoons will cover our withdrawal, then follow on as quickly as they can."

Eustace Ponks helped Rosey Bianco work at repairing Basset two. The damage was surprisingly minor for the force of the explosion—for a crew of mechanics working in a fully equipped shop with the proper tools and parts—but it was quite a job for field conditions at night, with the possibility of enemy interference at any minute.

More than the fender had been crumpled. The drive wheel's mounting had been bent, and there was also damage to some of the linkage for two of the sleepers—wheels that were merely there to keep the tread in place, not to drive it. The tread itself was damaged; three sections had to be replaced. Every Havoc carried a stock of extra tread links though. *That* was almost routine maintenance. Before they could repair the damaged drive wheel mounting, a short axle connected to the drive shaft for the starboard engine, that corner of the gun carriage had to be jacked off of the ground, and even with the power hoist built into the support van, it was hard work.

While Eustace, Rosey, and one of Rosey's mechanics worked on the carriage, the rest of both crews were out in a thin defensive perimeter, watching for the approach of any enemy soldiers. No more had been found in a sweep of the area, but there were indications that there *had* been several more.

"You were born lucky, Gunny," Rosey said after they got the damaged sprocket wheel dismounted. "The shaft isn't completely wasted. Just a little heavier hit, and we'd have had to leave the Havoc and haul you boys back to be foot soldiers."

"Talk later, work now," Ponks growled. "I want to get rolling again as soon as possible."

"I can talk and work at the same time," Bianco shot back. "Not like some gun jockeys I could name. We've got an hour, maybe an hour and a half of work left here. If we've got to pull that axle to straighten it, we're here the rest of the night, and then some."

"Not on your life. Come daylight, we've got to be under better cover than we got here."

"Maybe."

CHAPTER
13

Lieutenant Keye walked away from Porter City with the first squad of his platoon. Joe stayed relatively close to the lieutenant—or rather, the lieutenant stayed close to Joe, using what breath he had to spare to brief Joe on what he expected from him as platoon sergeant. Joe had yet to turn his squad over to Ezra. Continuity was more important—or so Joe told himself. He had no doubt that he could function as platoon sergeant while still concentrating on "his" squad.

It's not really so much different, he thought. The lieutenant and Max had usually stayed fairly close to Joe's squad. First squad was, after all, *first* squad. A platoon was not all that large to start with, only thirty men, including the platoon leader and platoon sergeant, when the unit was at full strength. And 2nd platoon was far from full strength now. After less than a week on Porter, the platoon was down to twenty-four men, and two of those had been evacuated for medical treatment, leaving only twenty-two present for duty. First squad was the only one of the four in the platoon that was not missing at least one man, killed or evacuated.

Joe tried not to think about that.

"How much time you think we've got till the Heggies hit us, Lieutenant?" Joe asked an hour after the strike force had withdrawn from the barracks compound. Echo and George companies were marching hard. The men needed little urging. There was no talk of taking a break. That would come only when the men had to sit down or fall down. Everyone knew how much force the enemy might bring to bear on them.

Keye looked around. The two men talked over a private frequency, but Keye still looked toward Joe before he answered.

"I wouldn't count on another thirty seconds, Joe," he said. "I'm surprised they haven't hit us already. We'd have been sitting ducks in that compound, lit by the fires. We wouldn't have been able to see a thing."

Most of the men in both companies were carrying two rifles now, their own and a captured Schlinal rifle. The Schlinal weapon was a half kilogram heavier than the Armanoc, and the spools of wire were also each thirty grams heavier. The only men who were not carrying a spare weapon were the wounded, and the men carrying the litters with the most seriously hurt of their comrades. Others were carrying spare rifles for the stretcher-bearers.

"Probably not infantry, not at first," Joe said, almost an aside to himself. "Tanks or fighters, most like."

"Most like," Keye agreed. "I'd guess fighters. The country we're headed into is too rough for tanks to be much use."

They walked in silence for several minutes. At least Keye did not talk to Joe. The lieutenant seemed to be engaged in another conversation, but Joe could not hear what, or who he might be talking to. He guessed, correctly, that Keye was talking to Captain Ingels. Joe looked around, to make sure that the platoon was where it was supposed to be, the men minding their intervals, and keeping their eyes on the terrain around them. Echo Company was in charge of security. George Company was tending the prisoners.

"Joe?" Keye said when he had finished his conversation with the captain.

"Sir?"

"There's a low ridge about three klicks in front of the point now. An outlying ridge on the facing side of a horseshoe-shaped hill, higher ground just behind it."

"I remember seeing it on the mapboard," Joe admitted. The valley bounded by that hill had looked amazingly like an outdoor arena.

"Change of plans," Keye said. "George is turning the prisoners loose now, sending them back toward the city, without boots—or much else, the way I understand it. We're going to take up positions along that ridge. If the Heggies send infantry after us, we'll be in the best possible location to meet them. There's no easy way for the Heggies to get behind us, and we'll have clear kill zones in front. If they send tanks or aircraft, we're also in relatively good condition. Give the recon teams a chance to catch up with us."

"Just dig in and take whatever they throw at us?" Joe asked.

"That keeps us close enough to the city that they've got to worry about us, tie down at least part of the garrison in case we might make another raid. So we set up shop and wait. With luck, just until sunset tomorrow. Or sooner."

"Recall?"

"No word on that," Keye said. "But the captain wants to get us in defensive positions as soon as possible so we can arrange pickup for the wounded. Try to, anyway. Apparently, there's a flat spot on the high ground behind the ridge we're aiming for, room enough for a shuttle to get in and out. After that, we can always move if we have to."

If we're not pinned down, Joe thought, but he kept quiet about that. He felt uncomfortable second-guessing the captain, but they would be little more than ten kilometers from the destroyed barracks compound on that ridge.

"Be good to get some rest," he said instead.

"I heard that," Keye said.

After a short pause, Joe said, "I'm going to miss Max, Lieutenant."

"You and me both, Joe. You and me both."

"He was a good friend," Joe said more softly.

By the time the two companies reached the ridge above the horseshoe-shaped valley, they had been marching without a break for more than two and a half hours, pushing themselves hard over rough terrain.

There was a thin stream, just a trickle of water in some places, caught between the outlying ridge and the grade behind it. The central part of the draw was U-shaped and flat, with some grass but more small rocks covering it. At the far end, there was only a narrow entrance. Any enemy approaching the ridge would have to come into the U, with guns on three sides of them. The ground on the reverse side of those outlying spurs was too rugged for any sort of coordinated, massed attack on foot. The climb would be slow, and the Heggies who would have to make it would be excellent targets for marksmen on the high ground above them.

Joe was impressed. It *was* an excellent defensive position— almost a textbook example. If they had searched an entire world for a place to stand off infantry attacks by a much larger force than their own, they could hardly hope to find a location better suited. Joe saw that as soon as the platoon was in position, near the right flank, close to the "bottom" of the U. There was solid rock in front of them and behind them. There were notches and irregularities in the rock along the ridge, excellent touches for an infantryman worried about cover. The hollow behind the ridge consisted of bare rock along the top of the outer ridge, with pockets of soil and a few thin patches of grass in the lower reaches, flanking the thin stream at the bottom of the notch. The only real danger in the position would be from mortar rounds dropped into the hollow, funneling shrapnel up on either side.

But, Joe thought, *it would be difficult for Schlinal forces to get close enough for that*. He looked over the edge of the rock at the long valley, and nodded to himself.

"It *is* a good spot, Lieutenant," he told Keye. "Long as they really can't get in behind us, above us."

"That would be hairy," Keye agreed. "But there aren't any handy access routes, except for this one, and we're sitting across that. From the map shots I looked at, there's no way they can get tanks within two kilometers of us except straight up the valley. They'd have to land shuttles to get men behind us easily, or quickly, and the captain is sending two thirds of the Vrerchs we have left up to the top of the hill to make that difficult."

"There's something else we need to talk about, Lieutenant," Joe said after looking around him. "Goff." Kam was twenty meters away, and they were talking over their private radio channel. Still, Joe led the lieutenant farther away.

"A problem?" Keye asked.

"A serious one, I'm afraid. Goff tries, none harder, and he's got all the skills, but . . ." Joe shook his head. "He sees a little blood and he spends the next half hour puking, past when he's got nothing left to come up. He's just not cutting it, Lieutenant, and he knows it. Combat is eating the hell out of him."

"We can't do much about that now," Keye pointed out.

"I know that, sir, but as soon as possible, we need to get him away from combat, 'fore he eats his carbine, or does something else really stupid. He can't take much more. Like I said, he tries, but the way he gets, I'm surprised he's lasted this long. He wants to do the job, but I've had to keep him damn near in my armpit just to make sure he didn't fall apart."

"You think the skull jockeys can straighten him out for us?"

Joe hesitated, then shook his head again. "No, sir, I don't think he'll ever make it in a combat unit. Maybe they can fix his head so it doesn't eat at him that he failed. But for this, he could be the best I've got."

"But the way he is, he's a danger to himself and the men around him—that what you're trying to tell me?"

"Yes, sir. That's what I'm saying. I've done everything I know how to, but it doesn't get any better. In fact, he seems to be getting worse every time. I don't think he can handle much more." Joe repeated that final thought consciously, knowing that the lieutenant would realize just how desperate he thought Goff's condition was.

"Keep somebody with him at all times. As far as possible. I'll talk to the captain when I get a chance. I don't know about evacuating him with the wounded though. That might make it even harder for him."

"Yes, sir, it might." *Or he might fall apart on us completely the next time there's a little gunfire*, Joe thought. He kept that notion to himself. He would watch over Goff personally, as he had been.

"What's the watch schedule, sir?" Joe asked then. "Alternate fire teams?"

Keye nodded. "Until something happens. You'd better bed down with the first shift. You're looking a little ragged."

Joe didn't bother to argue.

Eight Schlinal Boem fighters came out of the north, an hour before dawn. Moving at low speed and medium altitude, they were not spotted until their target acquisition systems locked on to the first Wasps and Havocs.

A depleted Blue flight was flying air cap over the Accord foothold on the plateau when the attack came. Only four Wasps were left of the six that Blue flight had brought down into Porter's atmosphere. Two planes and one pilot had been lost in a week of fighting. After being in the air an average of sixteen hours out of every twenty-four, all of the remaining Wasps of the 13th's squadron needed extended periods of maintenance. There had been no catastrophic failures yet, but nearly every pilot had reported that warning lights were coming on during some maneuvers. But until the campaign ended, the ground crews could do nothing but make patchwork repairs, just enough to keep the Wasps flying for another day . . . or another hour.

Zel Paitcher and Slee Reston were flying a loose figure-eight pattern along the northern half of the Accord's hold on Porter when the attack came. Moving in opposite directions, the two Wasps were able to keep watch over more area at one time. Zel and Slee, like all of the remaining pilots in the air wing, were also in need of extended periods of time on the ground, to catch up on sleep and get their minds fresh again, but like their Wasps, the flyers would have to wait until the campaign ended for that.

All eight enemy fighters came directly at Slee and Zel, at full acceleration, and the first enemy missiles were launched almost instantly once the Boem target acquisition systems locked on. Only two Boems fired at the pair of Wasps. The Schlinal pilots might be aggressive this time out, but they were not wasteful of rockets. Both Blue three and four were targeted, Zel from ahead, Slee from behind. At the angle of approach, Zel was able to get his own lock on the missile headed for Slee, blowing it apart with his cannons. That blast radiated enough heat to draw the other missile off course. While Slee turned toward the oncoming Boem fighters, Zel went through

the full menu of countermeasures to keep the other weapon
from regaining its lock.

Then he too moved toward the enemy flight.

The remaining two Wasps of Blue flight were forty
kilometers away—more than a minute and a half at their
best speed. In air combat, ninety seconds is an eternity.

"Get in the middle of the Boems," Slee told Zel. "That
way, they can't get too fancy without endangering their own
planes."

"Right behind you," Zel said. He had already switched his
weapons selector to rockets, ready to loose a spread at the first
targets his system locked on to. Then he would switch back to
cannons. Designed primarily for ground cover missions, the
25mm guns were not particularly well suited for air-to-air combat, but in these close circumstances, there was little choice.
The guns did have the virtue of putting concentrated amounts
of firepower into a very limited area. Even reinforced plane
armor could be damaged by that sort of assault, especially at
extremely close range.

The eight Schlinal fighters broke into separate pairs, giving
way before the counterattack of the two Wasps. Antigrav aircraft—and like the Wasp, the Boem was an antigravity drive
fighter—were the ultimate in mobility. A skilled pilot could
move his fighter around in three dimensions with an ease that
would astound anyone who had not done it for himself. By
reversing the directional push of the antigrav drive, the Wasp
pilot could also reverse his direction quickly, or change altitude
with equal acceleration, even flip the fighter end for end or turn
it upside down much faster than any plane that depended on
traditional notions of aerodynamics for lift. The limiting factor
was the gee-load that the pilot could stand. Slamming a Wasp
into a full reversal of its gravity field could press a pilot against
his restraining straps with enough force to dislocate bones. Or
worse.

The challenge was to learn to outwit the opposing pilot, to
guess which way he would go before he knew himself.

As this uneven battle was joined, Zel lost sight of Slee for
seconds at a time. The heads-up display on his canopy provided
a constant reference, but there was too much going on for Zel
to always have actual eyeball contact with Slee's Wasp. In the
middle of the flight of Boems, each of them worked to reduce

the odds. Zel and Slee did have one very slight advantage to partially offset the numbers. They had more targets, and only one friendly craft to avoid. But their ammunition was limited.

"Going to have to break this off soon," Slee managed to say about forty-five seconds after the fight had been fully joined. "I just shot off my last rockets, and I don't have more than another twenty seconds on my guns."

"Ditto that," Zel said, just as he fired his last pair of rockets. Between them, they had managed to bring down three of the eight enemy fighters, but it was getting more difficult to maneuver. The Schlinal pilots were learning to cope with their tactics.

"Let's lead them toward the others," Slee said, turning his Wasp even before he finished speaking.

Lead them without getting far enough ahead to make a missile shot tempting, Zel thought. That would be a monumental task, edging south, drawing the Boems along without giving them a clear shot.

"Our best bet, I guess," Zel conceded. His target acquisition system locked on to another Boem. The Schlinal pilot jerked sideways, flipping his Boem upside down and dropping five-hundred meters to evade a rocket that Zel no longer had to fire. And he was far beyond the effective range of the cannons in his Wasp.

Neither Zel nor Slee was expecting help before the other two Wasps of Blue flight could arrive. They were nearly as startled as the Schlinal pilots when three planes of Red flight appeared on the scene, still climbing, attacking the Boems from below. With the numbers momentarily even (even though Zel and Slee were virtually out of ammunition), the Schlinal attack grew more disjointed. Two of the Heggie pilots decided to grab as much altitude as they could, retreating straight up, then turning back toward the north.

"Red leader, this is Blue three. We're about dry. Think you can handle them until our other two boys get here?"

"Blue three, that's affirmative. Hurry back or you'll miss all the fun."

Fun? Zel thought. But he headed for the LZ just the same.

The attack on the ground started almost as the attack in the air was breaking up. This was no probing raid, as the first

Schlinal attack on the perimeter had been. This assault was
in force, hitting at three different points along the perimeter, a
total of perhaps three short battalions of infantry supported by
Nova tanks as well as the Boem fighters. As many as sixteen
Schlinal aircraft eventually joined in the fray. Though their
losses quickly ran over fifty percent, the surviving Boems did
not abandon the attack until they were out of ammunition or
running short of power for their antigrav drives.

The 13th had been anticipating the attack. Recon patrols had
come close to contact with two of the attacking battalions.
The fronts in the sectors facing those units had been quietly
strengthened during the night. The most imminent danger was
on the front that the third Schlinal battalion assaulted. Bravo
Company held that sector, and they had only a few minutes
warning before the enemy was on them.

Van Stossen and Dezo Parks hurried toward that sector
with the headquarters security detachment. That only added
sixteen rifles, but there were few other reinforcements to offer.
Maneuvering back through the central portion of the land the
13th controlled, the remaining Havocs were firing as quickly as they could reload and acquire new targets, but there
simply were not enough howitzers to stop an attack by themselves.

"Be nice if we could get Echo and George back in a hurry," Dezo commented as they approached Lieutenant Jacobi's
command post.

"It would be, but I don't think we can manage. They're
having their own troubles. We're going to try to get one shuttle
in to evac their wounded, but I think that more than that is out
of the question just now. I can't even spare them Wasp cover
until this settles down," Stossen said.

"I know," Dezo replied. "I was just making up my wish
list. I'm afraid to even hope that our relief will show up in
the nick of time."

"You've been watching too many commando vids," Stossen
charged. There was still no word about the relief fleet. It certainly was not in-system. If it was, they would have been in
contact. And once they did jump in-system, they would need
eight hours to get into position to launch the air cover the 13th
would need to withdraw safely. And the new fighters would
need thirty minutes to get low enough to be able to take part

in the battle once they were launched. Infantry reinforcements would take even longer.

"I kinda like the happy endings." *Ones where you don't run out of ammunition before you run out of enemies*, Dezo added to himself. That did not seem likely this time.

Stossen pulled out his mapboard and started comparing what he saw on that with the reports he was getting from the various company commanders. Half the Wasps—half the *remaining* Wasps—were on the ground getting fresh batteries or replenishing their munitions. Dealing with the air attack had kept most of the Wasps out of ground cover missions. Even after they took off again, there was still enough air activity to keep them occupied. Only in the most desperate of circumstances could Stossen pull one or two of them away to make a quick strafing run on the attacking Heggies, or a rocket attack on Nova tanks—on their way to meet the Boem fighters.

"Jacobi, I hope you haven't forgotten how to fire a zipper," Stossen said when he had a break from his radio conversations.

"I hope so too, sir," Jacobi replied with an earnestness that might have elicited a laugh in other circumstances.

"I think it's all time we got a piece of this." Three more rifles? Stossen's shrug was microscopic. He knew that he had no business going to the barricades and working like a mudder himself. He had broader responsibilities . . . but those would scarcely matter if the line broke now.

"You did good, Goff," Joe told the shaking private. "Now just stay calm." He thought that, this time, Kam might even avoid the sequel to each of the earlier skirmishes. There were no bloody corpses close at hand. Second platoon had taken no casualties in this fight, and the Schlinal casualties were all more than eighty meters away, some *much* farther away.

"Yeah, I don't have to puke this time," Kam said through obviously clenched teeth. "I haven't eaten anything in hours. Long as I starve myself, I'll be okay."

Joe sucked in a deep breath and held it for a moment, more concerned at the bitterness he heard in Goff's voice than at what had happened the other times.

The Schlinal infantry had tried one direct assault, into the valley and up the 40-degree slopes that bounded it, but the

combination of long-distance artillery and the wire guns of the
Accord soldiers above had turned back that assault, inflicting
heavy casualties on the Heggies. The remains of three Schlinal
Nova tanks, destroyed as they supported the infantry attacks,
effectively kept any more of the armored vehicles from entering the valley below the positions held by Echo and George
companies. One of the disabled tanks was still smoldering.
Fifteen kilometers away, more or less, three Havocs of Basset
Battery continued to bombard the Schlinal armor and infantry.
At least two Novas had left, moving at what had to be close to
their maximum speed on such broken ground, no doubt hunting
the artillery that was hitting to such effect. If any other Novas
remained in the vicinity, they had stopped bombarding the
ridge. Joe doubted that there were any left nearby.

The only thing missing from the Schlinal attack had been
Boem fighters. Joe did not know that there was also a battle
going on up on the plateau at the same time, and that the
enemy's available fighters were all busy there.

Joe had used a Schlinal rifle against that first assault, and
he had suggested that the rest of the platoon do the same.
"Save the weapon you're familiar with for when things get
close," he advised. Even Lieutenant Keye had accepted his
recommendation—and made it an order. He had also passed
it along to Captain Ingels, who then issued the same order to
the rest of the strike force. *Use the enemy rifles first. When
you run out of ammo for them, throw them away—that much
less weight to tote around when we leave this place.*

The frontal attack had ended ten minutes before.

"They might try it again," Ingels warned over the channel
that linked him with all of the platoon leaders and platoon
sergeants. "I imagine they'll *think* about some sort of flanking
movement first, but there's no easy way for them to do that,
no way that we can't counter. But they will attack again. If
it doesn't come sooner, expect it when the shuttle's visible,
just coming in. That will be too tempting for them to pass
up." Three squads from the recon platoons were out watching
the most likely routes for any attempted flanking movement.
If it came, the recon teams were equipped to slow the enemy
down long enough to allow reinforcements to reach them. But
if the enemy got too close, or those missing Schlinal Boems
turned up, the shuttle landing might have to be postponed.

"How long till the shuttle arrives?" one of the platoon sergeants asked.

"It's on the way now. Twenty minutes. The rest of the 13th is under attack on the plateau, so we're going to have to do without any air cover. If the shuttle spots enemy fighters in the air, they'll abort the landing, stay high until the Boems have to return to base."

"Do we have a wide enough cordon to keep the shuttle safe?" Lieutenant Vickers asked.

"I don't think anything but a Boem could get close enough in time," Ingels said. "Maybe a tank, but I think the rest of the Novas pulled out. In any case, we've done all we can as far as LZ security is concerned. We put much more up there and the enemy'd be able to overrun our positions here."

Joe more than half tuned out the conversation at that point. He lifted his head to look down into the valley. There were still bodies out there, but none of them looked as though they had moved since the end of the fight. If any of those men were merely wounded, they were not making any noises that Joe could hear.

Second platoon was back on half-and-half, one fire team from each squad in position on the crest of the ridge, watching, the other back and below, eating or seeing to their equipment. The fight was too recent for anyone to be sleeping yet. That could not come until the adrenaline of battle had a chance to dissipate.

"I want platoon sergeants and squad leaders to check on the ammunition their men have left," Ingels said. It was enough to pull Joe's attention back. "Our own zippers and the captured rifles. I want to know just how much resistance we have left." *How long we have before we're no better then cavemen with fancy-looking clubs.*

Those orders marked the end of the radio conference. Joe relayed the order to 2nd platoon's squad leaders. "Ezra," he added over a private channel, "you handle first squad. Time you get used to it."

"I'll do the inspection," Ezra said. "Can't get used to thinking of myself as squad leader yet."

"This is how it happens, Ez." Joe's tone didn't invite any continuation. He really did not think of himself as platoon sergeant yet either. That would require dealing with the idea of Max's death. There was no time for that now.

Joe walked along behind the outer ridge, stopping to talk with men in each of 2nd platoon's squads. He knew everyone in the company, not just in his own squad or platoon. To a greater or lesser extent, he had worked with everyone in Echo Company, even the recruits who had only reported to the unit two weeks before the 13th shipped out for this campaign. No one questioned his new role as platoon sergeant. That was the way of the military. No soldier was irreplaceable. Joe had been the senior squad leader in 2nd platoon. It was obvious that he would move into the higher slot if it became vacant. Chain of command. When one link was broken in combat, everyone lower in the chain moved up one link.

The vacancies at the bottom were filled from outside, afterward. Sometimes by people like Kam Goff. Joe was saved from dwelling on that as the reports on ammunition started to filter back from the squad leaders.

"Shuttle's coming in now," Lieutenant Keye told Joe. "It'll be in range of enemy ground fire in two minutes, if they've got anyone in position. Get everybody on the line, ready. They may attack again when they see the shuttle."

"Yes, sir." Joe clicked over to the platoon frequency and passed the order along. Then he moved back up to the ridge himself, fairly near—but not *next* to—Lieutenant Keye. This was no time to take a *management* position behind the lines. Every man with a rifle would be needed up front if an attack came. But it would never do to have the platoon leader and platoon sergeant close enough together that they might be taken out by one rocket or grenade. Having two links disappear from the chain of command at once might disrupt the platoon too much at a critical moment.

Joe lifted his visor and rubbed at his face with both hands, vigorously. His cheeks were rough from three days growth of beard and a layer of dirt that washing with a cup of cold water could never hope to remove. When he moved his visor back into position, he actually felt a little better—if not rested, then at least ready to stay alert for a time.

Two rifles. Joe set his Armanoc a little to the side, within easy reach, loaded and ready for action. He had a Schlinal rifle at his shoulder though. "Use the enemy weapons as long as you've got ammo for them," he told the platoon. "Throw it away when the Heggie wire is gone. Then you've still got your own zipper." Repeat everything important, as often as necessary. It wasn't absentmindedness, it was intentional. After a week of too little sleep and too much danger, no one's mind was at its sharpest.

Joe had one full spool of wire in his Heggie rifle, and another six spools for it in a pouch on his hip. But there was only one power pack for the rifle, the one already in the receiver. He was uncertain how long the Schlinal power packs were good for, but the tiny gauge next to the selector switch showed that it still retained eighty percent of its juice. *Should be enough*, he thought. Hoped.

This time, the Schlinal assault was presaged by the arrival of a half-dozen artillery shells—tank rounds. They carried smoke and feathery bits of metallic chaff. The smoke would cut down on visibility. The hot bits of metal foil would confuse infrared vision systems that could peer through the smoke. A moment later there was a volley of rocket grenades, dozens of them, scattered across the valley and up on the slope below the ridge where the Accord forces waited. Some of the grenades were shrapnel. Others were smoke or white phosphorous, more attempts to limit the visibility of the defenders.

"Hold your fire," Joe said over the platoon circuit. "They won't be coming until the barrage lifts. We've got the ground. Wait for the order."

The tanks came back, Joe thought. If they had ever actually left. But they were still keeping their distance. The rounds were falling down in the valley, or near the bottom of the slope. They were not reaching the defenders behind the ridge. It brought a grim smile to Joe's face. He tried to judge how many tanks were firing into the valley. It had to be at least four—maybe six, he decided. After another couple of minutes, Joe heard rifle fire coming from farther off to the right, out beyond the shoulder of the ridge, where one of the recon platoons was operating.

"That's not here," Joe reported over the platoon link. "Don't let it worry you." He looked to make sure that Goff was close to him, and not falling apart.

Kam's entire body was shaking, but he was at his post, rifle muzzle and eyes looking over the lip of rock into the valley below.

Hang tough, rookie, Joe thought. Then: *You're really not a rookie anymore. You've seen all the shit.* For as long as he dared, Joe stared at Goff, willing him to hold out through this fight, the way he had held out through the others. And then he had to look away. He was platoon sergeant now; he was responsible for a lot of other men.

The Schlinal infantry entered the valley. The shooting began.

CHAPTER
14

It was devilishly hot working under the thermal tarp, but the tarp was essential. Basset two had gone to ground before dawn, accompanied by the support van and its detachment of mechanics and security troops. The vehicles were twenty meters apart in a grove of stunted trees with sparse foliage. The trees provided little protection against even visual detection. They could not begin to mask the thermal signature of the gun carriage with its twin engines.

The Havoc had been unable to risk anything near its rated top speed as it worked its way back toward the plateau. The rear drive wheel on the right tread had been repaired, but not to the satisfaction of Eustace Ponks or Rosey Bianco.

"That axle's too badly damaged for field repairs," Rosey had said after the earlier work had been completed. "All we can hope for is it gets you back to camp. We should be able to salvage a part from one of the guns that went belly up." At least five Havocs had been knocked out of action by enemy fire. Some would have parts that could be cannibalized. "If not, maybe we can get a part down from the ships. I think there are a few spares."

"I've got to have good tread under us tonight," Eustace said. "Listen at this. Can we switch axles?"

"What d'ya mean?" Bianco asked.

"Say we take the axle from one of the sleepers and put that on the drive wheel, reverse them. The sleeper, even if it goes, won't cripple us. We'll still be able to move. Worst that might happen is we might throw the tread a few times."

Rosey leaned back and stared at Ponks as if the gunnery sergeant were out of his mind. Then, after a long moment, Rosey nodded. "It might work," he allowed. "Not according to the book, it won't," he added, "but since you got me here to make the switch, it just might work."

It scarcely mattered to him that the axles were not even the same diameter. The sleeper axle was a centimeter thinner than the rod that held the drive wheel, but with a little work, a little imagination, and a few pieces of scrap metal, they just might be able to do it.

"Take us most of the day, I think," Rosey said. Without the equipment of a full motor pool, it would be rough work indeed.

"Mark your targets, damn it!" Joe roared over the platoon frequency. A shout insured that everyone would at least hear him. "Don't waste your wire. We've got to stretch it a long ways yet."

He tried to follow his own advice, but it wasn't easy. There were hundreds of Heggies advancing into the killing zone of the valley, moving forward with their heads lowered and their backs hunched, as if they were more afraid of what was behind them than what was in front of them.

Maybe they are, Joe told himself. Maybe the stories he had heard about life in the Schlinal military were true, that the men were literally driven at gunpoint into combat, that anyone who hesitated or tried to retreat was summarily shot.

Joe had heard too many tales about life in the Hegemony, most told by people who had absolutely no way to know if what they said was even vaguely true, for him to accept any of the stories at face value. Even before the war, the Hegemons were *The Enemy*, and little good was published about them in any of the data banks that Joe had had access to on his homeworld of Bancroft. Now that hostilities were well under way, the Accord Defenses Forces certainly did not go out of their way to tell soldiers anything favorable about the Hegemons or their "minions."

Joe shook his head to clear his mind of the distractions. He didn't want to waste thought on anything about the enemy but what he could see through his gunsight. *Don't think of the Heggies as human. Don't do anything to personalize them. They're just targets you have to knock down in order to move on to the next task. If you think of them as people, just like you and your men, you can get as messed up as Goff.*

The Schlinal rifle, though heavier and longer than the Armanoc, seemed to lack nothing in workmanship. It didn't boast the laser sights of the Accord zipper, but those sights were rarely as valuable as the ADF's brass hats seemed to think. Using the laser to mark a target too often made the *shooter* a target as well.

This was not like shooting on the firing range in garrison. Despite his admonitions, Joe could never lose sight of the fact that the targets he was aiming at were live men, soldiers fighting for their worlds, or for the Hegemony, following orders—perhaps not entirely of their own volition. At the sort of range they were at when they entered the valley, body armor was moderately effective. It took a concentration of wire, and a little luck, to bring down a soldier at anything beyond two-hundred meters. Even at half that distance, good body armor could deflect quite a bit. But no body armor covered every square millimeter of a soldier. There were gaps at the neck, between helmet and jacket, at the hands and wrists, and where boots met trousers. There were also weak points in the battle dress sometimes, places where repeated flexing had weakened the layers of net armor. Men died in combat, even when the texts said that they shouldn't.

There was little return fire reaching the men on the ridge. The Heggies were too far away for accurate fire at the angle they had to shoot at, much too far away for men who were themselves being shot at. Whatever tanks the Heggies had backing them up, or forcing them on, even that fire was less than devastating. Most of the rounds continued to hit well down on the slope, doing little but showering the men above with secondary debris from the blasts.

"Blind men could shoot better'n that!" Joe mumbled to himself at one point.

But there was *some* accurate fire, even if that looked as if it might be pure luck. Over toward 4th platoon, Joe saw one tank round explode almost precisely on the ridge line, blowing a small gap in the rock. Fourth was too far away for Joe to get any sense of casualties, but there was a sudden hollow feeling in his solar plexus: men *must* have died in that blast.

Fortunately, that was the last tank round that came in. Joe could hear heavier artillery rounds exploding farther off, beyond the shoulder of the hill. It sounded like heavy artillery, and that meant that at least some of the Havocs had taken the Novas under fire again.

"Hit 'em hard," Joe whispered. His heart was beating faster than normal, but that was always the case in combat. Even at a time like this, when there was only minimal danger, there was always that edge of fear. *All it takes is one lucky shot, and I can die as easily as anyone else. Will I know it's coming?*

For Joe, fear had never been a serious obstacle. The fear was always there, on one level or another, but he trained hard to do the best, safest job he could. The results were beyond his control then. All he could do was work as smart as he knew how, make it as hard as possible for any enemy fire to hit him.

He ducked below the ridge line and turned to look up toward the top of the hill. Though he could neither see nor hear it, he knew that the shuttle must be on the LZ above by now. Maybe it had already taken the wounded aboard and lifted off again. There were no enemy fighters visible, and that was perhaps the best news of the day. A lander would be no match for a fighter. A shuttle was no match for one soldier with a shoulder-operated rocket launcher even. The four-kilo warhead on an infantry rocket could bring down a shuttle with ease.

Joe fed the last spool of wire into his Schlinal rifle before he moved back up to look down into the valley. A few more seconds of fire there, and then he would have to switch to his own carbine. He didn't have all that much wire left for it, either, maybe eight spools total, adding together the partials. That wouldn't last long if the enemy kept coming.

"Sir," Joe said on his link to Lieutenant Keye.

"What?" was all Keye said in return.

"We need to start cutting back hard on wire. Until the enemy gets a lot closer, I think we should have half the men hold their fire."

"Hang on." The pause was long enough for Keye to check with the captain. "Right. Go with it," Keye told Joe. Within a minute, the entire strike force had the same orders. The volume of fire coming off of the ridge was cut in half.

The sudden decrease in gunfire sounded painfully obvious to Joe, but there was no response from the Heggies coming toward the slope. They did keep coming. Fewer of them fell. But they showed no sign that they recognized that decreased fire was the reason.

"Goff, you holding up?" Joe asked over a private channel. At the moment, the squad's first fire team was the one back off of the ridge not engaged in the shooting. Kam turned to look toward his sergeant before he answered.

"So far, Sarge. So far." He went no further than that. He was holding up because he was almost totally disengaged from the fighting. Most of the time up on the line, he had kept his eyes closed. Only rarely had he pulled the trigger on his zipper, and even then it was without aiming, without *looking* at the enemy below.

Joe nodded, exaggerating the gesture to make sure that Kam saw it. "You're doing good, kid. Just keep at it."

"I'll try."

Joe reminded himself to have a talk with Ezra as soon as there was a break in the fighting. Ezra had to know about Goff, had to be prepared to work with him, and to watch him, now that Joe had the entire platoon to worry about.

The leading elements of the Schlinal attack were getting close to the base of the hill below the Accord line. To Joe's eye, it looked as if fully two thirds of the attackers had fallen crossing the valley. The ones who had made it to the base of the hill were the ones who were both lucky and smart, the ones who knew how to take advantage of what little cover the approach offered. With the enemy right below them, the men on the ridge had to expose themselves to bring their weapons to bear.

That gave the enemy better targets.

More as an experiment than anything else, Joe took his next-to-last grenade, pulled the safety pin, and hurled it out in a high arc. He watched as it bounced once, thirty meters down and twenty out, then sailed over four Heggies. They scattered, going down against the rock, drawing in limbs and heads, but the grenade went off in the air, above them, scattering the shrapnel over a twenty-meter diameter.

Three of the men got back up, and Joe could see blood on two of them. One went back down almost immediately, rolling until his body was stopped by a rock. Joe closed his eyes for an instant—more than a simple blink. He couldn't see the faces of the men below. Those were concealed by the visors on their battle helmets. But in his mind, he *could* see faces twisted by shock and pain, and death's blank stare in the eyes of the one who had not gotten up. And he felt himself falling and rolling, the way the second man had done, falling in death.

It was a new feeling for Joe. When he opened his eyes again, Joe looked toward Kam Goff. He saw that look on Goff's face as well, though it too was hidden by a visor.

Can that crap! Joe told himself, trying to work up anger to shove aside the twinge of fear. He blinked several times, rapidly. *Don't go metaphysical. It'll screw your mind as bad as his.*

Joe had switched over to his own rifle a moment before. Now, he switched on the laser sights—for the first time in ages, except on the practice range—using the infrared beam. He lined up targets carefully, giving each just the shortest possible burst of wire, moving back and forth across his fire lane methodically. The Schlinal soldiers were close enough now that wire could do damage even through body armor, and careful sighting could give Joe a better than average chance of finding the gaps in that position.

A second wave of Schlinal infantry entered the valley. This detachment was much larger than the first, perhaps two full companies. They took the ridge under fire immediately, close to two-hundred weapons firing on full automatic. Not all of these guns were wire-throwers. There were some slug-pushers as well. Along with the renewed rifle fire, there was also a new flurry of rocket-propelled grenades, some of which reached the hollow behind the ridge.

"This looks like the real thing," Lieutenant Keye told Joe. "Good thing we had half the men saving their ammo."

"I'd suggest holding back a little longer," Joe said. "Get the men back in position, sure, switch fire teams so we don't run half the men dry, but wait until the Heggies get close enough for every centimeter of wire to count before we pull all the guns into action."

"That's what I was about to tell you, Joe. The captain's already given orders to switch teams on the line. He repeated the order to conserve wire," Keye added. "To make sure we've got targets in the sights."

Joe slid back from the edge of the rock, issuing the orders over the platoon channel and watching while they were carried out. Perhaps if he had not been down out of the line of fire, he might not have noticed the new fire coming from above. The troops who had been sent up to guard the LZ on top of the hill were lined up along the crest now, getting their piece of the action.

I guess that means the shuttle's been and gone, Joe thought. Protecting the lander had been the primary mission for the troops sent up to the crest. *Too bad we couldn't all get on it.* Joe's stomach tightened up suddenly. He pressed his left hand against his gut, taking a slow, almost painful breath as he did.

Don't tell me it's getting to me now, he thought with some alarm. Though the rational part of his mind insisted that it wasn't so, deep inside, Joe harbored the belief that Goff's problems might be contagious, that they might infect everyone who came in contact with him.

Joe closed his eyes for an instant, longer than the last time. He took a deep breath, then opened his eyes and looked up at the sky. The morning was less than half over, and unless the captain changed his mind, they were going to stay where they were until dark.

If we last that long. The thought startled Joe. Echo and George companies, with their attendant recon platoons, remained in good shape, so long as they did not run out of ammunition or face a massive air attack. Ammunition might be a problem, but there was still no sign of enemy air activity. The Boems had not come after the shuttle. It seemed unlikely that they would come after a couple of companies of infantry after the shuttle had escaped. Where they were, the strike force could easily hold off heavy odds, as long as the enemy had nothing but infantry, or tanks that would not get close enough to do really extensive damage.

Until we run out of wire. Joe's mind came back to that limit. He knew how short of wire his men were, how short they had

been before this latest firefight erupted. Fairly soon, many of
them might start running dry.

"Lieutenant, if we don't break off this fight pretty damn
soon, all we're going to have left is expensive clubs, no matter
how tight we are with wire."

On the plateau, some of the men of the 13th had already
been reduced to using their wire carbines as clubs, not because
they were out of ammunition, but because the enemy had
closed to the point where much of the fighting was hand-to-
hand. The Armanoc was not equipped for bayonets. In Accord
military doctrine, bayonet fighting was out of the question.
*That sort of situation simply does not occur often enough to
warrant the training and equipment expense.*

Bravo and Charley companies were the hardest pressed.
Around the rest of the perimeter, the morning attacks were
being beaten back, in heavy fighting, but at a distance. One
Schlinal commander, however, had managed to get a full
battalion (or what was left of it after the early stages of the
assault) right into the Accord lines. If they had received even
modest reinforcements, another company or two of infantry,
or even a handful of Nova tanks, there would have been no
stopping them. The Accord positions could have been split,
and each segment mopped up at leisure. A decisive defeat was
that close for the 13th.

But reinforcements did not come for the Schlinal force, and
slowly, Van Stossen managed to draw in units from other
portions of the perimeter—a platoon here, a squad there, to
reinforce Bravo and Charley. At the point of the breakthrough,
the Schlinal battalion could not retreat. They had to stand
and fight. And they *did* fight, even when the flow of battle had clearly turned against them. The battalion did not
surrender the way the garrison of Maison had. It fought as
long as the companies had enough men to retain a sense of
unit cohesion. Only in the last stages did significant numbers
of Schlinal soldiers start to throw down their weapons and
surrender.

Van Stossen was drained. He slumped slowly to the ground
and could do nothing for several minutes but lean back against
the cone of dirt around the base of a tree and suck in one

labored, painful breath after another. He could not have lifted a hand to defend himself. The left side of his shirt had been sliced open from armpit to waist. A thin line of blood showed how close the colonel had come to dying. He scarcely recalled that duel, or the way he had driven rigid fingers into his assailant's throat, hitting the gap below the Schlinal helmet to crush the man's windpipe. He had followed up perfectly on that move, getting closer to get one arm behind the man's neck while his other hand shoved the head up and back, snapping the spinal cord and finishing the job.

Now, all he could think about was finding air to breathe.

"It's just about over, Colonel," Dezo Parks said. He was also breathing heavily, but he could still get the words out. He had a couple of advantages over Stossen. Parks was five years younger, ten kilos lighter, and he had stayed more active as ops officer than Stossen had as C.O. He tilted the visor up on his helmet and leaned forward, using his carbine almost as a crutch. "There are still a few pockets of resistance, but we broke the attack."

"Cost?" Stossen scarcely managed to get the one word out. He had *thought* that he was in perfect physical condition, as fit as any of the men under him. After all, he had always taken calisthenics with the men and walked the same twenty- and thirty-kilometer hikes in training. He might be past forty years of age, but in the long run, that was still young, less than a third of the way through the average life expectancy on his homeworld. But the bedlam of the past three hours had changed his mind.

"Too soon to know." Parks paused before he continued. "I know that we lost at least three Havocs and two Wasps. Beyond that . . ." He shrugged. "It's going to take time to get casualty figures."

Stossen's breathing started to get a little easier. After a moment he sucked in one especially deep breath and let it out slowly.

"The strike force is in trouble too, last I heard," he said. That had been—what? Thirty minutes earlier, an hour? "Hang on a second." Stossen pulled his visor down and talked to the Wasp squadron commander. Then he lifted the visor again. "We've only got two birds with juice and munitions to send to help Echo and George. It'll be at least fifteen minutes before we can send another pair. The rest will have to stick around to harass the Heggies up here."

"I called CIC five minutes ago," Parks said. "There's still no word on our relief. Nothing coming in-system that they can detect."

"I want every last bit of munitions left on the ships," Stossen said. There *were* reserves up in the fleet, but it still might not be enough. "Every spool of wire, everything else, even emergency flares. And I want it now. We'll try to time things so we have all of our remaining Wasps on hand to protect the shuttle, shuttles, whatever it takes."

"One will do it, I'm afraid," Parks said. "You want me to set it up?"

Stossen nodded. "Any wounded who need evac can go back on that shuttle."

While Parks made the call to CIC, Stossen took a long drink of the tepid water in his canteen. The water was nearly at body temperature, but it tasted strangely appealing. He could almost imagine that it was a fine red wine, an old claret from a special year. *That's crazy*, he told himself. *It's really getting to me.* He leaned back and rested his head against the bole of the tree, dreading what he had to do next. In turn, he called each of the company commanders. Two of the 13th's line companies had changed commanders during the battle—the hard way. Company-grade officers, lieutenants and captains, often showed the highest casualty rates. But *someone* was always in command, at every level.

"Two hours."

Stossen opened his eyes, startled by Parks's voice.

"Two hours?" He repeated it as a question.

"Two hours to get a shuttle down with all our reserve munitions." Parks shook his head and squatted next to the colonel. "Too bad we don't have slingshots. There are plenty of rocks around."

"We may get down to that. For the moment, let's pull in the perimeter—a hundred meters, all around. Tell the companies to find the best defensive positions they can. Pull Basset Battery back from the strike force. They're to return here at their best possible speed. We have to hold what we can up here." *Even if it means abandoning Echo and George and two recon platoons.*

"There's still that store of arms we left in Maison," Parks said. "If we could get those . . ."

"Try to put together a good contingency plan for that. Maybe tonight." Stossen paused, then added, "If the Heggies haven't moved back into Maison."

"I'll see what the satellite coverage shows, Colonel."

CHAPTER
15

The Schlinal attack just fell off, ending without any great fanfare. There had been no decisive turn in the battle against them. All they faced was the same problem as they had at the start. The surviving troops in the valley merely made an orderly withdrawal.

Captain Ingels dispatched half of his recon force to harass them, and to make certain that the enemy was leaving—and not merely regrouping for another assault. Work parties were sent down into the valley to collect weapons and ammunition from the dead and wounded. Little could be done to help the Schlinal wounded. Medics gave first aid, bandaged wounds, and administered painkillers and nanotech repair machines, but the medics knew that, for the most part, their efforts would be wasted unless the Heggies returned to collect their wounded.

"No choice," Ingels told First Sergeant Izzy Walker. "We can't carry them with us, and I'm not going to ask for another shuttle landing to evacuate Heggies."

Walker had not suggested otherwise. Under the best of conditions, the 13th was just barely able to think of civilized niceties of that nature. The 13th would lose a considerable portion of its mobility if it were to carry equipment and noncombat personnel to meet every possible contingency. For a detachment operating alone, far too close to the center of the enemy's power base on the world, it was impossible.

"Leastwise, we don't have any new wounded of our own who won't be able to walk," Walker said. "We come off lucky that way, Captain. Looks like nine dead, and maybe three dozen wounded, but none of the wounds are serious." The characterization of "not serious" was easy for someone who had not been wounded himself. Those with the wounds might disagree. Walker shrugged. "Not if we don't ask too much of them and get help in a day or so."

The dead were already being buried, not the easiest of tasks in the rocky terrain that the strike force occupied.

"We can ask for another evac shuttle if we have to," Ingels said. "Maybe tonight." He had expected that another shuttle run would be needed. The possibility that it might not was a minor relief.

"For now, we're going to move. I don't want to wait for dark. The more distance we put between ourselves and those Heggies, the better I'll feel." Not that they could put *too* much distance between them, not without new orders. The strike force had to remain close enough to Porter City to be seen as a threat to the Schlinal garrison. That was the entire point of this foray, not just one raid on a kaserne. The Schlinal garrison would scarcely be affected by the damage the strike force had done so far. It would only be an annoyance—except to those Heggies who had been killed or wounded.

"The men are pretty beat, sir," Walker said. "I don't know how much more they have left to give right now."

"Five klicks," Ingels said. "That's where the next decent defensive position is according to the mapboard." He had spent some time looking over their options. "We get there, and the Heggies don't attack, we'll let the men rest. All night and most of tomorrow, if we aren't recalled before then." All of his plans had to be qualified by that. Not knowing what new orders he might receive was annoying, but—this time—not particularly unwelcome.

"Yes, sir. I'll get the men formed up for the move."

There were more than a few audible groans as the word was passed to each of the platoons. No one enjoyed the thought of another hike. Most of the men had counted on having until dark, at least, before they would be on the move again. Infantry welcomed the dark, looked forward to it. Even when friends and enemies alike were equipped with efficient night-vision systems, the darkness gave some cover. The best night-sight gear, such as that which the Accord Defense Forces used, only provided seventy percent of daylight visibility.

Sore feet and legs were asked to carry everyone again. Five kilometers, over rough country: it took the strike force three hours to cover that distance, more than twice what it would have taken if they had been fresh.

It was hard to keep the men together during this march. After days in the field with minimal rations and major exertions, stragglers were a constant problem, and there were no pickup vans trailing along to collect them. They had to be urged on—prodded, cajoled, or threatened—by their mates as well as by the officers and noncoms. If they fell behind, the only pickup would be by the Schlinal forces, and no one wanted to trust themselves to the suspect mercies of the enemy.

The start of the march was difficult enough for most of the men. They had to climb to the top of the hill. Though the route was well defined, it was steep. After they crossed the top, they had to follow the recon platoons down a steep draw on the far side. That was too narrow, and treacherous, for anything other than single file, and it took a considerable time to move four-hundred men down it, slipping and sliding repeatedly.

The narrow draw opened into a long, narrow valley with slopes rising on both sides—steeply on the left. The bottom of the valley was rarely as much as twenty meters wide, and it was exceptionally rocky—scree, loose rocks from pebbles to boulders the size of a small truck—strewn around haphazardly. That was especially hard on feet that were already aching, and the uneven going pulled at the muscles in thighs and calves. Smaller rocks gave way underfoot. A few times, rocks larger than a man were dislodged to tilt or slide a meter or two.

After two kilometers of that, the strike force had to climb another slope, to reach a pass between two more rocky hills.

That opened up into a higher valley, a large bowl-shaped depression that had survived long enough to collect soil to support the growth of small trees. Once inside that wooded area—it was hardly large enough to term it a forest—Captain Ingels called a halt.

The men moved into defensive positions. Most of them were ready to collapse from fatigue, but there was work to do first. Holes had to be dug. Dirt and rocks had to be piled up. Men had to be reminded to eat. Exhaustion might seem more important than hunger, but they needed the nourishment, scant as their resources had become.

Even then, only half of the men could be allowed to sleep at any one time. The squads were matched off, one fire team on guard, the other to sleep. The first changeover would be made in two hours. After that, the intervals would be stretched by half. And, just maybe, everyone would have a chance to catch up on their sleep before the next march . . . or the next fight.

Eustace Ponks rode with his teeth gritted against the vibration he felt coming from the right tread of Basset two. The tremor had been there since they started moving after their repairs, just before sunset, and the vibration was beginning to get more pronounced. Eustace knew every sound and movement that the gun made, and this new sound did not bode well. They still had two-hundred kilometers to go to reach the escarpment, and there was a long, difficult climb when they did. He had already had Simon cut back on their speed. Basset two was doing no more than forty kilometers per hour now, scarcely enough to give them time to get to the top of the escarpment by first light. If that vibration continued to get worse, they would have to slow down even more. *That* might leave them out in the open, either at the rocky perimeter of the rift valley or on the road climbing to the plateau, in daylight— where they would have no room for evasive maneuvers in case of attack.

"The rest of the battery will probably pass us in an hour or two," Simon said. The recall order for the Havocs had gone out early in the afternoon, while the repair work to Basset two was still going on, but the move was not scheduled to start until dark, when the guns and their support vans would have some hope of moving unobserved. Basset two had started back

ahead of the others because of the damage it had suffered. But
a full day's lead would be lost because of the time they had
spent working on the drive wheel, and because of the slower
speed they were being forced to hold to now.

They'll pass us, Eustace thought, but there was nothing the
others could do to help Basset two move any faster. For a
time, the others would be in range to throw in a few rounds
if they were attacked on the ground, but they would not stay
close. That would simply present a more tempting target to
any enemy aircraft that might happen to spot them, and the
Havocs were not anti-aircraft weapons. They would be plump
targets, ripe for the picking. In any case, the rest of the battery
was needed on the plateau. *Not baby-sitting a cripple.*

"At least some of us will get back in time to lend a hand,"
Eustace whispered, not really caring whether or not Simon
heard him. A little louder, he said, "You feel that vibration?"
He had asked that question a dozen times already.

"I feel it," Simon replied. "If it busts, it busts. There's
nothing more we can do about it. Rosey said it's a miracle
we're even running. Just hope it gets us close enough that we
can make it the rest of the way on foot if we have to."

"Can that talk," Eustace said, too sharply. His voice sof-
tened somewhat when he added, "This old girl will get us
there. We just need to pamper her a bit. Try cutting another
klick or two off the speed."

"You're the boss," Simon said, resigned. He adjusted the
throttles on both engines just a fraction.

Once the Havoc was running at its new speed, Eustace
listened intently to the sounds the treads made for a moment.
"Maybe that *is* just a hair better," he conceded. "It should still
get us up to the top before sunrise." He hoped.

Al Bergon had a busy hour after the strike force made camp.
While the others were digging in, he made the rounds of first
squad, and second squad as well. Everyone had blisters or
badly strained muscles. Ezra Frain had managed to twist his
knee. By the time he was able to get off of his feet and stay
there, the knee had swollen up. Ezra was in considerable pain
but refused to admit it until he was alone with the medic. Even
then, he whispered.

"I didn't think I was going to make it," he told Bergon.

"It's a miracle you did. Next time, let me know right away. We could have taken two minutes to put a soaker on it. You'd have had a lot less pain, and it would heal a hell of a lot faster."

"Yeah, well." Ezra let his voice tail off. He did know better—it was the same sort of thing he had told Joe Baerclau when the sergeant hurt *his* leg—but it was always easier to give advice than to take it. With the pain, Ezra had not been thinking straight. "Long as we don't have to start off again for a couple of hours."

"Couple of hours? You'd better hope we have at least eighteen hours before you have to start walking again. That knee's in bad shape. You may have torn cartilage or muscle. I can't tell for certain. Right now, we've got to get you to Doc Eddles. Maybe he can come up with something more than I can."

"I'll be all right," Ezra insisted.

"Don't try to hand me that load of crap, Corp. If we had an evac shuttle coming in, you'd be on it. No shit. Doc Eddles would back me up in a second, and the lieutenant wouldn't try to stop it. And don't even *think* about putting any weight on that leg. I'll get a couple of guys and we'll carry you to the doc. You just wait where you are."

Bergon stood, but did not actually have to go anywhere. He called for Mort and Kam, and the three of them moved Ezra to where Doc Eddles had set up shop. Mort headed straight back to the rest of the squad. Al stayed with Ezra so he would have a chance to tell Eddles what he had found. Kam started to leave, but stopped a few meters away. He looked back toward Al.

"Okay, Kam. I'll be with you in a minute," Bergon said.

The whole squad knew that Goff was having trouble, though they tried not to let him see that they knew. Al, Mort, and Ezra had been sharing the duty of watching over Kam, and it really did not matter if one of them happened to be occupied for a few minutes; the rest of the squad was also watching. Kam hadn't realized that he was never out of sight of at least one of the others. They never called it a *suicide* watch, did not even think of it in those terms, but they knew that Goff was in danger, and they were determined to do what they could to help him through it. He was part of the squad.

Al briefed Doc Eddles on Ezra Frain's condition, then hurried over to Goff.

"Something I can do for you?" Al asked as casually as he could manage.

"I don't know." Kam had his visor up, and he whispered so softly that Al had to pay particular attention to be certain that he heard what Kam said. "I'm not sure there's anything anybody can do."

"Let's take a walk." There was too little room in the patch of woods to get out of sight of everyone, but they could manage a little privacy.

"Talk to me," Al said when they were finally out of earshot of the men around the dispensary.

Al sat, and gestured for Kam to get down as well. Goff hesitated, then more or less collapsed onto his rump. His head hung forward for a moment. Al waited without moving.

"I was wondering if Doc Eddles might have something to help me," Goff managed after a minute.

"Help you how?" Bergon asked.

"Deal with all this." Kam made a wild gesture with one hand. "You know what it's been like for me. I see somebody dead, see a little blood, and all of a sudden I'm puking my guts out. But that's not the worst part. I'm scared crazy. I can't sleep. I hardly dare close my eyes for all the terrible things I see. I don't know how much longer I can take it." More softly yet, he added, "I really don't."

"I can give you a sleep patch," Al said, speaking slowly while he tried to think what else he might be able to do. "That puts you so deep you won't dream." *Or won't remember what you dream if you do,* he qualified silently. "Just getting some undisturbed sleep should help. The human mind can do a lot for itself, if it gets a chance. A mild tranquilizer to help the other. But it can't be too much, Kam, you know that. We're stuck out here. You've got to be able to march with the rest of us. I know it's rough, but you *are* making it. You're doing your duty. You're doing the best you can, and that's all anyone can ask."

Kam shook his head. "I'm just going through the motions. I couldn't—*couldn't*—actually shoot *at* someone. Not anymore. I'm just making noises with my zipper. I think Sarge knows."

Probably, Al thought. "Don't worry about that. If it was ticking the Bear off, he'd let you know fast. Let's get back to the squad. I'll give you a patch so you can get some sleep before we hit the road again."

The next attack started with a dozen Schlinal snipers sneaking close enough to work on the strike force. The Heggie shooters had all managed to get past the thin cordon of sensors that the strike force had planted without setting off any warning. There had been too few of the remote bugs to adequately cover the perimeter, and the men of the strike force had been too tired to do their best work in any event. Sudden gunfire two hours before dawn woke everyone immediately—except for the two men who were struck by the first volley of fire, and those men who had required sleep patches for one reason or another.

Al Bergon came awake instantly. He rolled onto his stomach in the slit trench and lifted his head just enough to see over the dirt he had piled up around his hole. Though someone else had started it while he was treating the injured, Al had widened the hole and made it deeper, to give himself room for a patient.

Kam Goff was in a trench three meters away—with a sleep patch on his neck. No shooting in the galaxy was likely to wake him until the patch had run through its six-hour dose, or until it had been removed. Asleep, Goff had no way to defend himself, nor would he be able to respond to orders.

Al rolled out of his foxhole and crawled to Goff. Keeping himself pressed as close to the ground as possible, Al reached in and ripped the sleep patch from Kam's neck. Goff would still need time to wake, but yanking the patch was the first step. A stimulant patch was the next. Before Al could bring his arm back to his side to reach for the new patch, he was hit in the elbow by a slug.

The pain was so intense that he was even unable to scream. Then, there was a brief numbness, an instant of relief as Al's nervous system overloaded on pain and he came close to passing out. Then the pain was back, growing, and blood welled out of the shattered arm.

"Sarge, I'm hit," Al reported. He sounded almost calm. "At Goff's hole." Then he did faint.

Tod Chorbek and Wiz Mackey spoke at the same time. Wiz finally took over. "We can get him, Sarge. We're not all that far off."

Joe's instinct was to tell them to stay put, but he didn't. They could not—would not—leave their medic out in the open. He would have gone after any of them, no matter the risk.

"Be careful," Joe told the volunteers. "Stay flat. Drag him back to his hole."

Wiz and Tod scuttled across the ground as if they were trying to break speed records. Neither man had his rifle or pack harness, so they weren't slowed by gear. When they reached Bergon, each man grabbed a leg and they dragged him back to his own foxhole. Twice Joe saw dirt kick up within centimeters of one of the men as bullets struck—heavy slugs, not wire.

"Can't anybody see who's doing that shooting?" Joe demanded, frustration pulling his voice up a half octave. "Give them some covering fire."

After a few more rounds had hit, Joe thought he had an idea of the direction the shooting was coming from. He fired two short bursts, and told the rest of first squad to use his vector to guide their own. "Put some wire out there!" he shouted into his radio. He was on the platoon channel though and it was the whole platoon that started shooting into the trees.

They might not have hit the sniper—a slug-thrower had a much greater range than a wire gun—but there were no more incoming rounds while Wiz and Tod were dragging the medic in.

"His elbow's been shattered, and he's lost a lot of blood," Tod reported. "Our medic needs a medic, like *now*."

The medic from third squad, the only other one left in the platoon, got on the radio to say that he was on his way.

"Stop wasting wire!" Captain Ingels said on his all-hands channel. "Third and 4th platoons. Left and right. We've got maybe a dozen snipers out there. First recon on the south. Let's get them fast."

"Kill the engines," Eustace Ponks ordered. Simon hit the switches. Basset two was at the base of the road that climbed the escarpment.

"We've got less than an hour till first light," Simon reminded the gun chief after the engines fell silent. "The way we've been going, that's just barely enough."

"I've got to look at that tread," Eustace said. "That vibration is driving me crazy. I keep thinking we're going to lose the drive wheel any second. That happens at a bad place on this road, we go right off the side. You want to chance that?"

The climb would be dangerous enough as it was. The people of Porter had never anticipated that heavy artillery pieces would be using their road from rift valley to plateau. The route had been blasted out of the stone. Some of the switchbacks were cut back into the side of the escarpment, and most had little room to spare for a vehicle the size of a Havoc self-propelled howitzer. The weight of the vehicle meant that there was also a danger that it would crack off part of the roadway . . . and fall to the base of the wall with the rock.

"You lookin' at it ain't gonna stop the vibration," Simon said. "There sure ain't no time to do any more *work* on it. We either make it or we don't. We either drive the old gal up this road, or we walk it. Either way, don't make no sense to stop and stare at that damn wheel again."

Eustace felt a flash of anger, but he bit back any immediate retort. He looked across the gun barrel at Simon for a moment, knowing that the driver was right—and hating that.

"Okay, let's go. But *slow*. Maybe you got your wings polished, but I don't."

Simon laughed and started the engines again. He adjusted the idle until he was satisfied with the sound, then eased both treads into gear. The Havoc edged forward. Simon rotated the throttles forward, slowly.

"I'll get us to the top," he said. "Hell, this ole gal survived a direct hit from a rocket. Ain't nothin' gonna stop her now."

Rosey had already started the support truck up the road. Near the first switchback, he had stopped, waiting to see what Eustace was going to do with the howitzer. Once the gun started moving again, the truck also resumed its progress. The truck went first: that was in case something did go wrong. The gun would not take out the truck on its way down.

"Some guarantee you give us," Eustace had mumbled, but the trucks had all gone up ahead of their guns—the rest of the battery was already on the plateau—and they had followed the Havocs down the other day.

The rough road never climbed at more than a 27-degree angle. A Havoc in good condition would scarcely have balked at 45 degrees, up or down, but climbing a steep slope with a jury-rigged drive wheel might be asking for too much trouble. The extra burden on that axle . . . Eustace shook his head. *I wouldn't even think about trying anything more than 30 degrees*, he lied to himself.

Before long, Eustace found himself holding his breath again, as if that might make it easier for Basset two to make it up the narrow road. He kept his eyes on the outside monitors, jerking away from them only long enough to look out directly through one of his periscopes. He had two of those, fore and aft, each capable of turning through 210 degrees, providing overlapping fields of view.

The first switchback was only twenty meters above the floor of the rift valley, two-hundred meters from the start of the slope. The builders had taken advantage of a natural ledge that angled gently up to the first switchback.

Simon had to reverse the right tread for the turn. There was not enough room to go around the curve simply shifting the transmission for that tread into neutral. Eustace held his breath again. The turns were the most likely places for the drive wheel or tread to come off, or for the axle to snap.

Basset two made the turn without difficulty. Eustace detected no change in the vibration coming from the drive wheel. But he didn't relax after the gun was moving straight again. Each subsequent turn would be higher, some at a steeper grade.

Sweat started to form on Eustace's forehead. By the time Basset two was halfway up the escarpment, the sweat was flowing into his eyes, stinging, but he didn't wipe it away. When he didn't have anything else to do with his hands, he held on to the arms of his seat as if he were afraid of falling out.

Where the road reached its steepest grade, the pitch of the vibration from the right tread increased in pitch and volume. The shaking became gross, not subtle, as if the drive assembly were tearing itself apart. Yet again, Eustace held his breath, trying to hold the repairs together by willpower.

"Slow it down, just a mite," he told Simon, softly, his voice strained.

Simon didn't bother trying to change Ponks's mind. Obediently, he eased off on the throttles, just a hair, slowing the gun by perhaps no more than a half kilometer per hour. The gun was already barely creeping. The slope had eaten most of the power the engines were putting out on the reduced throttle settings he had been using before.

"Planes on the scope," Eustace announced a moment later, followed almost instantly by, "Wasps. I've got the recognition signal."

"Hope you're sending our RS too," Simon said under his breath.

"Loud and clear," Eustace said. *Be hell to get shot off this wall by our own birds.* There was enough danger in the climb without that.

The Wasps flew on until their signal was hidden by the lip of the plateau.

"They didn't seem to be in any particular hurry," Eustace said. "Must not be any Heggies close by."

For the next twenty minutes, the men rode in silence. Then, "Last switchback coming up, boss," Simon reported. "After that, it's smooth sailing. The road bends back and gets almost level."

Eustace didn't need the travelogue, but Simon couldn't hold back.

"Don't relax yet, Simon," Eustace said. "We're near the top, sure, but that just means we've got farther to fall if something goes wrong."

"You want to get out and walk?" Simon demanded, his temper finally beginning to frazzle. "You can get out and I'll chase you the rest of the way to camp, goose you with the gun every time you slow down."

"Simmer down, and keep your mind on your driving." Eustace regretted his own show of temper almost instantly, as did Simon. But as was usually the way between them, both men simply went silent. For the rest of this ride, there would be no conversation that was not absolutely required.

It didn't matter. Five minutes later, Basset two had success-fully made the last turn and was moving away from the edge of the escarpment. Even if the drive wheel gave out now, it would only mean a short walk. There would be no fall in their metal cage.

CHAPTER
16

In a few hours, the 13th Spaceborne Assault Team would have been on Porter for eleven days. The days, and nights, were getting no easier for the strike force west of the capital city or for the bulk of the 13th on the plateau. The Schlinal garrison had not attempted any additional full-scale attacks on either element of the invading force, but there were almost continuous harassing attacks against one or the other.

The strike force consisting of Echo and George companies and the 1st and 3rd recon platoons was on the march again, moving northwest, away from Porter City—but without getting closer to the territory controlled by the rest of the 13th. A second shuttle had managed to get in just before sunset the previous afternoon. That lander had taken off several more wounded and had brought in two cases of wire—the last ammunition available for the strike force. At that, it had amounted to only two spools per carbine. That would not last long in a serious fight.

Joe Baerclau put one foot in front of the other. Thinking

beyond that was becoming difficult. He scarcely recalled the previous step or imagined a future that held the next one. From time to time, as he happened to think about it, he did look around to see how the platoon was moving, or to tell the squad leaders to keep close track of their men, but the most routine duties had become infinitely complicated for a mind numbed by too many days of little sleep, short rations, and long hikes. Movements were leaden, tortured. Even the occasional moments of attack no longer excited the men. They went through the defensive routines with all the life of zombies. They tried to eliminate the attackers, or stalemate them, and the march would go on.

And on.

Kam Goff had taken on the duties of squad medic after Al Bergon was wounded. Al had been evacuated to the hospital ship. Kam was scarcely qualified to act as medic. He had only the same cursory training in first aid that all recruits went through, but he could doctor blisters, and that was the main call on his services. Beyond that, he could bandage a wound, or wrap a knee or ankle in a soaker . . . and direct the injured man to Doc Eddles.

The new duties appeared to have helped settle Kam's anxieties. They gave him something to think about besides his fear, and the way that combat paralyzed his mind. When he was going to help a buddy, or working with a wounded man, he did not have the reaction he had had to walking up and seeing the dead or wounded before. There was a little color back in his face, and only the exhaustion he shared with everyone else seemed to dull his reactions.

"We'll take fifteen here."

Captain Ingels's voice over the noncoms' circuit startled Joe. He passed the word to the platoon and blinked rapidly several times, as if just waking from a vivid dream. *I must have been asleep on my feet*, he thought. He stood motionless, his body swaying as if he were about to fall.

That would be the easiest way to get to the ground. Even that idle thought couldn't bring a smile to his face.

"Take a little care for your positions," he told the platoon. "Don't get caught with your butts in the air. We can't tell when we'll get another attack."

Then, at last, Joe sank to the ground. For a moment he just

let his head sag, the chin strap of his helmet on his chest. He closed his eyes and took a deep breath, on the verge of falling asleep. But there was no time for sleep. Fifteen minutes. *Fifteen minutes*. Not long enough to sleep. Too long to stay awake.

"Joe?"

"Yes, Lieutenant?" Joe had to shake his head to get his mind working again.

"One more hour. That's what the captain says. Then we find a place to stay put for at least four, maybe all day." Lieutenant Keye sounded as tired as Joe felt.

Joe looked around, trying to spot where Keye was. He had lost track of the platoon leader, and that was a bad sign. Everything seemed to be a bad sign lately.

"Another hour's going to be rough on everyone, Lieutenant, including you and me."

"I know, but it's going to take that long to reach a place that'll give us some security. And space for pickup, just in case. No, there's no word yet, either on relief or on a ride back to the plateau." He paused. "At least, no word *we've* been told about." Keye cursed himself silently for rambling. He might be as tired as his men, but it was still bad form to show it so clearly.

"Better be soon, Lieutenant. Another day and we'll be out of food as well as everything else."

"They're getting short on the plateau too, Joe. We're going to organize a couple of hunting parties, if we can, after we bivouac for the night. Maybe after we've all had time to get a little sleep."

"Hunting parties?"

"Recon will handle that. Most of those snipes have been hunters since they learned how to walk."

Fresh meat would be a treat, Joe thought. "Take a lot of meat to feed everybody," he said.

"Every little bit helps," Keye said. "How's Goff holding up?"

"Pretty good now, sir. We're still keeping watch on him, but there's been no sign of trouble since he started handling the blister detail."

"Remember that," Keye said before he signed off.

• • •

"Can't help you this time, Lieutenant," Roo Vernon told Zel Paitcher. "That entire port drive has to be replaced, and I can't do that here. Not now, at least. That's a three-man job, and we'd have to bring the replacement drive down from the ships. Even if the colonel okayed that, it'd take three, four hours of work once we got the parts. And without a clean room to work in . . ." He shook his head. "Be better just to slide the bird into one of the heavy transport lifters and do the work back in the hangar, on the ship. And we can't get one of *those* down here without more security than we've got. Sorry, sir."

Zel wanted to scream his rage, his frustration, but he didn't. If the bird couldn't be repaired, it couldn't, and no amount of shouting would change that. Still, for a long moment, he could do nothing but stare at Roo, his body trembling with pent-up emotion. Then the emotion seemed to drain away, suddenly, and his body went rather limp. He took a deep breath and let it out slowly.

"I know you've done your best, Chief," Zel said. Under his breath, an intense "Damn!" slid out.

"We've got one other bird in the same shape out of Red flight," Roo offered. "Short as we are, maybe the colonel will authorize bringing down the repair parts. I'm sure he wants as many of them flying as possible."

"But you don't think it's a good idea to try the repairs here."

"Not the best, no, sir. I wouldn't guarantee the work for more than ten hours of flying time 'less we do it in a clean room. An' *that's* pushing it. Get dust and organic molecules in there, fouling things up. The control circuits can be mighty touchy about that. You saw what happened before, sir. We got something in your bird and it shut right down. You were lucky, sir. It happened on the ground last time. This might be worse. A little speck of dust caught in the wrong connection can raise the heat 20 degrees in no time at all. Use the bird hard and you can go right on by the safety limits, not even know what's happened until you get drive failure. Temperature fault like that, you couldn't even count on 'jecting safely." Roo paused for a moment, trying to come up with some way to make the lieutenant feel better about his plight.

"'Nother day or two, likely everybody be grounded," was the best he could find. "We're down to the scrapin's on muni-

tions now. Won't any of it last much longer. Your plane, sir,
I'll have to get in and strip what ammo you're carrying so
we can keep another bird flyin' that much longer." Privately,
Roo doubted that the ammunition would last even one more
full day. If the Heggies made one more determined assault on
the 13th, the remaining Wasps would run dry in short order.

Zel looked at the ground. He was out of the air, probably for
the duration of the campaign—unless a couple of other pilots
had to be grounded with planes that were still airworthy, and
that was highly unlikely.

"I guess that makes me a mudder," Zel said eventually.

" 'Fraid so, sir," Roo said, sympathy in his voice. "Other
pilots who lost their birds, colonel's took 'em right into the
HQ detachment." Roo failed to suppress a chuckle then. "He's
got the highest ranked rifle squad ever, I think."

Zel looked up then.

"Sorry, sir," Roo said quickly. "I just couldn't help myself."

Zel was slow to say, "That's okay, Chief. If it wasn't me, I'd
probably be making the same sort of comments." He *had* made
the same sort of comments, talking to Slee about the three
other pilots who had lost their planes but remained healthy
themselves.

"This campaign can't last much longer," Roo said, trying to
be conciliatory. "Relief be here soon, maybe afore the day's
gone."

"I'll believe it when I see it," Zel said. He shook his head.
"Talk to you later, Chief. I'd best go report to the colonel. If
I can find him."

"Last I heard, sir, HQ was still up by Bravo Company," Roo
offered.

The Schlinal commander on Porter had not bothered to
return a garrison to the city of Maison. There would be time
for that later. After the Accord troops were destroyed, the
people of Maison would be next on his list of *Things To
Do*. They had to have helped the invaders. At a minimum,
they had permitted the Accord to attack and destroy or capture
the troops stationed there. He did not know yet which was the
case. Either way, it really did not matter. In any case, the punishment for Maison would be severe, and extended. But . . .
later. After the burr of the Accord had been eliminated from

Porter, he would think about punishment for Maison. Anticipation was half the fun. The Accord: the Schlinal commander did not assume that they had merely killed all prisoners out of hand, as he might easily have done in similar circumstances. After all, they had turned loose the prisoners they had captured in Porter City. Without weapons, helmets, boots, or *clothes*, true, but they had not harmed anyone after capture.

"It's not as if I actually *need* the men they left in Maison," he reasoned.

He still had more than sufficient troops for the job. It was just a question of bringing everything together in just the right way at just the right time. Soon, the Accord would be low on ammunition and food. Even with all of his satellites out of commission, the commander could still tell how many enemy ships were over his planet. There had been no reinforcements, no additional stores of ammunition coming in-system. Or food. The invaders would be easy pickings when they got hungry and short of wire. The Schlinal commander had no delusions about the quality of his troops. They would not have been assigned to garrison duty on a world like Porter if they had been first-rate combat soldiers. Most were conscripts. Many were too old and out of shape for the front lines. But they had the numbers, they had the weapons, and they had more than enough ammunition to deal with the enemy. After all, no more than two thousand or so could have landed, and they *had* taken casualties. The Schlinal commander had no idea how many casualties, but that there were *some* was obvious.

Soon, the commander promised himself. Eleven days was too long as it was. If he let this incursion go on much longer, his superiors would ask too many uncomfortable questions. In the Schlinal military, *questions* could be hazardous to an officer's career . . . not to mention his health. The delay meant that he would need a "glorious" victory. He would have to completely obliterate the enemy. That way, he could always rationalize the time by saying that he had merely been toying with them, experimenting with methods, preparing himself and his troops for future engagements.

He smiled. Yes, that would go over well with the field marshal, and the baron.

Tomorrow night, he decided with a self-satisfied nod. After another thirty-six hours of softening up, the enemy should be in just the shape he wanted. His troops ought to be able to simply walk over them. Both units, the one in the valley, and the larger one up on the plateau. The smaller force, the one that had raided the capital, was nearly to that point now, from appearances. They had been reported using captured weapons, and abandoning them once they were empty.

"Easy pickings indeed," the commander whispered.

With that decided, he rang for his batman, and for breakfast. He had a good appetite this morning.

Six Havocs made the trip back to Maison under cover of darkness. Thirty men from the 2nd recon platoon met the howitzers outside the city and confirmed that the Heggies had not returned. After that, it was a matter of an hour's work to load the weapons and ammunition that had been left for the residents of Maison. The locals also provided more than a ton of foodstuffs, mostly vegetables and fruit, after they learned that the 13th was low on rations.

"We're in this together," the acting mayor of Maison told the senior officer. The acting mayor was under no delusions as to what the fate of Maison would be if the 13th was destroyed. The reason he was *acting* mayor was that his elected predecessor had been hung in the town square as an example, for some unexplained infraction of Schlinal rules. "We'll do whatever we can."

"Damn delivery truck," Eustace Ponks mumbled under his breath. "Spend a day and a half repairing the ole girl and they turn her into a *delivery* truck."

Simon pretended not to hear. That was better than rekindling the tirade that had started within seconds after they received their orders to be part of the mission to Maison.

The damaged drive wheel and axle had been replaced with parts scavenged from a wrecked Havoc. The job had still taken more than eighteen hours of concentrated work. The jury-rigged repairs made in the rift valley had caused additional damage. Halfway through the new repair process, Rosey Bianco had come within seconds of throwing up his hands and giving up. Eustace had taken the mechanic aside and spent ten minutes convincing him to stick with it. Neither man would talk about what was said in that conversation.

It gives us a chance, Simon thought—collecting the captured weapons and ammunition, that is. If the infantry ran out of wire, the Havocs would not last long. Artillery and infantry, and even the air wing, were all dependent on each other. The flyers needed safe places to land for fresh batteries and ammunition. The Havocs needed safe areas as well, and infantry to keep the enemy from destroying them like bugs. A Havoc had little defensive capability. It was pitifully easy to knock out. The more ammunition the mudders had, the longer the Havocs would have some sort of haven. Of course, the Havocs themselves might soon run out of ammunition. They were down to just the rounds they carried with them now. Basset two was down to eighteen rounds. In a hectic fight, they might run through that many shells in ten minutes. After that, Basset two would be nothing more than an expensive battering ram. Or a delivery van.

Might as well start now, Simon thought. But he knew that Eustace would never see it that way.

Kam Goff woke feeling halfway rested for the first time since landing on Porter. Even after sleeping with the knockout patch that one time, he hadn't felt really rested. Of course, he had been wakened prematurely from that sleep. But this time, he woke on his own, quickly, fully. He felt exceptionally clearheaded, also for a change. Under other circumstances, he might have gotten rapidly to his feet, ready to face a sunny new day. But that could never happen again, not unless he found a magic potion that allowed him to forget everything he had seen and done on Porter. And Kam did not believe in magic.

The bright alertness of waking refreshed quickly dulled as the events of the last eleven days reimprinted themselves on Kam's mind. It always came back—the killings, the blood, numbness, vomiting—all of it, down to the looks his comrades gave him when they thought he wouldn't notice.

He always noticed. After several minutes, Kam finally sat up and looked around. They had made camp in a narrow canyon this time. He actually grinned at the thought that it could be a death trap. Enemy gunners on top of the canyon walls, shooting down: that would be a real slaughter. If the recon squads patrolling above were overwhelmed quickly, or missed spotting an enemy force, Echo and George might simply cease to exist.

The countryside had become distinctly foreboding during the night's march, but it was only now clear just how foreboding. Up above this canyon, there seemed to be no trees at all left. There were rock-strewn vistas that might have come from an airless moon. Rarely was there any greenery visible, only in sheltered nooks, mostly along the few watercourses. The occasional bird stayed far overhead—scavengers looking for a meal. More rarely they saw a small animal, usually at a considerable distance. Most of those animals were the small hopping reptiles one of the men had jokingly termed a bunnysaurus. They did make decent eating, though they tasted nothing at all like rabbit.

There was a thin stream running through this canyon, never more than two meters wide and sixty centimeters deep. The current was swift though, and the water clear and cold and pure. Doc Eddles had found no worrisome contamination with his field tests. In many ways, the water was even purer than the recycled fare they had know aboard ship coming to Porter. It certainly *tasted* better.

I wonder if there are fish in it? Kam mused. He wasn't even sure that Porter had fish or recognizable analogs. Many worlds did, and many that had no native fish had imported them from Earth (or one of the other worlds with piscine fauna) to stock their waterways. He had seen pictures of beautiful, exotic species from dozens of worlds. As a child, Kam had once had a terrestrial aquarium, stocked solely with genuine Earth species. That hobby had lasted for nearly a year before the last of the fish had died, from some complaint he had never been able to identify.

Kam got to his feet and stretched, twisting his body and moving from side to side. He looked up at the sky. The sun was shining in a cloudless sky. At least the portion of sky he could see between the canyon walls was cloudless. Despite the burden of his memories, Kam felt as at ease with himself as he could remember ever feeling. There was a measure of comfort to everything now, and had been since he had taken over Al's duties and made his other decision. He had finally come to terms with his failings. He knew what he had to do, and he knew that he could do it.

A beautiful day, Kam thought. *A beautiful day to die*. If he could escape the watching eyes of his comrades long enough. He had noticed them tracking him, every second of every hour. He suspected that they even stood guard over him while he was asleep. It didn't matter. He would find his opportunity. And then he could *really* rest.

CHAPTER
17

Corporal Dem Nimz of the 3rd recon platoon led his squad back into the canyon bivouac. The recon platoons were organized differently from the line companies. Each recon platoon was divided into twelve-man rather than seven-man squads. Within those squads, the troops were divided into three 4-man fire teams. Recon soldiers normally operated in smaller units than line troops did, most often without backup from air or artillery. Recon soldiers tended to be more independent by nature, more difficult to fit into the normal garrison discipline of the military. But the nature of the men, and the nature of the assignments they drew, also brought a certain amount of consideration. It was rare for them to be pressed to act like drill field soldiers.

The sergeant who had commanded Nimz's squad on landing had been killed the first day, on a patrol far beyond the lines. Nimz still had eight men left, including himself. The squad worked its way down a narrow pathway along the canyon wall. When they entered camp, they headed directly toward Captain Ingels's command post on the far side of the canyon, under an overhang that gave the area the appearance of a cave mouth.

"I didn't want to say anything over the radio, sir," Nimz said when he was face-to-face with the captain and both men had their helmet visors up.

Ingels raised an eyebrow in surprise. "You ambushed a short company of Heggies. What happened then?"

"We caught 'em fair, sir, and didn't lose a man doin' it," Nimz said, nodding at the satisfying memory. "They walked right into our kill zone, an' we did 'em up proper. Three splat guns." He smiled broadly. "The body count was ninety four, including three wounded Heggies who couldn't make it another hour. Far as we could tell, no one escaped. I'm pretty sure o' that, sir, but not full one hundred percent. Maybe ninety-nine point five." Nimz had to restrain himself to keep from laughing, still on a high from the ambush.

"So, what was the problem?" Ingels kept his voice even. He had dealt with recon types often enough. He had even done a short tour as a recon platoon leader before deciding that he fit in better with a line company—that is, before deciding that he really didn't belong with the crazy reccers.

"The Heggies know we're short of ammo, sir. *Know it.* Plain and simple, no doubt at all. We took ninety-four rifles. The most any of the dead Heggies had was two full spools, plus whatever was already in the magazine. An' no spare power packs. One of the wounded managed to talk a little before he died. Said their officers got orders that they weren't to go into combat with any more ammo than that. Their reserves were being held back, out of our reach."

For a moment Ingels simply stared at Nimz.

"We brought back the rifles and wire," Nimz added. The captain's silent stare bothered him in a way he really couldn't understand.

"Every little bit helps," Ingels allowed. He sighed. "But if they know we're hurting . . ."

"Yes, sir," Nimz said, mostly to prevent another lengthy silence. "You see why I didn't want to put that on the radio."

"You did right, Corporal. Thank you. Get your men fed and settled down for a rest. We'll get the weapons distributed."

Ingels stood motionless and watched while Nimz rejoined his men and led them off toward a space a little farther upstream.

North. Anyone who thought much on the subject wanted to be upstream of everyone else. The stream might have been pure when the strike force arrived, but the presence of so many dirty humans would not leave it that way for long.

After two or three minutes, Ingels lowered his visor and said one word on a private channel. "Vic."

"Yes, Captain?" Lieutenant Vickers replied.

"Come see me, soon as you can."

Ingels lifted his visor again, walked over to the stream, and looked down into the water. He knew that he had to pass the intelligence on to Colonel Stossen—over the radio, despite the sensitivity of the information—but he wanted a moment to think through what he would say first. He knelt slowly and dipped his hands in the stream and splashed water against his face. Then he dipped again and took a long drink. He had a canteen cup on his belt, but this was quicker and, in a way he did not try to understand, more satisfying, even if it was far less efficient.

If only wire flowed like water, there for the taking.

Joe Baerclau had a dull ache in his lower back that simply would not go away. He had even had Doc Eddles take a look, but all the doc could do was to put a soaker over it, and even that did not seem to help, or help much. The ache was still there, a constant reminder nagging at Joe's attention. The ache even disturbed his sleep, insinuating itself into his dreams, keeping him from the deep oblivion his exhaustion merited. *Keep me on my toes,* Joe told himself, trying to find something positive in the pain. *I get too deep asleep, I might not wake up if we're attacked.* There was really little chance of that, but it did address one of Joe's constant worries in a combat situation. From experience, he knew that he would never sleep that soundly. If there was any gunfire at all around, it would snap him right out of sleep, ready to return fire or do whatever else the situation might demand. But he always worried about it.

After the strike force made camp during the night, Joe had stayed up for the first two hours, sharing that watch while the ache in his back increased. Then he had settled down to get some sleep. He had managed nearly four hours before the ache finally woke him. He was free to go back to sleep now, if he wanted, if he could. It was nearly noon, and the strike force was planning to stay put until dark, unless the colonel decided to send the shuttles for them, to take them back to the plateau.

Until the shuttles come. As far as Joe had heard, there was no decision on that yet. The Heggies were attacking, off and on, up on the plateau. The raids seemed to be nothing serious, just enough to keep the men there busy, and to make the air space over the 13th too dangerous for shuttles. Boem fighters, Nova tanks, infantry raids against one section of the perimeter or another, in and out, back and forth, jumping around so that the 13th never knew where the next strike would come from. Facing tactics of that sort was particularly unnerving. It was worse than facing constant pressure in one place. All the spyeyes the 13th had strung around Porter didn't seem to do much good. The 13th got warning when the Boems or Novas came on, but rarely more than a couple of minutes. And infantry movements were rarely noted in time to give a warning before the shooting started.

They could lift us back to the ships, Joe thought, knowing that the colonel would attempt that only in the most dire of emergencies, unless their relief force showed up. But *that* news would certainly have been released as soon as the colonel knew about it. Joe was almost certain of that. That kind of news would be too good for morale for the colonel to keep it secret.

Wouldn't it?

Joe was bone-tired, but he had chosen not to try to sleep. Instead, he had taken time to talk with each of the fire teams in the platoon, sometimes to individual soldiers. Though he had known everyone in the platoon, in the company, before Porter, he had only been a squad leader then. Now he was platoon sergeant, even if only temporarily, and responsible for more men. He had done all of the normal things in the last few hours, said whatever he thought might boost the men's spirits, even a little, while he warned them to be particularly sparing of ammunition and food, and to drink plenty of water while they had such a good source at hand.

"Don't get dehydrated," he had warned them. That was too easy to do. Even when it caused no trouble in the field, it could complicate the procedure of getting back "to human" when they finally left Porter. Even if a soldier did not suffer injury or illness on a campaign, he would still need a certain amount of convalescence time afterward. That was something that was too rarely understood by the men—and even by some of the officers who ought to know.

Joe had returned twice to Goff during the last three hours. He spent more time with Kam each time than he did with anyone else. Kam seemed different. Joe wasn't sure that he could define the difference exactly, and he didn't know what to make of the new Kam Goff. *Being our medic has brought the best out in him,* was as close as he could come, and he felt uneasy about that assessment. He toyed with the idea of suggesting that Goff transfer to the medical corps. Perhaps he would be unable to handle permanent assignment as a combat medic. Medics were, after all, simply riflemen who accepted the additional duties. But as an orderly in a hospital ward, he might do well. Maybe he could even take training as a medtech like Doc Eddles. That way, Goff could, perhaps, keep a decent opinion of himself after Porter.

After Porter. Joe shook his head. It was becoming increasingly difficult to think of any future after Porter. They had already been on-planet twice as long as they had anticipated, with no word yet about when they might finally get off. *After Porter* was a dream, maybe even a hallucination.

"Baerclau."

"Yes, sir," Joe replied automatically at the sound of Lieutenant Keye's voice.

"As it stands now, we're here until sunset. The colonel's ordering down shuttles to take us back to the plateau then."

Joe nodded to himself. "Guess that's the best time, sir. Like when we left." Dawn or sunset, times when the sun was low in the sky.

"Get the men up," Keye said. "We've got a little perimeter duty ahead of us. Up top. We're to go out three klicks to the northeast and set up a line of bugs. We *do* have bugs left, don't we?"

"Yes, sir. That's one thing we're not short of." Joe suppressed a sigh. "I guess it is our turn for a little work, Lieutenant."

Keye chuckled. "You could say that. Get 'em mounted up. Fifteen minutes."

Joe relayed the orders to the squad leaders. He had to remind himself to let Ezra handle first squad. If Joe kept butting in there, Ezra would have that much more difficulty getting the men to think of him as their squad leader.

Fifteen minutes passed quickly. Those men who had been sleeping were wakened. Nearly everyone took the opportunity to take long drinks of the cool water from the stream and to refill their canteens. Some of the men ate part of a meal pack. For three days, they had been making one pack last for two meals. A few had started stretching their rations even more on their own initiative; those were mostly veterans. It made for hungry moments, but postponed the time when they might run out completely.

Echo Company's 2nd platoon was not the only one setting out on the same sort of mission. Altogether, five platoons were positioning sensing devices. If there was any Schlinal activity around, the sooner the strike force knew about it, the better. If necessary, the shuttles could be warned off, told to stay out of the atmosphere and wait for the danger to pass. Or the LZ could be adjusted to set the shuttles down farther away from the Heggies.

Northeast, Joe thought as the platoon started to climb out of the canyon. *At least that's in the direction of the rest of the regiment.* It might take four hard days to walk back to the plateau, but if worse came to worst, they could do it.

First squad led the way, more by default than from any conscious decision. Mort Jaiffer had the point, followed by Goff and Ezra Frain. Joe followed first squad, and Keye followed second squad. The "path" up the canyon wall was merely a series of ledges, each higher than the last, narrow, but not so narrow that there was any real danger of anyone falling off. Moving from one ledge to the next could be a little touchy. Three of them required each man to set his rifle on the rock above and hoist himself up with both hands. With a little help from the man before, and a boost from the next man in line, it went a little faster.

There was no real concern about an ambush at the top of the canyon. The recon platoons had a perimeter staked out to prevent that. A canyon might be a dandy place to hide from prying eyes, but it could be a death trap if proper care was not exercised. Captain Teu Ingels was not the kind of commander who missed elementary precautions.

Three klicks out, three klicks back, Joe thought as he reached the top of the canyon wall. His mind gauged that distance in aching muscles and sore feet. He turned slowly, eyes slightly squinted, trying to see everything within line of sight, on the ground and in the air. He was pleased at what he saw—or, more accurately, did not see. There were no planes in sight. While Wasps might have been morale boosters, it was even more heartening that there were no Schlinal Boems around. Nor were there any Nova tanks or enemy infantry visible. There was no gunfire coming in or going out. The platoon almost might have been alone on the world.

"Last time I tried to plant a row of bugs, you know what happened," Joe said when Lieutenant Keye stopped next to him.

"Don't go borrowing trouble, Joe."

"All those rocks and crevices, a couple of regiments could be hidden," Joe said. "Fifty tanks, four or five thousand men."

"If there were anywhere near that many Heggies around, you think we'd have lasted this long?"

Joe hesitated before he said, "Naw, I guess not. Still, you got to worry 'bout what *might* happen, or you forget to do the things that could save your butt."

"If there were any real numbers out here, we'd know about them, Joe. Between the spyeyes and the reccers, we'd *know*."

Joe laughed, but without humor. "I know that, sir, but if I don't have *something* to worry about, then I have to worry about nothing. I don't feel right 'less I'm worrying about something or other."

"You're starting to sound like Max."

Joe faced the lieutenant squarely, but did not speak.

"Sorry, Joe," Keye said after a moment. "I know how close the two of you were."

Joe shook his head. "I just can't get used to him being gone sir, not yet. I just wall that off, I guess."

"Let's get moving."

The platoon moved by squads, in four separate columns. As close as the terrain permitted, the columns stayed twenty-five to thirty meters apart. Within the columns, the men kept their spacing as well. They were too tired to bunch up. It was in forest that intervals were most difficult to maintain, and there was not a single tree to be seen, not even any of the scrub trees that had been most common in this area of Porter. The only significant greenery of any kind was a prickly grass whose fifty-centimeter blades had serrated edges. That grass seemed nearly sharp enough to cut leather. At least the grass grew only in sparse patches. It could almost always be avoided.

The hike out was uneventful. Lieutenant Keye kept the pace easy. After eleven and a half days on Porter, no one was capable of much speed in any case, especially not Keye. He told himself that he was finally beginning to feel his age, and he couldn't get far from that thought afterward. It was a thin excuse.

The men moved with instructions to watch the ground carefully for any sign that there had been soldiers across it recently, but no one saw anything that indicated that humans had *ever* trod any of this ground. On a world like Porter, that was eminently possible—even within sixty or seventy kilometers of the capital.

Once they reached their destination, the squads fanned out and planted thirty of the electronic devices, twenty-five meters apart in a shallow arc, deviating only for the needs of the terrain. Joe personally directed the placement of most of the snooper bugs. After they were all in place, Joe and the lieutenant went out beyond them, to make sure that the devices would not be spotted too quickly by a Schlinal force moving toward the strike force's positions. Then, after the platoon was far enough behind the line of bugs that they wouldn't set off alarms themselves, Joe activated them remotely.

"Okay," Keye said. "Let's get back. We don't want to be late for our ride."

The platoon had not made a hundred meters back toward the canyon when rifle fire started, coming from the east, on their left.

The fire was far from heavy. Even as he dove for the ground, Joe guessed that no more than a half-dozen rifles were active. But two men from fourth squad, the squad that had the left flank, went down heavily from the first bursts of wire. Their squad leader crawled toward them while a dozen others from the platoon returned the fire. It only took a moment for the squad leader to learn that one of his two men was dead, the other only injured.

"Slack off on the wire," Keye ordered the platoon. "Third squad, go around the left. Second, take the right. First and fourth, hold your fire unless you have a clear target."

Joe got behind a rock that was just high enough to give him a good kneeling position so he could fire over the shoulder of the stone, using it as a stationary rest for his rifle. He glanced around, trying to fix everyone's position in his mind. He could tell, vaguely, the area where the ambush was located. The Heggies had picked their position well. They had cover on at least three sides. Joe couldn't tell what was behind them. He guessed that they had decent cover from that angle as well.

"I think it's just a squad, Lieutenant," Joe said. "Not enough guns for anything larger."

"I hope that's all it is," Keye replied. "And not just the advance squad for a larger unit."

"You know, all the bugs in the galaxy won't do much good if there's an enemy force already inside the electronic perimeter," Joe said. "Any chance of getting an air search to make sure the circle's not contaminated?"

"I doubt it, but I'll make the suggestion," Keye said. "See if you can spot any of the Heggies out there while I talk to the captain."

Joe took out his power binoculars and started to scan the rocky area that seemed to be where the wire was coming from. At the range he was searching, the glasses had the theoretical capability to detect something as small as a one-half-by-four-centimeter blade of grass moving in the breeze. The computer module of the binoculars was equipped to do the kind of scan that Joe needed. It would flag anything that looked like battle dress or a gun, as well as movement too minor for a human to notice without help. It could even identify a burst of wire in the air under near-perfect conditions.

"Spot them?" Keye asked.

"Yes, sir. There are only four of them firing now, 130 meters out, about 12 degrees right. Second squad is within 50 meters of them, and it doesn't look as if they've been spotted by the Heggies."

"Warn them that they're getting close," Keye said.

Joe did that, then asked, "What about the air search?"

"Not until the shuttles come in. They'll be doing a close scan as they approach. If they see too much . . ."

"We walk back," Joe said, finishing the statement.

We don't have enough rations to make it on foot, Keye thought, but it wasn't something he felt compelled to talk about. Joe could see that for himself. They weren't finding enough game to make the difference. Four-hundred-plus men needed a lot of feeding, and the very presence of so many intruders drove the game farther off.

Joe leaned forward, resting the binoculars on the rock in front of him. He forgot his conversation with the lieutenant and started directing second squad's movements. He had a better view of what they were getting into than they did. At the same time, he moved third squad closer from the other side, watching the angles so that the two squads would not be shooting at each other by mistake. The exercise fully occupied his mind.

"The Heggies are trying to withdraw," Joe said after a couple of minutes. "Second squad, turn 45 degrees right, third, 45 left." He told each squad how far they were from the enemy and where the other squad was. "Careful with your fire."

A dozen meters from Joe, Lieutenant Keye was also watching the maneuvering through power binoculars, but he left the directing to Joe. Having two spotters try to control the troops could only lead to confusion.

Second squad was closest, by twenty meters. They were the first to take the Heggie patrol under fire. When the Heggies moved, trying to get away from second squad, they walked right into the path of third squad. The fight lasted less than two minutes from the time second squad opened fire. The two squad leaders reported only a minute after that. They had seven bodies, all Schlinal—seven rifles, thirteen spools of wire, and three Schlinal RPG launchers, with a dozen rounds for them.

"Bring the munitions along," Keye ordered.

"That gives us a little more firepower," Joe commented. "I still wonder if we shouldn't be looking for good-sized rocks for throwing. It may come to that."

"Let's hope not," Keye said. "Have everyone take a good look around. I'd hate to find that more Heggies snuck up on us while we were preoccupied with one squad."

"Yes, sir." *I should have thought of that,* Joe thought, angry at himself for the oversight. It was too easy a mistake, one that could have proved deadly.

"I want every Wasp we've got left in the air to cover the shuttles," Stossen told Parks. "If it's still possible, I want them all to have a full load of munitions as well."

"We can manage that," Dezo said. "We're down to eight airworthy Wasps. The last report I had, we had munitions to fill their cannon magazines twice and maybe two full loads of rockets each. We've even got a couple of bombs left."

"All these petty raids. I don't think that the Schlinal commander is just out to annoy us. It must be leading up to something."

"They obviously know we're short on ammunition," Parks said, not for the first time. Even before the report from Captain Ingels, that had seemed clear. "They're probably trying to deplete our stocks as far as possible before they move in full scale again."

"Much longer, and it won't take much of a 'full scale,'" Stossen said. "If we've got any mines that haven't been planted yet, get them out before sunset. I can't help thinking that tonight is the night. The Schlinal commander waits much longer and he'll have trouble explaining why."

"Every mine we've got is out and armed," Parks said. "We laid the last of them last night. About half are set on automatic. The rest are controlled from the perimeter."

"Is there anything I've forgotten?" Stossen asked. "Anything at all we can still do to help ourselves?"

Parks shook his head. "If there is, I can't think of it. Unless, of course, we were to try to withdraw to the ships, and I don't suppose our orders permit that."

"They don't." *Just as well,* Stossen thought, *it would be too tempting.* A withdrawal without cover would be difficult at best, perhaps deadly, but even under a worst-case scenario, he might be able to save half of his command. If they were overrun by the Schlinal army, there was little chance that any of them would make it off-world again, at least not as long as the war lasted, and with hundreds of worlds involved in the fighting, one way or another, the war could easily continue for generations.

"How about a *partial* withdrawal?" Parks suggested. "We're bringing five shuttles down to pick up the strike force. We could just as easily send those men up to the ships instead of bringing them here. Consolidate ammunition and have one shuttle drop that here. Keep us fighting a little longer, perhaps."

That's certainly not covered in our orders, Stossen thought. He took a moment to mull over the idea. Two companies, two recon platoons—or what was left of them. *It would at least leave a cadre to rebuild the 13th from.*

"It is tempting," Stossen allowed. A mental toss of the coin. *I could support the decision before a court-martial if I had to.* It seemed unlikely that he would get a chance to face a court-martial if things went badly on Porter. After another moment, he shook his head.

"Too tempting." He hesitated before he added, "But, no. Maybe it would be the smart thing to do. But we're going to stand or fall together. Having those men back here could make the difference. I can't take that chance."

"I didn't think so, but I had to make sure you looked at the option."

"Headquarters has to know our situation, and just how long we can hold out," Stossen said, half under his breath. "They'll get to us if we just don't give up on ourselves."

He had to believe that, but it was getting more difficult every hour.

CHAPTER
18

Five Accord shuttles came in from the west, low, just enough before sunset to keep Porter's sun firmly behind them during the last stages of their approach. Even the troops they were coming to pick up had difficulty seeing the landers until the last minute before they settled down on flat ground a half kilometer from the canyon. The shuttles came in fast, settling to the rocky ground and swinging open the troop bay doors almost before they came to a halt. Echo and George companies were ready to swarm into the landers. The two recon platoons boarded last. Until the two line companies started filing in, the recon platoons formed a last perimeter guard. They had the last of the strike force's Vrerch missiles. The men carrying them had the launchers on their shoulders, ready to fire instantly against any Schlinal Boems or Novas that might appear.

But there was no attack on the strike force as it got ready to leave.

"Hurry it up," one of the pilots told Captain Ingels. "You've got enemy troops within five kilometers, moving this way."

"Another thirty seconds," Ingels replied. "How large a force?"

"Rough guess is three companies of infantry and a full battalion of armor. With that much on the ground, they'll have air cover timed to get here when the ground forces do, and I want to be *far* out of here before then."

"Okay, the last recon squads are coming through the doors now," Ingels said as they reported to him, then, "Button 'em up. We're ready."

Some of the last troops aboard had no time to strap in before the shuttles lifted off and accelerated back toward the west, away from the approaching Schlinal ground troops and their anticipated air cover. In one lander, two men managed to break arms in falls. There were dozens of less serious injuries. But men helped each other, and soon, everyone was in place—except for the medics who were treating the two broken arms. Those men would get a longer ride. They would be carried on up to the ships after the rest of their mates were deposited back on the plateau.

Captain Ingels linked to Colonel Stossen to report on the enemy movement toward the location they had just left.

"We've got 'em moving toward us also," Stossen said. "You're going to be coming in hot, just like the first day. Out as fast as possible, ready for anything. We want to get the shuttles out of the way before the attack breaks. If we can." The earlier sunset where the bulk of the 13th was had given the enemy more time to move into position.

"This the main event?" Ingels asked.

"Looks like it, Teu. Hang on, I've got another call coming in." He wasn't off the channel long. "We just had two mines go off. That means that the leading elements of the enemy attack are within two kilometers of our perimeter. You're going to be landing near the cliff. I don't want to get the shuttles any closer to the fighting than necessary. It means another forced march for your men when you get here. I need you on the line right now."

"Just tell us where, Colonel."

"I'll let you know as soon as I can."

Ingels alerted Lieutenant Vickers, the platoon leaders, and the noncoms. There was little time for details, because by the time the sergeants and corporals had passed the word to their men, the shuttles were popping up over the edge of the escarpment, moving toward touchdown.

"Everybody out!" Ingels shouted into his radio on the all-hands channel. "There could be enemy fighters over us any second."

The landing drill went smoothly. As soon as the last troopers were out, save for the casualties being lifted to the fleet, the doors closed and the shuttles lifted off at full acceleration, reaching straight for orbit and their hangars aboard the transports.

Colonel Stossen ordered the two line companies northwest, the recon platoons due north. "Quickly, if you please," Stossen finished, the tone of understatement giving the officers on the other end of the conversation a chill.

None of the troops were up to a real double time, but Ingels kept the pace as rapid as he dared, as fast as he himself could manage, something approaching quick step—drill-field speed.

Echo Company had not traveled far before they heard the sounds of combat, the mixed wire fire of Accord and Hegemony weapons, the occasional crump-crump of artillery or rockets, and the higher-pitched blast of grenades or mortar rounds. The farther they went, the louder and more pervasive the sounds became, and not simply because they were getting closer to the action. The volume of fire was increasing steadily.

"Remember, wire discipline," Joe Baerclau warned his platoon while they were on the move. "Don't touch the trigger unless you have a target in your sights. We don't have wire to waste." That was an understatement of such dimension that it caused him to shake his head in wonder. *Wire to waste*. No matter how stingy they were, they were going to run out of wire before this fight ended. Joe had absolutely no doubt of that.

Joe looked to see where Goff was. Keeping track of Kam was becoming instinctive. Joe scarcely needed to think to look for him. Kam was keeping up with the squad, but he was near the rear of the group. Mort Jaiffer was staying close, hanging back, talking to the rookie as they moved.

One more fight, kid, Joe thought as he looked at Goff. *If we make it through this one, we're all home free.* And if they didn't make it, it wouldn't matter much whether or not Goff held up.

Twelve days of occupation had brought changes to the area surrounding the original LZs. Much of the ground cover had been trampled into mulch. Trees that had been damaged had been felled afterward, the wood used for fires and for shelter. Latrines had been dug; with chemicals added to neutralize odor and bacteria. A number of tents had been erected, not as quarters for the troops—everyone slept in the open, in their slit trenches—but to hold stores and to provide places for the medtechs to work. There had been no significant rain during the 13th's time on the plateau, but there had been heavy dew almost every night, and an occasional mist, normally just around dawn. But, generally, the weather had been almost perfect, if a little warm—a rare event in the mind of any mudder.

Joe used the time spent crossing the Accord's ground to check with the units on the section of line toward which Echo Company was hurrying. None of the noncoms he talked to had more than a second to tell him that it was hot and getting hotter—the fight, not the weather. Schlinal troops were coming on in waves, with air and armor backing them up. The Heggies were moving slowly but steadily, taking advantage of whatever cover they found to edge in closer, unit by unit. There were no wild charges against the line this time, but the more methodical, persistent advance would be even harder to throw back. *If* it could be thrown back at all.

An arc of eighteen riflemen and three splat gunners—covering slightly more than a semicircle, with the open section toward the escarpment—provided one last barrier in front of the 13th's command post. Over the last two days, those twenty-one men had dug in with some zeal, throwing up dirt ramparts around their positions, reinforcing their foxholes with tree trunks, and cutting clear kill zones in front of them. The riflemen had only the wire in their zippers and one spare spool apiece. The splat guns had only enough wire to last ten seconds of continuous firing. None of them were firing now. The battle was too far away for them. Their job was to watch, and wait.

One of those riflemen was Zel Paitcher, pilot without a plane. He didn't mind not shooting. He wasn't especially good with a rifle. That sort of weaponry had been neglected totally in flying school, and pilots were not required to periodically qualify with infantry weapons. Most of them were unlikely to go searching for opportunities to use those weapons. It would have been considered almost déclassé in the ready room. If any Heggies got close enough for him to actually have a chance of hitting them with a zipper, Zel was unsure that he would be steady enough to shoot at them. But he no longer had a Wasp to fly, and the colonel had no use for idle hands. Well, Zel's hands might be idle at the moment, but with a purpose. If the entire 13th failed to stop the Schlinal attack, Zel and his companions were expected to do the job, to keep the enemy away from their commander. For just as long as they could.

Colonel Stossen stayed away from the front lines this time. In fact, he stayed in or very near his CP. Too much was happening for him to allow himself to get sidetracked by the fight on any one portion of the perimeter. The 13th finally had a solid command post, split logs laid across a bunker dug into the dirt, anchored by three trees that were still standing. The log roof was covered with nearly a meter of dirt and rock. In addition, the bunker was—somewhat—camouflaged with leaves and small rocks. The bunker would not be proof against a direct hit from a tank's main gun, or a bomb or rocket from a Boem, but the fortifications would stop wire and hide the residents from casual discovery by visible or infrared light at any distance.

Stossen kept telling himself to stay inside the bunker, but he was less than proficient at obeying his own order. Every few minutes, it seemed, he would duck outside to take a look toward one section or another of the perimeter, propping power binoculars on the roof of the bunker, or leaning against a tree. It bothered him that he was having so much difficulty steadying the glasses. His hands and arms had developed a palsied shaking the night before, and the trembling had only gotten worse through the day.

"CIC has everything from here, up to the minute," Dezo Parks reported. He had been sitting cross-legged in a corner of the bunker for the last forty-five minutes, making certain that none of the 13th's data, mostly action and casualty reports, would be lost, no matter what happened to the men and their equipment.

We'll go out in proper military style, Parks thought. He had given up hoping for any reprieve. Even if the relief fleet entered Porter's system that very instant, it would still take eight hours for them to get in position to provide any help to the men on the ground. Dezo Parks doubted very much that the 13th had eight hours left.

Stossen nodded absently. He was listening to a report from the commander of Fox Company.

"They claim to have knocked out four Novas," Stossen said. "Digby has moved his men up to the Novas and taken over their automatic weapons. None of the tank cannons seems to be operational. Or Digby doesn't have anyone who can figure out how to operate them."

Parks managed a short laugh. "Can't have everything. What kind of infantry are they up against?"

Dryly, Stossen said, "According to Digby, *dead* ones."

"The strike force units are reaching their positions now," Parks said. Like Stossen he was monitoring outside calls while their conversation continued. "Echo and George at least. Haven't heard from the two recon platoons yet."

After several minutes of silence between the two men, Stossen said, "The Heggies won't back off this time. They mean to finish the job."

"I know," Parks replied. "With a little luck, I figure we might hold out for another three or four hours. Not much more than that if they continue to press the attack. If we had more wire, more of all munitions, it might be different, but . . ."

Stossen didn't reply. After a short hesitation, Parks spoke again. "I know the answer to this, Van, but I'm your exec now, so I have to ask. Our chances of beating back this attack appear to be slightly less than nil. Do we fight on, or do we try to arrange surrender terms?"

Stossen lifted his visor to stare at Parks.

"I told you, I have to ask," Dezo said.

Stossen nodded. He took a deep breath before he answered. "The 13th does not surrender while we have a weapon or a man to wield it. Not to Schlinal troops. Anyway, they don't like to take prisoners."

Echo Company moved into positions that had been prepared in advance. Alpha Company had dug two sets of primary and secondary defense lines. Until Echo arrived, Alpha had spread out to cover twice as much front. The two platoons that had been covering Echo's section of the perimeter moved out as soon as their replacements arrived. The men of Echo had no time to spend getting acquainted with their new digs though. There was activity beyond their front.

The field of tall grass that had occupied Joe and his men the first morning on Porter was a half kilometer to their left now, and even farther out beyond the reduced perimeter that the 13th was now defending. Echo was well back in the trees now.

The Schlinal troops were moving forward with great deliberation, taking their time, sliding along the ground from one tree to the next, digging in—if minimally—and pouring fire into the Accord lines. After checking with one of Alpha's platoon sergeants, Joe learned that the Heggies had advanced no more than fifty meters in the hours since they arrived to start the battle.

"They figure they got all the time they need now, sir," Joe told Lieutenant Keye after relaying that information.

"Maybe they do, Joe."

"If they've got as many troops out there as we've been told, they could run over us in minutes. Not like the Heggies to be so careful of their mudders."

"They're just waiting for us to run out of wire. That has to be it. The Heggie C.O. wants a real walkover." Keye made no attempt to hide the bitterness he felt. So long a road to end like this.

"Sir?" Joe hesitated before he continued. "What do you figure happened that they didn't come back for us?"

Lieutenant Keye stared at Joe for a minute, then shook his head. "I don't know. Maybe the main task force got beat bad, or bogged down. I hate to think that they abandoned us, for *any* reason, but—even more than that—I hate to think that we might miss pickup by no more than a matter of days, or hours."

"You think they're still coming?"

Keye nodded. "They'll come, soon as they can." *Even if it's too late to help us.*

First squad had been reorganized as a single fire team during the shuttle ride back from the valley. With Al Bergon wounded and evacuated, and Joe Baerclau serving as platoon sergeant, there were only five men left in the squad—really only four effectives. Kam Goff found himself sandwiched between Mort and Ezra, with less space on either side of him than normal. Kam doubted that the arrangement was as accidental as it was made to appear. There had been no relaxation in his mates' observation of him. He had never had a moment to himself. Even a latrine trip was never made alone.

They know I'm useless for fighting. Kam took no offense at that, and he was beyond sorrow or self-pity. He knew he was useless. His comrades obviously worried that he might try to kill himself. At least, everyone did make a pretense, not saying or doing anything openly to make the situation more painful than it was for Kam. He had the spool of wire in his rifle, but no spares. Those had been distributed, on the sly, to the others in the squad. Ezra had taken care of that, personally.

At least I don't have to worry about finding a way to end it anymore, Kam thought. A wry smile found its way to his face. He was glad for the visor on his helmet. No one else could see his expression. *The way this is shaping up, the Heggies will do me the favor soon enough.*

Basset two still had eleven rounds of ammunition. After that, it would be useless, except to protect its crew against enemy wire. Wire was about all that the armor would stop. At the same time, the gun was a magnet for heavier enemy munitions. Once Basset two ran out of ammunition, the crew would be safer abandoning their ride and taking their chances with enemy wire. Each of the four men had an infantry helmet close at hand now. With all the casualties the 13th had taken in its twelve-plus days on-planet, there were plenty of spare helmets.

Eustace had virtually stopped talking since the Havocs had returned from Maison with the captured enemy weaponry. He broke his silence only when it was absolutely essential, and then he kept his words to a minimum. Simon had never seen Eustace like that before. He didn't seem to be angry, at least not at anyone in particular. Angry at life in general . . . or at the way it might end soon . . . was the way that Simon interpreted it, with a shrug. There was always the chance of death in combat. Havoc crews had the odds against them.

But that was different. Either death came or it didn't. Here, on Porter, death seemed to be waiting for all of them. They would run out of ammunition. The infantry would run out of ammunition. Inevitably. Then the Heggies would do whatever they damn well pleased.

Simon had a fatalistic appraisal of what that would be. He had already made his peace.

For the most part, the shooting coming from the 13th was limited to the men with Dupuy RA rifles. They were the only ones who still had a—relative—abundance of ammunition. In the line companies, two Dupuys were assigned to each platoon, one for every fifteen men. The recon platoons were rather more heavily equipped with the sniper rifles, two for each twelve-man squad. The Dupuy could not fire on full automatic, which cut down on its rate of fire, but at ranges under three hundred meters, the rocket-assisted slugs could penetrate any body armor in the galaxy, or shatter a helmet— and the skull beneath it. Striking before their rocket assist ended, the slugs might be still accelerating when they hit. The men chosen to use the Dupuys were usually the best marksmen in each platoon. Their efforts helped to keep the Schlinal advance slow. With little need to worry about distance or windage, they needed very little in the way of a target, and as soon as one of them caught a Schlinal mudder in his laser sights, the trigger went back.

The Dupuys made a distinctive sound. Back in his bunker, Colonel Stossen paused to listen to them. He had been critical of the Dupuys in the past, touted as a long-range weapon— unlikely ranges for the most part. But they were finding a better purpose now.

It was ninety minutes past sunset when Stossen received the call from CIC.

"Colonel, we have the relief fleet in-system. They just emerged from hyperspace, not ninety seconds ago."

At first, Stossen didn't reply. He couldn't. The thought of help coming, just hours too late, was too much for him. He bit at his lower lip, hard enough to draw blood. *Too damn much!*

"Colonel? Are you there?"

"I'm here," Stossen replied. The taste of blood in his mouth was a surprise. He found it difficult to speak over the growing feeling of emptiness in his gut. *So close. So far.* He wanted to cry, but knew that he would not. Could not.

"They're in-system. Can you hold until they get to you?"

Stossen looked at Dezo Parks, who was also listening to the conversation. Parks shook his head. He held up a hand with four fingers extended. *Four hours.* And both men knew that even that was an overly optimistic estimate.

"Negative, CIC," Stossen said. "We'll be lucky if we can hold out another four hours. I wouldn't lay odds on it. We're too close to dry on ammunition, and we're facing a major enemy offensive at this moment. If the Heggies press it, we could be gone in two hours. Or less."

"I'll pass that information on to the relief fleet, Colonel. Hold on, sir. We're all with you."

CHAPTER
19

Van Stossen hesitated for nearly five minutes before he broadcast the news of the relief fleet's arrival to the rest of the 13th. Through most of that five minutes, Stossen and Parks merely stared at each other. At one point, Dezo said, "You can't hold back that information, sir. Knowing that help is coming might make the difference." He didn't really *believe* that, but it was a chance, more chance than they had otherwise.

"It's more likely to destroy their spirit completely when they realize how just-out-of-reach help is," Stossen suggested. When Parks started to reply, the colonel waved him silent. "I know, Dezo. I'll make the broadcast. But I also know what the news has done to me. As if I'd just been sucked dry and hung in a museum in an exhibit called 'They Almost Made It.'"

"We're not dead yet," Parks pointed out. "You know the heart our boys have. As long as they know help is coming, at least some of the 13th might survive. Hold an LZ for the relief. Nobody's going to just lay down and die. Even if we can't hold the lines, some of our lads might get away, hide until help gets here."

"It might come to that. Is there anything left we can do that we haven't done already?" Stossen asked, suppressing a sigh with difficulty. "Any way to give us those extra hours?"

"I don't know. We shortened the lines. We've got a second line of resistance prepared for when we have to abandon the first, even shorter. That helps concentrate what firepower we have left. Mines, out in front of the primary LOR, and on that line as well. I think some of the men have prepared a few more, ah, primitive surprises for the Heggies as well." Dezo paused, and cocked his head to the side. "You want to consider something *really* insane?"

"Right now, I'd even consider witchcraft."

"Something just came to me. We could bring down a half-dozen shuttles, not to escape in, but to form one last barricade, a final redoubt."

"One last place to fall back to?"

"Something like that. Granted, we'd probably lose most, maybe all, of the shuttles we use, but—*just maybe*—they might buy us a little extra time."

"Let me think about it for a minute." While he was thinking, Stossen broadcast the news of the arrival of the fleet to his troops—just that the fleet was there and moving toward their aid as quickly as possible.

"Hold on, men," he concluded, his words almost a prayer.

"Why do I feel like a fraud?" Stossen asked when he lifted his visor and turned to face Parks again. Before Dezo could think of a reply, there was another call from CIC.

"Colonel, the admiral says he's going to try something to get to you quicker. If it works, you'll have Wasps over your position in three hours, troops forty minutes after that."

"*How?*" Stossen demanded.

The watch officer in CIC hesitated before he answered. "I know this is going to sound crazy, Colonel, but this is what I was told. Part of the relief fleet is going to make another hyperspace jump, coming out near our position up here."

"Can they do that?" Stossen asked, his eyes going wide.

"I don't know. The manual says it can't. I don't think it's ever been tried, but honest to God, Colonel, that's what the admiral himself told me, personally. I asked him to repeat what he said, and it came out the same both times."

"Can they do that?" Stossen asked Parks after unlinking from CIC.

Dezo shrugged. "I don't know any more than they do. I'm not all that current on that sort of thing. But what I'm thinking is that the admiral's more likely to lose ships and men. Still, maybe it does offer a little hope."

"I don't know much about flying a starship either," Stossen said. "What I *do* remember is that both ends of a hyperspace transfer have to be so far away from any planetary mass or ships get ripped apart, all the way down to their constituent atoms."

"With a massive release of energy," Parks added, nodding as much to himself as to the colonel. "Comparable to a fair-sized matter-antimatter annihilation. That's what the texts say. I have no idea at all what the safety margin is."

Both men were silent for a moment. Then Stossen said, "Either way, I think we can forget about bringing down those shuttles."

Parks let out a sigh. "Yeah. Probably wasn't such a good idea anyway. Most of them probably would have been shot down before they landed anyway. Wouldn't do us much good that way, and we might lose men on the ground as well."

"Let's just hope we last until they get here," Stossen said. Silently, he added, *If they get here*, unaware that his executive officer was thinking the same thing.

"Three hours," Parks said. "That's sure better than eight."

The Schlinal troops brought up their own sniper rifles. Though the attackers did not have the benefit of prepared positions, the heavier slug-throwers did make life a little more chancy for the 13th.

If a battle absolutely has to be fought, most soldiers prefer it to be at night. The green glow of objects in infrared sights comes to look as normal as the bright lights of day. A different set of sensory responses are needed. Light and shadow take on distinct meanings related more to hot and cold. The overlay of two night-vision systems in the optics of Accord helmets could, at its most extreme, resemble an activity that people from thousands of years in the past might have recognized— watching a primitive 3-D film without the special filter glasses that brought the images together. But experience made that double vision more helpful than any practical amalgam.

Shortly after the men of the 13th received the news that the relief fleet had finally come in-system, the Schlinal forces made their first straight-up assaults on the Accord lines. Those early attempts were tentative, probing attacks made on various sectors by small units and quickly abandoned when they met stiff answering fire. Echo Company beat back one of those probes without taking any casualties.

"Mind your wire," Joe said over his platoon circuit as soon as it was clear that the Heggies were withdrawing. The colonel's second message, that the relief fleet might actually get to Porter sooner than expected, came during the fighting. It was enough to make everyone take notice, if only for a fraction of a second.

"Don't go shooting at their backs," Joe said. That was no gesture of civilized sportsmanship, it was necessary frugality. New hope brought new worries. Every additional second that the wire lasted brought them one more second closer to help. That thought came and came again, quickly obsessing Joe and many others on the line.

"Squad leaders, check ammunition," was Joe's next transmission. Check and recheck; do everything possible to drive home the continued need to be as sparing of wire as possible.

Tod Chorbek and Wiz Mackey had devised their own private system for stretching their ammunition. They took turns firing, never both at the same time. Though it was not something they had ever drilled at—neither had ever suspected that it might someday be necessary—the two young men knew each other so well that they fell into an easy rhythm and hardly needed to look at each other or talk about the changeovers to make it work. From the beginning, their alternation went smoothly.

Kam Goff kept his head down, mostly, or looked around to see if there were any casualties who needed his help. He no longer needed to see death to feel the reactions he had experienced during his first views of violence on the battlefield. Each burst of wire, from either side, reimprinted the pictures in his memory. His stomach twisted and lurched, but did not expel its contents. He was far beyond that.

Why does it do this to me? He had asked himself that question hundreds of times since coming to Porter. He still didn't have the slightest clue. No one else in the platoon reacted the way he did. As far as he could see, no one in the entire 13th did.

Why me? He did make an effort, one last attempt to assert some measure of self-worth. Two different times, he put his eye to the sights on his zipper and fired off short bursts. There were no living targets in his sight picture either time, but there was enemy activity "out there," and no one who wasn't looking through his eyes could know that he was shooting at nothing. He was shooting. He actually managed to make his finger squeeze the trigger and then release it. He did not freeze up. The first time, he was so astounded that he had to do it again just to convince himself that he had actually done it.

Mort Jaiffer looked to his left when he heard Goff's zipper fire. For a moment he simply stared, also surprised that Kam was actually taking part in the fray. Looking past Goff, Mort saw that Ezra had also noticed. On a private channel, Mort reported the event to Joe Baerclau. "Maybe he's gonna make it after all," Mort said.

"Let's hope so," Joe replied. *For his sake, if nothing else.* With relief on its way, maybe the 13th would survive the night. If it did, if Goff did, perhaps he would be able to hold his head up again. If he didn't, at least he would go out knowing that he had learned to handle his fear.

Joe had no time to waste thinking about Goff though. Nor could he really afford to waste time on the other thoughts that kept nagging at him. *The relief fleet is here, but they can't get to us in time.* The irony of it all left a sour feeling in Joe's stomach. To fight, perchance to die. That was always the lot of the soldier, and Joe had no illusions left about that. But to fall hours, maybe only minutes, before help arrived . . . that was hard to accept.

Maybe. That one word became a sort of shorthand for thoughts that there simply was no time to think through in detail. *Maybe we'll fall, but maybe we can hold out. Maybe they'll get here in time after all.* The colonel had come back on to tell them that the admiral in charge of the relief fleet was going to try something that might get them to Porter sooner than *The Book* said they could. Maybe that—whatever "that" was—would work; maybe it would not.

"And maybe pigs will fly," Joe mumbled as he raised his rifle. A Schlinal helmet had just come into view.

Slee Reston was the last Wasp pilot in the air. During his last two flights, he had been wingman to Red three. They had been forced to defend themselves against Schlinal Boems while trying to get in as many strikes as they could against the infantry and armor closing in on the 13th. After Red three shot off his last rockets and emptied the magazines on his cannons, Slee had covered him while he made his run back to the LZ. But Slee still had ammunition—rounds for his cannons, at least—and he was not about to land with ammunition still aboard, not where there would be no more flights on Porter.

As soon as Red three was on the ground, Slee swiveled Blue three and headed for the nearest point on the line where there was currently heavy fighting, in the northwest sector. Slee talked directly to the company commanders along the area he was headed for, looking for targets. Everyone had targets they wanted him to hit. As soon as Slee had a fix on friendly positions, and distances to the nearest Heggies, he banked right and made his run parallel to the front, spraying the trees that mostly hid the enemy from him.

If I get one Heggie for every hundred rounds . . . He didn't expect any better than that—couldn't really expect *that* level of performance. Even with the enemy clearly visible, formed up in ranks on a drill field, he would scarcely expect to get one hit for every hundred rounds. In actual combat, one kill for a thousand rounds was more realistic. But realism was too hard to bear just now.

A blinking red light told him that he had less than five seconds worth of ammunition left. He took his finger off of the trigger and started to make a 180-degree turn to run back along the front. He was halfway through the turn when another warning light came on, this one to warn him that a missile had locked on to the Wasp.

Slee turned to race away from the missile, dropping the last of the chaff his Wasp carried. There were no decoy drones left. Slee ducked past the missile and resumed his strafing run, but a second missile locked on. This time, Slee was too low to have any chance to evade the rocket. His guns were dry, so he couldn't even attempt to shoot it down.

There was no need for hesitation. Slee banked back toward the 13th's lines. One hand lifted the lid on a panel and armed the ejection controls. Another panel slid open and Slee hit the red button. The escape pod had scarcely cleared before the missile hit Blue three. The force of the explosion boosted the ejector pod a few additional meters. Slee blacked out momentarily. By the time he came to, the pod's parasail had been deployed and he was drifting behind Accord lines, with enemy small-arms fire dinging off of the pod.

The remaining Havocs flitted from deep cover to deep cover. With the reduced area that the 13th was defending, there was less maneuvering room than any of the gun crews liked, but at least the Schlinal force had still shown no use of long-range counterbattery fire, and the Havocs were still far enough from the front that there was little danger from infantry rockets. The crews of the Havocs were most concerned about not attracting enemy aircraft. They moved after each round, but they did not move as far or as fast as they would have if the enemy had brought up an artillery battalion.

There were no massed artillery barrages in this fight. Each gun crew hoarded their few remaining rounds as long as they could. Fire missions called in from the 13th's command post or from the line companies were handled with single-shot responses—if they were handled at all. As long as the coordinates provided were accurate, one high explosive plasma round could be sufficient. Against a Nova tank, one hit was all that was needed. The Nova's armor was nowhere near sufficient to stop the bite of a Havoc.

"We've got one frag and two HE left," Jimmy Ysinde reminded the others in Basset two.

"I know," Eustace replied. "And we've got a mission for the frag now." He watched his controls while Jimmy loaded and Karl Mennem dialed in the coordinates and adjusted the elevation of the gun.

"We've got missions for the last two HE too," Eustace announced while the others got ready to fire off the last fragmentation round.

"Locked in," Karl announced.

"Fire!"

Simon had Basset two moving before the last echoes of the shot abated.

"Take us closer to the lines," Eustace told him.

In the rear compartment, Jimmy and Karl worked to ready the next shot. It went just like a drill. The crew of Basset two had some of the best times of any artillery crew in the fifteen SATs. Simon brought the Havoc to its new heading. Karl locked in the target, and Eustace gave the command to fire. After this round. Simon merely moved the Havoc forward 120 meters.

"Fire!"

The last round went out.

After the last echoes of it faded from inside the crew compartments, Simon stared across the gun barrel to Eustace. Eustace stared back.

"Infantry time?" Simon asked. The Havoc was moving. Even though they had no more ammunition, they had to move the gun away from its last firing position.

Eustace growled under his breath. He knew what they were supposed to do, but he didn't like it any better now than he had when the order was given.

"We can at least ride a little closer to the lines," he said. "Slowly."

"No new word on the relief fleet yet?" Dezo Parks asked. He had been away from the CP for nearly a quarter hour, taking a look himself at one sector of the fighting.

Van Stossen shook his head. "No. They haven't emerged from this last jump yet. If they have, they haven't made contact with us or CIC." *The ships could all be lost by now, on whatever the admiral thought he could do.* He didn't bother to add that.

"I didn't think so," Parks said, knowing that the question had been unnecessary in the first place. Stossen would have cut him in on the call, or relayed the news as soon as it was over.

"What's it like out there?" Stossen knew what he was hearing from the various company commanders, but that was never the same as a firsthand look. A report from his second in command was as close as he was going to come though.

"As tight as you'd imagine," Parks replied. "We're still holding the outer line, all the way around, but we can't do that much longer. I'd advise bringing the men back to the secondaries now."

Stossen nodded. Better to do it voluntarily, before there were any breakthroughs. "I've been waiting for you to get back before I gave the order." He hesitated, then said, "This is going to be one of the hairy spots."

It was Parks's turn to nod. Taking men from prepared positions, ordering them to fall back to a second line of resistance in the face of enemy pressure, could bring disaster if the Schlinal troops were prepared to take full advantage of the opportunity.

"We can't avoid it," Parks said.

Stossen gave the order. Then he closed his eyes and prayed.

Most of the men in the 13th had been anticipating the order to pull back. The actual timing was a matter of some local control. No company wanted to be left out in front of the units on their flanks, so they coordinated—as best they could—with the companies to either side to insure an orderly withdrawal.

In the 2nd platoon of Echo Company, Lieutenant Keye moved back with the third and fourth squads. Joe followed with first and second. The Schlinal forces facing them reacted to the move faster than most of their comrades. They started forward, picking up their rate of fire, trying to turn the Accord withdrawal into a rout. But Echo Company was ready for them.

"Now!" Joe told the squads he was with.

First and second squads had been especially parsimonious with wire for the last half hour. Now they made up for it, returning fire in a volley, each man going through nearly a full spool of wire as they started to move back. Except for Kam Goff. He did manage one short burst—that went nowhere near any of the enemy—then turned to help Tod Chorbek. Chorbek had gone down ten meters from Goff.

Wiz Mackey was with his friend, trying to pull him along toward the secondary positions. Carrying Tod's rifle and firing his own, Wiz had forgotten all about conserving wire. He could scarcely think beyond what he was doing. His best friend had been hit; there was blood oozing through Tod's

uniform and net armor, *liters* of blood, the way it looked to
Wiz. He had to strike back at the enemy with everything he
had . . . *while* he dragged Tod to safety.

Wiz was so preoccupied that he didn't even notice Goff
at first. He resisted when Kam moved to take over carrying Tod.

"Wiz! It's me. You handle the shooting, cover us. I'll get
Tod back to the line."

For just an instant, Wiz took his eyes from his shooting. He
started to nod to Goff but had no chance to complete the gesture. A heavy burst of enemy wire struck the group, wire from
a splat gun. Goff dove forward, taking Wiz down with him and
Tod, covering them. But all three of them had already been hit.

"Sarge! To your left," Mort Jaiffer shouted. Joe's head
turned that way. He saw the men down, still being struck
by Schlinal wire.

The rest of first and second squad were halfway between
the two defensive lines. The Heggies were near the now abandoned outer line. Joe—and most of the men with him—stopped
moving toward the secondary line. They took what momentary
cover they could, looking to see if there was any hope for the
men who had been hit.

Joe called each on the radio, using both the squad channel
and private links to each helmet. There was no response—no
words or groans, nothing.

"It'll take all of us to get them," Ezra said. "Can you cover us?"

Joe didn't answer immediately. *They've got wire left,* took
over his thoughts, but even that trove did not make it possible
to get to the men. The Heggies were advancing, and they were
closer to the fallen men than he was.

"Sarge?" Ezra asked over the radio.

"No." The word hurt. "We can't. They're dead, Ez. All we'd
do is lose more men. Back to the secondary line."

"Sarge . . ."

"No!" Joe repeated. He raised his rifle and let off a long
burst at the nearest group of Heggies, but that did little to
ease the guilty ache he felt as he guided the rest of his men
back to the new line of resistance.

As the Schlinal advance reached the abandoned outer line
of defense of Echo Company, First Sergeant Iz Walker pressed

three keys on a small detonator, setting off the string of mines that had been planted along the company's perimeter. The Schlinal advance stopped. Walker saw at least thirty men go down, but he couldn't tell how many of those had been struck by shrapnel, and how many had simply dropped to find cover. For a moment, smoke obscured the outer line. It gave the remaining elements of Echo time to get behind the secondary line and position themselves to resume firing.

"Check your wire!" Joe told 2nd platoon. His voice rasped now. His throat was irritated by the thin layer of smoke and fumes that hung over the battlefield, but the rasp came even more from having left three of his men behind.

He waited while the squad leaders checked with their men and passed the information back to him. Most of the platoon was on its last spool of wire. The few who hadn't yet put the last spool in their zippers were about to.

"You hear that, Lieutenant?" Joe asked on another channel.

"I heard," Keye replied. "The rest of the company is in the same shape." Both men assumed, without much fear of error, that the entire 13th was in an equal state. Perhaps some of the companies were already dry.

"How long?" Joe asked, knowing that Keye would interpret the question correctly.

"I don't know," Keye replied. "I haven't heard a word on the new fleet in forty minutes or more."

Basset two came to a halt fifty meters behind the secondary line. The crew bailed out of their hatches almost as quickly as they had when it was hit. A Havoc would still be a prime target for any enemy armor, or for an infantryman with a shoulder-operated missile launcher, and no one counted on being lucky a second time. Eustace had already warned the commander of Echo Company that they were coming. Now he led his men toward the new command post of Captain Ingels.

"There are four of us with RA pistols," Ponks told the captain. He was wearing an infantry helmet now, but the visor was up. "Where do you want us?"

"The line is twenty meters that way." Ingels pointed. "Wherever you can find a place. Glad to have you aboard. Just wish you still had ammo for that big gun of yours."

Ponks bared his teeth. It was no grin. "You're not the only one, Captain."

"A rifle and wire frees up, put somebody on it," Ingels added, his voice cold. If a rifle became available, it would only be because its previous owner was no longer able to use it.

Eustace nodded. "Kinda hope that doesn't happen," he said. Then he turned and left the CP. Gesturing to his men, Eustace led the way toward the line.

"Where do you want us?" This time, Ponks asked Joe Baerclau the question. Joe had been prone but rolled over on his side to look up at the newcomers. The artillery crewmen were kneeling, low, behind Joe and to his side.

Joe scanned the four men, and noted that they had side arms only. "Anywhere right along here'll do," he said. "I just lost three men, but out there." He pointed beyond the line. "So I don't have rifles for you."

"We'll make do," Ponks said.

Joe nodded. "I suspect you will, Gunny. But pull those visors down. That way, maybe you'll hold on to your faces awhile. And you'll be able to communicate with the rest of us."

Eustace flushed briefly but bit back any retort. He pulled down his visor. Simon already had his in place, but the other two quickly followed the lead of their sergeant.

Joe watched until the artillerymen settled down behind the low defensive ridge, then turned his attention back to the fight. Four pistols wouldn't add much to the platoon's firepower, but at this point, *any* addition was welcome. And when the Heggies got closer, those pistols might finally be useful.

The Schlinal troops facing Echo Company had not completely recovered from the volley of mines that had gone off in their faces. Firing remained light in the sector for the next quarter hour. Still, there was some wire, as well as other munitions, coming across, and the sound of fighting from neighboring sectors provided a constant background level of noise. A lot of debris had fallen from the trees to cover the ground, leaves and small branches. Here and there, even entire trees had been felled by the fighting. The infrequent raids by Boem fighters, and the somewhat more common shelling by Nova tanks, had done a lot of damage to the forest.

Looking through his binoculars, Joe saw that the Heggies were finally getting their act together again. Another line of them had reached the outer perimeter. They were on the far side of it, using the low mounds that the 13th had thrown up in front of their foxholes. At least, the slit trenches were on the wrong side of the mounds for the Heggies to use them.

While those troops picked up the rate of fire against Echo Company, more troops were advancing behind them.

"I think they're going to try a frontal, Lieutenant," Joe told Keye over their private link. "Looks like they're starting to get impatient."

"Give 'em hell, Joe," was Keye's response.

For about three seconds, Joe thought. That was about how long his wire would last. He looked left and right. None of the men close to him gave any sign of being completely out of wire, but none of them could have much more left than he did, and Joe suspected that most would have less.

A piercing whistle over his radio startled Joe so much that he almost jumped to his feet. Then the very excited voice of Colonel Stossen shouted, "They're here! They made it! Hold on, men. Just *minutes* now."

CHAPTER
20

"Minutes," Joe mumbled, "and me with seconds of wire." He closed his eyes for an instant and took a deep breath. Then he looked out toward the abandoned outer line of resistance again, wondering if he was too late to learn how to pull rabbits out of hats.

The Schlinal troops were crossing the outer line now. There appeared to be at least a full enemy battalion facing the remnants of Echo Company, and the Heggies were not being sparing of wire.

"Stretch the wire as much as you can," Joe said over the platoon channel. "Give us those minutes."

Echo Company hunkered down behind the defenses of their secondary lines and took the Schlinal fire. They returned less than a second of wire for every minute's worth that the attackers sprayed at them. Most of the shooting was, as usual, inaccurate, but so much wire was coming in that there were casualties, all along the line. With only one medic remaining in Echo Company, he couldn't possibly get to all of the wounded

If help did not arrive very soon, treating the wounded would become futile anyway.

But the attackers were also taking casualties. Men dropped as they crossed the outer defensive line. They dropped as they advanced across the mostly open space between that line and Echo's new positions. None of the Schlinal attackers had reached the inner line yet.

It was an impossible goal, but Joe tried to keep his touch so light on the trigger that he would shoot individual snips of wire, as if he had a semiautomatic slug-thrower. Even if the task had been possible, single pieces of wire could hardly be effective at any distance. But Joe was willing to try *anything* that would postpone the end of his ammunition.

He reached down to his side to make sure that he still had his belt knife. Once the wire was gone, it would be clubs and knives. *Not for long.* At that point, the Heggies would be able to stand off and shoot without endangering themselves.

"Minutes," Joe mumbles again. "*How many* minutes?" He glanced skyward, but he could see little through the night and the canopy of leaves and branches.

"Where are they?"

Almost as Joe spoke, help was there. Flights of Wasps were diving to attack the closest Heggies, all around the perimeter, while other flights of Wasps attacked the enemy's Boem fighters and Nova tanks. Even if he hadn't known that the 13th's Wasps were no longer flying, Joe would have known that these came from outside the regiment. There were simply too many of them, more than the 13th possessed at full strength. Just on the small sector of front that he could see, he could count eight Wasps all at the same time—more by their weapons than by seeing the planes. It was dark; the Wasps were invisible except for rare flashes. And he could hear the sounds of other Wasps farther off, their rapid-fire cannon chewing up the air and—he hoped—plenty of Heggies.

The noise level increased dramatically. Bombs and rockets and cannon. The line of the abandoned outer defensive line became a wall of fire, shrapnel, and slugs as the new Wasps used that line to guide their runs. Caught between that and the 13th, the Schlinal assault halted. Men went to the ground— dead, wounded, or trying to avoid those states. Few even tried to keep up any fire against the infantry in front of them.

"Watch for drops behind you," Colonel Stossen said on the noncoms' channel. "They're dropping crates of wire, Vrerchs, and grenades. Soon as you see something coming in, get men to it. Get that ammo divvied up and in use as fast as you can."

You bet! Joe thought. He looked skyward again. *Even if they drop it square on my head.*

Joe passed the alert to the men in the platoon. "Squad leaders, watch for the drops. Figure out who to send if one lands in your area."

If it lands in time. Joe felt surprise at his remaining pessimism. Just because reinforcements had arrived, there was still no guarantee that the 13th would make it through the battle. Until they had that ammunition in their guns, the men of the 13th would still be virtually defenseless. If the Wasps let up for even a minute, Echo Company might be overrun . . . and perhaps the rest of the regiment.

Joe heard the incoming ammunition drop before anyone on the ground could see it. The crate crashed through the trees with two antigravity belts strapped to its sides. Joe shook his head. He had never considered that sort of use for the new devices. But it did look effective. The belts' power gave out when the crate was less than two meters off of the ground. By that time, Joe had grabbed one of the artillerymen and was running toward the crate.

"First and third squads, get over here!" Joe called over the radio. "Second and fourth, wait until they get back, then we'll get you loaded up."

Despite the urgency, it still took several minutes to get the ammunition distributed and into use. Joe saw, or heard, several other crates coming through the trees along the nearest portions of the front. There would be no need to share this box with other companies. Men came from the other platoons of Echo. With a thousand spools of wire in the single crate, there was enough to give everyone left in the company six spools. There were also ten Vrerch launchers and six missiles for each tube, and two dozen disposable RPG units.

"Watch for more drops," Joe warned when he finally headed back to the line. They had enough ammunition to last for a time, but more would certainly be welcome.

For the moment, there was really little for the men of 13th to do. The Wasps were still active, crossing back and forth along the front. Joe set his men one simple task. If any of the Schlinal forces between the two sets of lines moved, shoot him. Then he told the squad and team leaders to watch the front beyond the outer perimeter, to look for more targets coming into range.

There were very few. The Schlinal attack had been broken.

Within another thirty minutes, the first elements of the 4th SAT were landing in the center of the territory that the 13th was guarding. Before the 4th's artillery landed, part of the 27th Light Infantry Regiment came in as well.

Van Stossen's command post got very crowded. Colonel Eggars of the 4th landed with the first shuttles, along with his staff. When the lead units of the 27th started to land, Brigadier Dacik arrived.

"What happened?" Stossen asked the brigadier. "What went wrong?"

Dacik hesitated before he met Stossen's gaze. "I'm not certain that anything really went *wrong,* except for some damn poor planning. We should have provided you with more stores. Other than that, things went exceptionally well."

"What?" Stossen shouted, unable to contain himself.

Dacik took a deep breath. "We took Devon so quickly that the high command decided to retake Porter as well. The delay was what we needed to assemble a few more units. Besides the 4th and the 27th, we have three more regiments ready to land tomorrow, and a second entire wing of Wasps. The bulk of the new forces will land in the valley as soon as they arrive, ready to take Porter City. The rest of the fleet is coming in more conservatively."

For a moment Stossen simply glared at the brigadier. Then he shook his head. "We've lost a lot of good men here. By the time we get the final count, I expect our total casualties, killed and wounded, will be fifty percent. Maybe higher." He tried, without much success, to keep his voice level. "You cut it too damn close . . . sir."

"I know," Dacik replied. "Unfortunately, the important decisions are still made by men who've never been in a situation like yours. In any case, once my people are all in position, the

335

...ved. You should be on the way home within
...olonel. Your men did one hell of a job."

...rly an hour after the first Wasps arrived before Echo ...pany was able to move back to the forward line and recover the casualties they had left there. Joe Baerclau was with the group that went to where Goff, Mackey, and Chorbek had fallen.

Goff and Chorbek were, as expected, dead, but Wiz Mackey was still alive. Barely. Doc Eddles had difficulty keeping him alive until he could be evacuated. But there were medics, and a surgeon—a full trauma ward—aboard one of the shuttles, and once Mackey and a dozen of the other most seriously wounded were in their hands, they all stood a better than average chance of recovery.

The fighting was over for Echo Company of the 13th—as far as Porter was concerned. They were among the first to be routed back to the center of the rapidly expanding perimeter that Accord forces controlled. A field kitchen was up and running by dawn and Joe and his men stood in line for their first hot, full meal since landing on Porter thirteen days before. In a few hours, they would be back aboard ship, heading for home.

There was no rejoicing. The men of the 2nd platoon sat around and ate. Of the thirty men who had landed, only fourteen remained together. The four-man crew of Basset two sat with them. No one talked much.

There wasn't a damn thing to say.